A STRAIGHTFOR\
TO
EMPLOYMEI

CW00972698

Vanessa Davie

KAREN LEIGH

STRAIGHTFORWARD PUBLISHING

First Edition

Published in 1997 by Straightforward Guides
London E17

Copyright © Straightforward Publishing 1997

ISBN 1899924 65 5

A CIP catalogue record for this book is available from the British Library

Cover design by Straightforward Graphics

Layout by Straightforward Publishing

Printed by BPC Wheaton Ltd, Exeter.

CONTENTS

INTRODUCTION

Chapter 1. Employment law. How it is administered 7

Industrial Tribunal
Employment Appeal Tribunal
Advisory, conciliation and Arbitration Service (ACAS)
Central Arbitration Committee (CAC)
Certification Officer (CO)
Commissioner for the Rights of Trade Union Members
Secretary of State for Employment
The courts
European Courts
Equal Opportunities Commission (EOC)
Commission for Racial Equality (CRE)
Health and Safety Commission (HSC)
Health and Safety Executive (HSE)
Commissioner for Protection against
Unlawful Industrial Action.

Chapter 2. The contract of employment 17

Definition of the contract
Form of the contract
Vicarious liability
Selecting employees
Rehabilitation of Offenders Act 1974
Continuous employment
Transfer of Undertakings

Chapter Three. Specific employment contracts 24

Directors and partners
Apprentices
Public Sector employees
Police
Armed Forces
Minors
Temporary employees
Probationary employees
Fixed term contracts
Government training schemes
People over retiring age

Chapter four. Terms of employment contracts 29

Significance of the terms of contract
Sources of the terms of contract
Minimum Statutory standards
Minimum terms orders
Express statements
Collective agreements
Works rules books
Custom
Duties of the employee
Duties of the employer.

Chapter Five. Renumeration 44

Wages Act 1986, Employment Rights Act 1996
Wages Councils

Guarantee payments
Suspension from work on medical grounds
Maternity leave
Insolvency of employer.

Chapter Six. Trade Unions 49

Listing
Independent Trade Unions
Recognition
The Political Fund
The Rule Book
Right to information
Closed shop

Chapter Seven. The Rights of Trade Union Members 55

Enforcement of Rule Book
Exclusion and expulsion
Discipline of Union Members
Commissioner for the Rights of Trade Union Members
Action short of dismissal

Chapter Eight. Industrial Action 59

Industrial action and the contract of employment
Go slow
Work to rule
Overtime bans
Blacking
Strike without notice
Strike with notice
Trade dispute

Industrial action and the economic torts
Liability
Loss of immunity
Picketing
Remedies

Chapter Nine. Discrimination in employment 68

Equal pay
Sex Discrimination Act 1975
Race Relations Act 1976
Disability Discrimination Act 1996

Chapter Ten. Termination of employment 74

Dismissal with notice
Summary dismissal
Employee leaving
Termination by agreement
Termination by frustration
Action for wrongful dismissal/damages
Specific performance
Injunction
Declaration
Written statement of reason for dismissal
Suspension.

Chapter Eleven. Unfair dismissal 81

Dismissal
Reasons for dismissal
Dismissal for trade union issues
Other reasons
Procedure for action

Chapter Twelve. Redundancy 89

Generally
Misconduct
Suitable alternative employment
Claiming redundancy payments
Consultation

Chapter Thirteen. Health and Safety 93

Health and Safety at Work Act 1974

Index **96**

INTRODUCTION

When I received the request from Straightforward Publishing to produce the 'Straightforward Guide to Employment Law' the main problem, it seemed to me, was how to produce a slim volume, readily accessible to the beginner, at the same time embracing the whole complex legislative framework including the recent 1996 changes.

I knew that the project would be an uphill task and this book is the outcome. I have spent many hours toiling away and I hope that I have produced a work which will be a more than adequate introduction for the student or lay person, in short for all those who wish to read an informed introduction.

Throughout, there are cases which serve to highlight main points of law. There is reference to the 1996 Employment Rights Act, which came into force on 22nd August 1996. This Act consolidated a number of existing Acts, including Employment Protection (Consolidation) Act 1978, Wages Act 1986 and Trade Union Reform and Employment Rights Act 1993.

The 1996 Industrial Tribunals Act also came into effect on 22nd August 1996, again with the purpose of consolidation rather than bringing into force new legislation.

In addition to the above, the Disability Discrimination Act 1995 came into force in may 1996, which places greater responsibility on employers to ensure that disabled people/ employees are not disadvantaged in the sphere of employment.

Also, the Asylum and Immigration Act 1996 received royal assent on 24th July 1996, which creates the criminal offence of employing someone who does not have immigration entitlement in the U.K. The maximum penalty is a fine of up to £8,000 for each worker employed.

Employment law has become increasingly complex and for the person who wishes a basic introduction and who wishes to know something of their rights this book should prove invaluable.

1. EMPLOYMENT LAW-HOW IT IS ADMINISTERED

Before the advent of the industrial tribunal system in 1964, labour law was regarded as an aspect of the law of contract, dealt with by the civil courts. Since 1964, the industrial tribunal system has grown and now encompasses other courts and non judicial bodies.

Most people with grievances relating to their employment will attempt to resolve these from within, utilising procedures set up by the employer. Usually, policy exists which will encompass most situations which may arise. However, in some cases, for example, where unfair dismissal is alleged, Industrial Tribunals are used.

Industrial tribunals

The industrial tribunals were established by the Industrial Training Act 1964 to deal with certain disputes arising under the Act. They have grown in power and influence and are organised on a regional basis with each tribunal consisting of a legally qualified chairman and two lay members appointed from a panel. The Industrial Tribunals Act 1996 is the current relevant legislation.

Industrial tribunals are empowered to deal with a wide range of matters arising from a number of legislative provisions, the most important being:

Complaints of unfair dismissal

Applications for redundancy payments

References regarding the written particulars of terms of employment

Complaints regarding guarantee payments

Complaints regarding suspension from work on medical grounds

Complaints regarding trade union membership and activities

Complaints regarding the time off work provisions

Complaints regarding the right to maternity pay and leave

Complaints under the Sex Discrimination Act 1975

Complaint under the Equal Pay Act 1970

Complaints regarding time off work for anti-natal care

Complaints regarding secret ballots on employers premises

Complaints regarding unreasonable expulsion from trade union membership

Complaints from trade unions relating to failure of consultation on employment

Complaints by trade unions relating to failure to consult them about transfer of undertakings.

The procedure in industrial tribunals is regulated by the Industrial Tribunal Act 1996. Rules provide for pre hearing of assessments of industrial tribunal cases at which the tribunal may warn either party to the proceedings that if he wishes to continue an order of costs may be made against him if he loses. The proceedings are intended to be relatively informal both in terms of the pre-tribunal procedure and the hearing. The reasons for the decision of a tribunal must be recorded in a document signed by the chairperson and he must state in this document whether the reasons are recorded in a full or summary form. Full reasons must be recorded in certain types of cases, for example, under the Equal Pay Act, Sex Discrimination Act or the Race Relations Act.

Appeals on questions of law lie in respect of most of the jurisdictions of the industrial tribunals to the Employment Appeal Tribunal, regulated by the Industrial Tribunals Act 1996.

In respect of most of the kinds of application which may be made to the industrial tribunals, before there is a hearing, an attempt is made to settle the matter by conciliation using the services of a conciliation officer.

Employment Appeal Tribunal (EAT)

The EAT was established in 1975. The legislation governing the EAT is now the Industrial Tribunals Act 1996. It consists of judges of the High Court and Court of Appeal one of whom is appointed president, and lay members drawn from a panel of persons having special knowledge of industrial relations.

The essential function of the EAT is to hear appeals on questions of law from the industrial tribunals on most of the jurisdictions exercised by the tribunals and to hear appeals (some on questions of law only and others on questions of law and fact) from the Certification Officer. The EAT has only limited jurisdiction allowing it to determine some applications for compensation following the refusal of a trade union to admit or re-admit a person to membership of a closed shop.

The EAT regulates its own procedure subject to the provisions of the ITA 1996. A party who wishes to appeal from an industrial tribunals decision must submit a copy of the full written reason for the decision in addition to a notice of appeal and a copy of the decision within 42 days. The EAT does, however, have a discretion to authorise the institution of the appeal before the full written reasons are sent if it considers it would lead to more "expeditious or economic disposal of any proceedings or would otherwise be desirable in the interests of justice". An appeal from the EAT on a question of law lies to the Court of Appeal and thence from the House of Lords.

Advisory Conciliation and Arbitration Service (ACAS)

ACAS was established in 1974. It is independent of Government and is managed by a council normally consisting of a full time chairman and nine other members, including three appointed after consultation with the representatives of employers organisations and three appointed after consultation with workers representatives. ACAS is based in London with offices based in regional centres. ACAS has the power to appoint staff, including conciliation officers, and to request other persons to perform services, eg, arbitration.

ACAS is charged with the general duty of 'Improving industrial relations by exercising its functions in relation to the settlement of trade disputes in particular the encouraging of collective bargaining and the development and where necessary the reform of collective bargaining machinery. ACAS draws the duties from s209 of the Trade Union and Labour Relations Act 1992. Its specific functions include conciliation in trade disputes, conciliation in individual cases, arbitration, advice, carrying out inquiries, disputes related to disclosure of information and codes of practice. (see below).

Codes of Practice

The publication and use of codes of practice is becoming of increasing importance in the regulation of employment and industrial relations. The status in law of codes is that, although a failure to observe any provision of a code cannot of itself give rise to legal proceedings, in proceedings before industrial tribunals and other bodies the provisions of a code are admissible in evidence and are to be taken into account in determining the question at issue. In Polkey v. A.E. Dayton Services Ltd (1987) the House

of Lords reaffirmed the importance of the appropriate codes in determining the fairness of dismissal.

ACAS has issued the following codes:

Disciplinary practice and procedures in employment

Disclosures of information to trade unions for collective bargaining purposes

Time off for trade union duties and activities.

Central Arbitration Committee (CAC)

The CAC was established in 1975 by the Employment Protection Act (now s259 of the 1992 Act) and replaced the Industrial Arbitration Board. Although independent of government and ACAS, CAC is served by ACAS staff. CAB has a chairman and members appointed by the Secretary of State for Employment.

The main function of CAC is hearing complaints following an employers failure to disclose information for collective bargaining purposes. There is no appeal from CAC but it is subject to judicial review if it exceeds its jurisdiction or powers.

Certification Officer

The office of CO was created in 1975 (EPA 1975 s7) The main

functions of the CO are to determine whether a trade union is entitled to a certificate of independence, to maintain a list of trade unions and employers associations and to perform certain duties under the Trade Union Act 1913 (amended) in relation to the political fund of the trade unions.

The Employment Act 1988 added two further powers in this respect. Section 16 created the right to complain to the CO (or the High Court) where a trade union member claims a political fund ballot has been or will be held otherwise than in accordance with the rules drawn up by the CO. S22 allows the CO to regulate his own procedure, including a power to 'restrict the circumstances in which the identity of an individual who has made, or is proposing to make, any such application, or complaint is disclosed to any person. The purpose of this is to prevent a complainant from being victimised. The 1992 Trade Union and Labour Relations Act now governs (s2 and 123).

Any appeals from decisions of the CO are heard by the Employment Appeal Tribunal.

Commissioner for the Rights of Trade Union Members

The Employment Act 1988 s 19 (now s266 of the 1992 Trade Unions and Labour Relations Act) empowers the Secretary of State for Employment to appoint a commissioner for the Rights of Trade Union Members in relation to the following:

A failure to hold a proper ballot before industrial action

The right to inspect a trade unions accounts and records

The recovery of union funds used to indemnify unlawful conduct

The restraint of trustees from acting unlawfully

A failure to comply with the CO's rules for conducting a political fund ballot

A failure to comply with the provisions of the Trade Union Act regulating election to a unions principal executive council

The misuse of union funds for unapproved political purposes

Such other matters as may be specified in an order made by the Secretary of State for Employment.

The Secretary of State for Employment

The main functions of the above are:

Approving agreements making provision for payments to redundant persons

Approving Codes of Practice and seeking Parliamentary approval for them

Approving dismissals procedure agreements

Receiving notification of proposed redundancies

Approving guarantee payments agreements

Reviewing various financial limits

Making regulations upon a wide range of matters

13

Issuing, after consultation with ACAS, Codes of Practice containing such practical guidance as he thinks fit for the purpose of promoting the improvement of industrial relations and keeping such codes of practice under review.

As with codes issued by ACAS, a failure to observe the provisions of such a code of practice does not of itself render a person liable to proceedings, but in any proceedings before a court, industrial tribunal or the CAC, a Code is admissible in evidence. To date, the Secretary of State has issued three codes of practice on picketing (limiting number of pickets),closed shop agreements and Draft codes for Industrial Action Ballots.

Powers of the courts

The most important matters with which the courts are concerned are actions by employees for damages following injury at work, actions in tort arising from industrial action, actions for breach of contract including breach of a covenant in restraint of trade and prosecutions under the health and safety legislation.

European Court of Justice

Because it belongs to the European Community, Britain is bound by the decisions of the European Court of Justice. The decisions are only relevant where there is a conflict between British and European law. An industrial tribunal, employment appeals tribunal or any court may (by virtue of article 177 of the Treaty of Rome) refer a case to the ECJ where there is a question of any conflict between the two sets of law. On of the major sources of reference to the ECJ has been the law on equal pay. However, in Pickstones v. Freemans PLC (1988) the Court of Appeal felt able to apply European Law directly without reference to the ECJ. In light of this decision, it can be argued that European law is being incorporated directly into English law without having passes through any parliamentary process.

The Equal Opportunities Commission

The EOC was established by the Sex Discrimination Act 1975s 53. It consists of between eight and fifteen commissioners in addition to its full time staff. The three general duties of the EOC are to work towards the elimination of discrimination in employment and elsewhere, to promote equality of opportunity between men and women and to keep under review the Equal Pay Act 1970 and the Sex Discrimination Act 1975. The EOC produces an annual report for presentation to Parliament and is also empowered to produce Codes of Practice.

The main powers of the EOC in relation to employment are to carry out investigations, in the course of which if it is satisfied that a breach of the Sex Discrimination Act or Equal Pay Act has occurred, it may issue a non discrimination notice against which there is a right of appeal to an industrial tribunal. The effect of a non discrimination notice which is kept on a register is that in the following five years the EOC may apply to a county court if it considers that a further breach of the legislation is likely. Further powers are to bring proceedings in respect of discriminatory advertising or instruction or pressure to discriminate and to give assistance to aggrieved persons. See Chapter   for a fuller exposition of the law.

Commission for Racial Equality

The CRE was established by s 43 of the Race Relations Act 1976. It functions in relation to Racial discrimination are similar to the EOC in relation to discrimination dealt with by the Sex Discrimination Act. See chapter   for a fuller exposition of the law.

The Health and Safety Commission

The Health and Safety Commission was established by the Health and Safety at work Act 1974. The HSC is responsible to the Secretary of State and has a number of duties, the main ones being to assist and encourage persons to further the general provisions of the 1974 Act, to make arrangements for research and the promotion of training and information connected with it, to act as an information advisory service, to submit proposals for regulations and to approve and issue codes of practice.

Health and Safety Executive

The HSE was established by s10 of the Health and Safety at Work Act 1974. The HSE is answerable to the Health and Safety Commission except as regards the enforcement of the health and safety at work legislation. The function of the HSE is to enforce the health and safety at work legislation by means of inspection of premises, the issuing of improvement and prohibition notices, prosecution etc.

Commissioner for Protection against unlawful Industrial Action

This is a post created by the 1993 Trade Union Reform and Employment Rights Act by inserting a new section into the 1992 Trade Union Act. The Commissioner has the power to assist any party who wishes to take proceedings on the basis that the supply of goods and services to him as an individual has been prevented or delayed by unlawful industrial action or that quality of goods and services has been affected (s235A). Such assistance may be in the form of bearing of legal costs and or representation, and in the form of an indemnity in respect of costs or liability incurred.

2. THE CONTRACT OF EMPLOYMENT

Defining a contract of employment

A contract of employment will use the terms 'employee' or 'servant' which distinguishes it from a contract of services under which an independent contractor performs services under contract for another person. legally, the contractor is self employed and the distinction between an employee and independent contractor is significant. Many Acts of Parliament and statutory regulations demand such a distinction. For example, part V1 of the Employment Protection (consolidation) Act 1978 (now 1996 Employment Rights Act) extends only to persons who are employees. Furthermore, the system of taxation is different as between self employed and employed persons.

In addition, the concept of vicarious liability normally extends only to the employer/employee relationship. Vicarious liability means that an employer is responsible for the legal consequences of act done by his employees during the course of work. There are also certain implied terms, such as rights duties and obligations which are implied into every contract of employment, but they do not extend to self employed. The question of whether the relationship of employer/employee exists is a matter for determination by the courts rather than relying solely on the description or label attached to the contract by the parties. Young and Woods v. West (1980): the Court of Appeal stated that whether a person is to be regarded as self employed or employed is a question of law not fact. The label which the parties attach to the relationship may be relevant to determining that relationship but it is not conclusive. The courts have developed several tests for distinguishing between employees and independent contractors.

The tests are as follows:

a. The control test. Does the person alleged to be the employer   actually control the employee in respect of the work done and the performance of that work. If the answer was in the affirmative the relationship of employer/employee was established.

b. The integration test. This test was first stated in precise terms by Denning LJ in Stevenson, Jordan and Harrison v. Macdonald and Evans (1952):

'One feature which seems to run through the instances is that, under a contract of service, a man is employed as part of the business, and his work is done as an integral part of the business: whereas, under a contract for services, his work, although done for the business, is not integrated into it, but is only accessory to it'

c. The economic reality test. In recent years the courts have used a more flexible approach which incorporates both of the previous tests. This is referred to as the economic reality test and means that factors such as control, integration and powers of selection etc are simply issues which contribute to the decision which must be based on all the circumstances.

   One important case was Ready Mixed Concrete (South East) Limitedv Pensions and National Insurance (1968). The worker to whom the case related was the driver of a lorry which he obtained on hire purchase from the company. He was required to paint the lorry in the companies colours and had to obey instructions from the company's servants. On the other hand, he could use substitute drivers if he was ill or on holiday and the contract stated that he was not to be regarded as an employee. In other

words, certain terms of the contract tended to suggest that he was employed whilst others pointed to him being self
employed. The question arose as to whether he was an employee. Held: there are three conditions which establish a contract of service:

a. The employee agrees to provide his own work and skill

b. There must be some element of control exercisable by the employer: and

c. The other terms of the contract must not be inconsistent with a contract of service.

In this case, a consideration of point (c) and particularly the question of the use of substitute drivers led to the finding that the driver was an independent contractor.

Recently, the tribunals and courts have tended to ask the single fundamental question: 'is the person who has engaged himself to perform these services performing them as a person in business on his own account'

Young and Woods V West (1980) is an important case in this respect. West worked for the appellants as a sheet metal worker, however choosing to pay his own tax and national insurance. He had no entitlement to holiday or sick pay. Following the termination of his contract he claimed to be an employee and pursued a claim for unfair dismissal. The Court of Appeal, applying the above test, said that it was impossible to regard West as being in business on his own account. Apart from handling his own deductions, and having no holiday or sick pay, Wests conditions were the same as other workers.

One of the many problems arising out of the distinction between an employee and an independent contractor is that, particularly in the construction industry, workers are often taken on the basis that they are self employed, although, to all intents and purposes, they may appear employed.

This is called the "lump" which means that the person contracting his services is paid a lump sum payment and takes care of his own tax, national insurance etc. The employer is absolved of responsibility for PAYE etc.

Since 1971, legislative provisions have existed whose purpose is to minimise the income tax evasion through use of a system of exempting certificates available only to genuine sub contractors. The most recent of these provisions are those contained in the finance Act 1979.

Form of contract

With two exceptions (merchant seamen and apprentices) there is no requirement that the contract of employment be in writing. However, this can lead to difficulties of providing proof and the contracts of Employment Act 1963 was passed (subsequently the 1972 Act) with the objective of ensuring that most employees were provided with some written evidence of the main terms of employment. These provisions were contained in part 1 of the Employment Protection Act 1978, now consolidated into the 1996 ERA which applies to all employees except registered dock workers, workers working wholly or mainly outside Great Britain, part time employees who do not have continuity of employment and Crown employees.

Section 1 of the 1978 Act states that employers to whom the Act relates must provide employees with a written statement laying out the following particulars:

Names of parties and date of commencement and the date on which the employees period of continuous service began: The scale or rate of Renumeration or the method of calculating it;

How often paid:

Hours of work:

Holidays and holiday pay:
Terms and conditions relating to sickness:
Pensions:
Length of notice entitlement when terminating contract, or, where the contract is for a fixed term, date of expiry of contract:
Title of job:
Disciplinary rules:
Grievance procedures:
Whether a contracting out certificate is in force relating to that employment.

There is a requirement to include a note in the written particulars specifying disciplinary rules applicable to the employee if the employer has more than 20 employees. The requirement to provide a note concerning the disciplinary procedure still remains.

The written statement is not a contract but is merely evidence of certain terms of the contract of employment. Nor are the statement of terms finally conclusive.

Vicarious liability

The basic principle of vicarious liability is that the employer is liable for the torts (negligence) of employees whilst employed by him (during the course of employment). The key here is 'during the course of employment'. AS Lord Porter said in Weaver v. Tredegar Iron and Coal Company Ltd (1940):

'The mans work does not consist solely in the Task which he is employed to perform, it also included matters incidental to that task. Times during which meals are taken, moments during which the man is proceeding to his work from one portion of his employers premises to another and periods of rest may all be included. Nor is his work necessarily confined to his employers premises'

Vicarious criminal liability

As a general rule an employer is not liable for the criminal offences committed by his employees during the course of employment. However, in modern times a number of statutory exceptions have been created to this rule, particularly as regards offences committed by the employees of corporate bodies, eg, under the Trade Descriptions Act 1968 and the Health and Safety at Work Act etc 1974.

Selection of employees

A number of statutory restrictions have been introduced which affect the employers right to employ who he chooses. The main ones are the Disability Discrimination Act 1996: the Rehabilitation of Offenders Act 1974, the Sex Discrimination Act 1975 and the Race Relations Act 1976.

Rehabilitation of Offenders Act 1974

The 1974 Act allows a person to 'live down' certain convictions after a specified period of between six months and ten years, depending on the conviction and sentence, a conviction is deemed to be spent providing no serious offence has been committed during the rehabilitation period. The Act provides that normally a spent conviction or failure to disclose it, is no ground for refusing to employ or dismiss a person or discriminate against him in employment. It should be noted that regulations under the Act means that it does not apply to a number of kinds of employment including teaching, medicine, accountancy etc.

Continuous employment

The concept of 'continuous employment is very important in that nearly all of the various statutory rights afforded employees are dependent upon the acquisition by the employee of two years continuous employment, as a minimum. The rules for computing the period of continuous employment are contained in schedule 13 of the 1996 Employment Rights (Consolidation) Act.

Employment is presumed to be continuous unless the contrary is shown. Any week in which the employee is employed for sixteen hours or more counts towards computing the period of employment. These don not include 'hours on call'. Sickness injury etc does not discount weeks.

One vital question is: can separate concurrent contracts, with the same employer, be aggregated in order to give a person continuity of employment? In Lewis v. Surrey County Council (1987) L had worked for the council since 1969 in three art colleges. L had separate contract for each college term and for each of the three courses. Each contract was confined to the particular department concerned. The contract merely specified the total number of hours to be worked. The House of Lords held that the contracts could not be aggregated as the legislation referred to only one single contractual obligation. The House of Lords did however indicate that L should have pleaded that the three contract amounted to one single contract.

Any week in which an employee is absent on account of a 'temporary cessation' of work counts in the calculation of a period of continuous employment. Any week during which an employee is absent counts towards continuous employment if, by arrangement or custom, the employment is regarded as continuous. Any week in which an employee is on strike, or absent from work because of a lock out, does not count in computing the period of employment but does not break continuity. If an employee is employed for more than 16 hours per week and then becomes employed for less than 16 hours but more than 8 hours, he will, for a further period of twenty six weeks, be treated as employed for more than 16 hours per week. If an employee has been employed for more than 8 hours per week, but less than 16, and has been so employed for five years, he is regarded as being continuously employed for that period.

Transfer of undertakings

There are various provisions dealing with the question of continuity of employment for the purposes of employment protection rights. The 1978 Act Schedule 13 and the Transfer of Undertakings (protection of Employment) Regulations 1981 deal with these. the net effect of the provisions is that where there is a transfer to a new employer, continuity is not broken.

3. SPECIFIC EMPLOYMENT CONTRACTS

Some groups of employees are in a special position with regard to contracts of employment.

Directors and partners

A company director is regarded as an employee for most of the statutory purposes if he has a written service contract with the company, but a non-executive director is not usually regarded as an employee. Whether such a service contract exists is a matter of law, to be determined by reference to the facts of the particular case. Thus, even the director of a one man business may be an employee. One important case dealing with the employment rights of directors is that of Eaton v. Robert Eaton and Secretary of State for Employment (1988). Eaton was the managing director of RE Ltd. When the company ceased trading, he applied to the tribunal for a redundancy payment. No payment was granted as there was nothing in writing to indicate that E was an employee of the company and since 1981 E had not received any financial Renumeration from the company because of its financial position. The EAT supported the decision of the tribunal as they could not find fault with the finding that E was an 'office holder' and therefore not an employee.

Partners

A partner in a firm is self employed. If a person is employed by partners, the relationship of employer/employee exists.

Apprentices

A contact of apprenticeship is an agreement whereby the apprentice binds himself to the employer to learn the trade. Such a contract must be in writing: Apprentices Act 1814. The contract may only be terminated by the employer if the apprentice clearly demonstrates an intention not to learn or for gross misconduct. Conversely, the apprentice may only terminate the contract if the employer fails to provide instruction.

Although apprentices are entitled to claim statutory rights of unfair dismissal and/or redundancy, the expiry of an apprenticeship contract is not of itself unfair dismissal or redundancy.

Public sector employees

In the case of crown servants, a relationship is enjoyed between crown and employee which is analogous to a contract of employment, subject to an implied right of the Crown to dismiss without notice. Employees of nationalised industries and local authorities are not Crown employees. Unless an Act so provides, it does not bind the Crown. A number of modern employment law provisions, however, have been extended to cover the Crown.

Police

The police are excluded from many of the statutory rights to which other employees are entitled, eg, the right to present a complaint of unfair dismissal. The definition of police service in the 1978 Act is wide enough to include police officers. One important case was Home Office v. Robinson and the Prison Officers Association (1981). In addition, the rights of police officers to be members of trade unions and to engage in industrial action are severely limited. However, as 'office holders' police officers cannot be dismissed without a hearing and have a right to reinstatement in the event of the dismissal being found to be wrongful.

The armed forces

The armed forces are excluded from the various statutory rights enjoyed by employees.

One of the questions which has been recently raised is whether or not a public sector employee is able to have the decision of his/her dismissal reviewed by the court through the judicial review procedure. As the normal route of Industrial Tribunal cannot be followed by an 'office holder' eg a police officer judicial review is appropriate to obtain a remedy as there is no alternative. The mere existence of a contract however will not stop a court from reviewing a decision where it thinks appropriate. One important case is McGoldrick v. London Borough of Brent (1987).

Minors

The ordinary rule of the law of contract is to the effect that a minor (person under eighteen) is bound by a contract of employment if the agreement as a whole is substantially to that persons benefit. In Doyle v. White City Stadium Ltd and the British Boxing Board of Control (1935) an infant boxer held a BBBC licence to box. After one contest he was disqualified and in accordance with BBBC rules his purse with held. He claimed that the contract was not binding on him so the purse could not be withheld. The courts held that the contract was substantially to his benefit so the BBBC was within its rights to withhold the purse.

In addition to common law there are some statutory restrictions covering minors. The Children and Young Persons Act of 1933 and the employment of Children Act 1973 regulate the employment of those minors below school leaving age (16). These Acts prevent the employment of any person under 13. Between the ages of 13-16 a minor may be employed in part time work subject to the restrictions as to the number of hours which may be worked and as to the time of such work. In addition, there are restrictions as to the employment in certain jobs, eg factories and mines. Between the ages of 16 and 18, minors are classed as young persons and in various legislative provisions restrictions are imposed upon the kind of work and the number of hours which such persons

27

may do. The Sex Discrimination Act 1986 removes most of the existing statutory provisions restricting womens hours of work. Clauses 4-7 of the Employment Bill 1988 (now 1996 ERA) seeks to modify the differences between working conditions for women. Clause 8 seeks to repeal the majority of decisions relating to employment of 'young persons'. The aims of these repeals is to remove restrictions on hours and holidays.

Temporary employees

Once an employee has completed the appropriate period for continuous employment (notably two years for unfair dismissal) he is eligible to claim the various statutory rights. An employee who is engaged expressly as a temporary employee to replace someone suspended on medical grounds or absent on maternity leave is not normally regarded as unfairly dismissed when the absent employee returns.

Probationary employees

An employee may be engaged subject to a probationary period, the employer retaining the right to terminate or confirm the contract within or at the end of the specified time. Once the employee has completed the stated time he is eligible to present a complaint of unfair dismissal. As with any other dismissal which is alleged to be unfair, the employer must show that he acted reasonably. Regular appraisals are seen as necessary evidence by tribunals in order to demonstrate that the employee under probation knew he may be dismissed.

Employees on fixed term contracts

Under such contracts employment rights depend whether the contracts can be aggregated in order to give the employee continuous employment. There is no statutory definition of fixed term contract. However, following the decision in BBC v. Dixon (1979) it is clear that a fixed term contract is not fixed if it contains a clause for early termination. A fixed term contact is one which expires on a particular date, rather than on the performance of a task or the happening of an event.

Government training schemes

The status of persons on these schemes depends on its nature. For example, Youth Training Schemes are aimed primarily at training as its objects are those of work experience and learning. Therefore a person on such a scheme is not an employee.

Clearly, if a person is an employee under the scheme then service with an employer will count towards continuous employment. However, in schemes where the person is not an employee, previous training will not count towards continuity.

Persons over retiring age

The law in this area has recently been changed because of the European Court of Justice decision in Marshall v. Southampton and South West Hampshire Area Health Authority. (1986) This decision meant that the equal treatment directive was directly applicable to state employees, but legislation was required to provide a remedy for private sector employees. The decision concerned men and women being required to retire at different ages which the ECJ held to be discriminatory. The response of the Government was to pass the Sex Discrimination Act 1986 which gave effect to the decision in Marshall but also made other amendments.

4. TERMS OF EMPLOYMENT CONTRACT

Significance of the terms of contract

In any dispute between an employer and employee, the terms of the contract are of considerable significance in that one party may have a right to take legal action against the other in respect of any breach of contract. Of more importance is the significance of the terms of contract when an action for unfair dismissal is brought. In such a case, although the question of whether one or more parties has broken the contract is of considerable importance, other considerations arise-notably whether the employer acted reasonably in dismissing the employee.

Prior to the introduction of the remedy of unfair dismissal, an employer could always terminate the contract provided that he gave proper notice. The employee would have no recourse in law.

Sources of the terms of the contract

The terms of the contract of employment may be derived from a number of sources: minimum statutory standards; express statements of the parties; collective agreements; works rules books; custom; duties of employees; duties of employers.

It should be noted that, by virtue of the 1996 Employment Rights Act , an employer is under an obligation to supply his employees with a written statement containing information as to certain terms of the contract of employment.

Minimum Statutory Standards

In effect all those statutory rights and duties which apply to the employer/employee relationship may be said to form part of every contract of employment except those to which the statutory provisions do not apply. With very few exceptions it is not possible for parties to contract out of statutory provisions.

Minimum terms orders

Certain bodies, notably wage councils, are empowered to make orders which take effect as part of individual contracts of employment and are enforceable as such. It should be noted that the powers of wage councils were limited by the Wages Act 1986, itself consolidated by the 1996 Employment Rights Act.

Express statements of the parties

Nature of express statements. an express statement, in this context, is a statement, either oral or written, made by the employer to the employee (or vice versa) concerning the terms of the contract. Such statements may include letters of appointment, formal contracts drawn up by the employer, verbal statements as to the terms and conditions of employment upon which the person is to be employed (as to wages hours holidays etc) or other statements.

If an express statement is made before the parties enter into the contract of employment, it forms part of the contract and may not be subsequently altered without the mutual consent of the parties. If one party deviates from the agreed pre-contractual terms, that party is in breach of contract unless the other consents to the deviation either expressly or by deviation.

Post contractual statements. Post contractual statements do not form part of the contract of employment unless the parties expressly or implicitly agree that such a statement doe~ become part of the contract. If an employee is employed upon certain terms which are not stated prior to the commencement of the contract and he is subsequently given a written statement which differs from the original terms the written statement does

31

not supersede the written terms because the written statement is not to be regarded as contractual but merely as evidence of the contract.

Collective agreements

The term 'collective agreement' has a particular definition in s 178 (1) of the Trade Unions and Labour Relations (consolidation) Act 1992 but in general terms it may be described as an agreement between a trade union and an employer or employers association which deals, amongst other things, with the terms and conditions of employment of employees of the employer who is a party to the agreement. A collective agreement must be considered at two levels:

a) its effect as between the parties to it;

b) Its effect upon the individual contract of employment of the employees who are the object of the agreement.

It has been estimated that 75% of all employees have their terms and conditions of employment determined by collective agreements and it is therefore important to know the extent to which as a matter of law, such agreements form part of the individual contract of employment. this is sometimes referred to as the 'normative' effect of collective agreements. Several arguments have been advanced to suggest that a collective agreement must automatically be regarded as forming part of the contracts of employment of those employees to whom the agreement refers; but these arguments have generally been refuted by the courts.

The correctness of this view has been put under pressure by the Court of Appeal decision in Marley v Forward Trust Group Ltd (1986) M was employed as a field supervisor in F's Bristol office. His terms and conditions of employment incorporated the terms of a collective agreement with ASTMS, and included both a mobility and redundancy clause, the latter allowing a six month trial period. However, the final clause of the agreement stated that the agreement is binding in honour only.

F closed their Bristol office and M worked in London, under the terms of the agreement, for a trial period. he found the job unsuitable and sought a redundancy payment. Both the IT and the EAT rejected his claim on the ground that the agreement was stated to be binding in honour only and was, accordingly, unenforceable. The Court of Appeal rejected this and held that the terms of an unenforceable collective agreement can be incorporated into contract so of employment and are then enforceable against the individual employee. The unenforceable nature of the agreement was limited to the parties to the agreement, in this case the employer and the union.

Express incorporation. It is fairly well established that it is possible to incorporate a collective agreement into an individual contract of employment if the contract expressly provides that this is to be the case. In National Coal Board v Galley (1958) it was held that a clause of a collective agreement which stated that colliery deputies would work 'such days or part days in each week as may reasonably be required by the employer' could be regarded as being part of the original contracts of employment because the contracts of the deputies referred to that collective agreement as being the source of the terms of the contracts.

It should be noted that the written statement supplied pursuant to the 1992 Act permits the employer to refer an employee to a document, such as a collective agreement, as being the source of certain terms of the contract of employment. The leading case on this issue is Robertson and Jackson v British Gas Corporation (1983). Two employees employed as gas meter readers were told, by letter, that incentive bonus scheme conditions would apply to the work. the employees were also given a

33

written statement of terms of employment which stated that the provisions of the collective agreement would apply to their renumeration-and that any bonuses will 'be calculated in accordance with the rules of the scheme in force at the time'.

The employers gave notice terminating the scheme on the ground that it had no legal force. No new scheme was negotiated and no bonus payments were received. The employees sued for loss of wages. Held; although the collective agreement was not binding between the union and employers, it had been incorporated into the contracts of employment. The employers could not unilaterally alter the scheme and therefore the employees were entitled to the bonus payments.

The importance of the case is that the letter of appointment was the contract and not the written statement. Therefore all the relevant documents are pertinent in determining this issue and it is clear that a 1192 Act statement is not necessarily conclusive.

A collective agreement may also expressly become part of a contract of employment by virtue of statutory provisions. There are a number of situations where this is possible:

a) under the 1992 Act. Provision is made for application to be made to the Secretary of State for the approval of dismissals procedures agreements. Such agreements, which replace the right to claim unfair dismissal for those employees covered, form part of the terms of employment of those employees within their ambit;

b) under the 1992 Act, a collective agreement may be made which substitutes for the right to claim a redundancy payment under the provisions of the 1996 Act, a right to claim under the collective agreement . If such an agreement approved by the Secretary of State, it forms part of the terms of employment of those employees to whom it applies;

c) under of the 1992 Act a collective agreement may be made which substitutes for the right to a guarantee payment under the provisions of the 1996 Act, a right to claim under the collective agreement. It should be noted that where the terms of a collective agreement are expressly incorporated and varied by consent between the unions and employers the new terms become incorporated into the individual contracts of employment; however, unilateral variation or abrogation of the agreement by one party does not have a corresponding effect on individual employment contracts;(Robertson a and Jackson v British Gas (1983).

Works rule-books

A works rule book can take a number of forms in so far as it may consist of an actual book given to each employee when he enters employment or at some subsequent date. These rules relate to disciplinary action, suspension, dismissal for conduct etc. Safety procedures are normally incorporated. S 3 of the Employment Rights Act 1996 states that an employer must give details of disciplinary and grievance procedures to an employee when taking up employment.

As far as the effect on contract goes, if the employer gives the employee the rule book, or expressly refers to it before a contract is signed then it is considered to be part of the contract. In Petrie v Macfisheries (1940) a notice was posted on the wall of the work place stating the circumstances in which sick pay would be paid. The plaintiff claimed that it was not part of his contract. The defendants case was upheld as the rule concerning sick pay was deemed to be incorporated into his contract as a result of his continued working at the place.

Not all works rules will be part of the contract, particularly where there are numerous rules contained in the relevant documentation, some for example may be out of date and inappropriate. This is well illustrated by the decision in Secretary of State for Employment v ASLEF (1972) a case concerning the rule book of British Rail, where Lord Denning said ' Each man signs a form saying that he will abide by the rules but these rules are in no way terms of the contract of employment. They are only instructions to a man as to how to do his work'.

Custom

Custom plays a significant part in employment law. It seems that there are four different categories of custom which may form part of a contract of employment.

a) Custom of a particular place of work.

b) Custom of an industry or trade.

c) Custom of a specific geographical locality.

d) Customary conduct of the parties to the contract of employment.

a) See Marshall v English Electric !1945)

b) See Sagar v Ridehalgh (1931) and Davson v France (1959)

c) Sagar v Ridehalgh

d) Mears v Safecar Security (1982)

Implied duties of the employee

Into every contract of employment are implied a number of obligations in so far as these are not inconsistent with the express terms of the individual contract of employment. These duties are based on principles developed by the courts in the decided cases.

Implied duties may be classified as follows:

a) to be willing and ready to work;

b) to use reasonable care and skill;

c) to obey lawful orders;

d) to take care of the employers property;

e) to act in good faith.

To be ready and willing to work

The fundamental duty owed to an employer by an employee is to be turn up to work and to work at the direction of the employer in return for wages. Two interesting cases have arisen in relation to this. Miles v Wakefield Metropolitan District Council (1987) M was a superintendent registrar of Births deaths and marriages, working 37 hours per week, three of which were on Saturday morning. As part of industrial action, M refused to carry out marriages on Saturday mornings, although he was willing to do his other work. Wages were deducted, M sued for lost wages and the employer won, with the House of Lords saying that where an employee refuses to perform the full range of duties and had been told that he would not be paid if he did not, then the employers were entitled to withhold the whole of his renumeration, (3Hrs) although he attended for work and carried out a substantial part of his duties.

To use reasonable care and skill

This has two aspects:

a) The duty not to be unduly negligent.

b) The duty to be reasonably competent.

If an employee is negligent during the course of his work, he may be regarded as being in breach of contract. In Lister v Romford Ice and Cold Storage Ltd (1957) a lorry driver, employed by the company, carelessly reversed his lorry and injured a fellow employee, who was his father. The employers paid damages to the father but claimed indemnity from the son, because of negligence. This was held to be the case.

Duty to be reasonably competent

If an employee is incompetent this may be a breach of contract. In Hamer v Cornelius (1858) this was held to be the case.

To obey lawful orders

An employee is under a duty to obey all the lawful orders of his employer, i.e. those which are within the scope of the contract. In Price v Mouat (1862) a lace salesman was ordered to card (pack) lace but he refused and was dismissed without notice. He claimed wrongful dismissal and this was held because the order was not one which was within the scope of his contract.

An employee, therefore, is not obliged to do any act which is deemed to fall outside the ambit of his individual contract of employment. The question of the introduction of new technology has caused problems here and must be linked to the scope of managerial prerogative in introducing new work techniques. In Cresswell v Board of Inland Revenue (1984) the Revenue wished to introduce a computer system to assist with the PAYE system. The majority of the work associated with the system had been done manually. Did the employers have the ability to change the nature of the working system Did the employers have the ability to change the nature of the working system? Held: employees were expected to adopt the new methods and techniques in performing their contracts if the employer provided the necessary training in new skills.

To take care of employers property

An employer is under an obligation to take reasonable care of his employers property. In Superflux v Plaisted (1958) the defendant had been in charge of a team of vacuum cleaner salesmen and had negligently allowed fourteen cleaners to be stolen from his van. Held: he was in breach of his contract of employment.

To act in good faith

This implied duty has several different aspects which together form the basis of a relationship of trust. There is the duty not to make a secret profit, i.e. not to accept bribes. This principal was clear from the case of Reading v AG (1951) which concerned a member of the armed forces, in which Lord Normand said:

---though the relation of a member of his majesty's forces is not accurately described as that of a servant under a contract of service--he owes to the Crown a duty as full fiduciary as the duty of a servant to his master--and in consequence--all profits and advantages gained by the use of his military status are to be for the benefit of the Crown'.

(1932). However, there is one important exception, namely where the employment of that particular person is made more hazardous by virtue of an undisclosed defect on part of the employee.

Covenants in restraint of trade

A covenant in restraint of trade is a clause in a contract which purports to limit an employees rights to seek employment when and where he chooses upon leaving his employment. This is usually done as a protective measure by an employer when he might suffer as a result of disclosure of confidential information or for other such reasons. There are difficulties however, in enforcing such covenants and the employer has to demonstrate that the covenant is justified. A court will look at such factors as time that the covenant runs, geographical area that it covers and public interest when considering the reasonableness of such covenants.

If a covenant is found to be unreasonable, the contract as a whole is not necessarily regarded as void, unless it is impossible to distinguish the covenant from the rest of the contract. If the covenant can be severed from the rest of the contract, without altering the nature of the agreement, the unreasonable clause may be struck out: see Commercial Plastics Ltd v Vincent (1965).

If an employer breaks the contract of employment by wrongfully dismissing an employee, the employee may disregard any covenant in the contract which purports to limit his right to seek employment elsewhere: see General Billposting v Atkinson (1909).

Patents

At common law, unless the contract dealt with the matter, an employee would not normally be entitled to the benefit of any invention made by him if to allow him to do so would be a contravention of the implied duty of the employee to act in good faith. The Patents Act 1977, ss-39-47, gives ownership of an invention to the employee inventor unless the invention was made in the course of the duties for which he was employed. Any disputes are dealt with by the patents court.

Duties of the employer

By virtue of common law, and a number of statutory provisions, employers have a considerable number of obligations towards employees. The main examples are:

a) to pay contractually agreed renumeration

An employer is under no obligation to provide work as long as renumeration is paid. This however, has been questioned in recent times, particularly in relation to skilled employees. Lord Denning said, in Langston v AUEW (1973): 'in these days an employer, when employing a skilled man, is bound to provide him with work. By which I mean that the man should be given the opportunity of doing his work when it is available and when he is ready and willing to do it'. Therefore, a failure to provide work of a nature that the employee is used to could be regarded as constructive dismissal.

There are three exceptions to the rule, one is piecework, the second is where the nature of the employment is such that the actual performance of the work forms part of the consideration supplied by the employer, the employee may be entitled to compensation over and above the contractual wages. These situations are sometimes referred to as 'names in lights' clauses. the other exception is when an employee is taking part in limited industrial action.

b) to observe provisions relating to sick pay

An employer may have an obligation by virtue of a term in the contract of employment to pay sick pay to employees. Such an obligation may arise as a result of an express term or an obligation may arise under an implied term. The principles governing the implication of terms relating to sick pay were discussed by the court of appeal in Mears v Safecar Security Ltd (1982) where it was held that there is no general presumption of an implied right to sick pay.

Since April 1983 all employers have had a statutory obligation under the Social Security and Housing Benefits Act 1982 to pay Statutory Sick Pay to their employees. The employer pays the employee his statutory sick pay and, until recently then recouped those payments through his National Insurance Contributions. By the Statutory Sick Pay Act 1994 only those employers who pay less than £2000 in National Insurance contributions can now recoup such payments.

In outline the scheme provides that a qualifying employee is entitled to SSP for the first 28 weeks of sickness and after that period he will receive state sickness benefit. Certain employees are excluded from the scheme, including pensioners, persons employed for less than three months, persons who do not pay NI contributions and persons who are not employed due to a trade union dispute at their workplace.

c) to treat employees with trust and confidence

In Courtaulds Northern Textiles Ltd v Andrew (1978) the EAT held'--- there is an implied term in a contract of employment that employers will not, without reasonable and proper cause, conduct themselves in a manner calculated or likely to destroy or seriously damage the relationship of trust or confidence between the parties' A series of cases have firmly established this principle.

d) to observe provisions relating to holidays

The written statement provided to employees under the 1996 Act ought to state the holidays to which the employee is entitled and whether the employee is entitled to holiday pay and if so how much. There are relatively few statutory provisions. Section 94 of the Factories Act 1961 provides that women and young persons who work in factories must have a holiday on bank holidays and the Wages Councils and Agricultural Wages Board have the power to fix holiday pay for workers in the industries over which they have jurisdiction.

e) to observe provisions relating to hours of work

The hours which an employee is required to work are determined by reference to his individual contract of employment and the written statement supplied to the employee ought to state these. There are certain statutory provisions, section 7 of the Sex Discrimination Act 1986 removes the majority of limitations imposed concerning the hours to be worked by women. Part V1 of the Factories Act 1961 limits the working day to no more than nine hours for young people. There are no general limitations on persons over 18, although certain specific restrictions exist in areas of particular work, eg, coach and lorry driving.

f) to permit employees time off work for public duties

The 1996 Act provides that an employer must permit an employee to have time off work for the purpose of carrying out work as:

a) Justice of the peace (work relating to this)

b) a member of a local authority

c) a member of a statutory tribunal

d) a member of a regional health authority or an Area or District educational establishment.

e) a member of a governing body of a local authority maintained educational establishment.

A number of categories of employees are excluded from this right, under the 1996 Act.

Under the 1996 Act a pregnant employee has the right not to be unreasonably refused time off work with pay in order that she may keep appointments for receiving anti natal care. Evidence of pregnancy and appointment must be produced if requested by employer.

g) to indemnify employees

An employer is under an obligation to indemnify his employees in respect of any expenses incurred in performing their duties under the contract of employment, for example travelling expenses. In certain circumstances however, the employee may be under an obligation to indemnify the employer for any loss sustained: see Lister v Romford Ice and Cold Storage Ltd (1957)

h) to provide references

There is no obligation on an employer to supply character references for employees although, in practice, employers normally supply them since failure to provide one speaks for itself. The legal effect of references means that if an employer does provide one, it ought to be correct for several reasons:

a) Defamation. If a reference is defamatory, the defamed employee may bring an action against the employer, although the defence of qualified privilege is available to the employer, ie, the employer may show that the statements were made without malice.

b) negligent misstatement. A person who acts in reliance on a reference which has been issued negligently may apparently bring an action to recover any loss sustained as a consequence.

i) to insure employees and other duties.

5. RENUMERATION

Renumeration

A number of legislative provisions exist affecting renumeration to employees and the way it is paid.

Wages Act 1986, consolidated by the 1996 Employment Rights Act.

The scope of this Act (1996) is wide. By S8 of the 1996 Act every employee who works eight hours or more a week has the right to an itemised pay statement. It must state the gross and net amount of pay and the amounts deducted and the purpose of the deduction.

The 1986 Wages Act, now consolidated by the 1996 Act defined wages in very broad terms. Wages means 'any sum payable to a worker by his employer in connection with his employment and includes any fee, bonus commission, holiday pay or other emolument referable to his employment, whether payable under his contract or otherwise...' However, a number of payments are specifically excluded and these include expenses and redundancy payments.

One of the effects of the 1986 Wages Act was to abolish the requirement that workers be paid in 'coin of the realm'. We now have the concept of cashless pay. The 1996 Act only allows deductions from wages if it made by virtue of a statutory provision or by a provision of the workers contract, or if the work has previously indicated his agreement in writing to it. There are much stricter controls on retail workers who are defined as being workers who carry out retail transactions directly with members of the public or with fellow workers. Under the Act any deductions in respect of cash shortages or stock deficiencies must not exceed one tenth of the gross amount of wages payable on that day. Also, any sum demanded of such a worker in respect of these losses shall not exceed the 10% figure.

Wages Councils

The original 1986 Act weakened the powers of Wages Councils, introduced originally by the Wages Councils Act 1979. The Secretary of State no longer has power to establish new wages councils.

Existing wages councils are, therefore, weak and limited to fixing a basic minimum hourly rate, overtime entitlement and a limit on deductions from pay that an employer can make for living accommodation. Section 12 (2) of the 1986 Act
removed young people under the age of 21 from the scope of the regulations.

Guarantee payments

Unless a contract of employment expressly or implicitly allows for it, an employee who is laid off is entitled to be paid during the period of such lay off. To be eligible to receive such a payment, an employee must:

a) have been continuously employed for at least one month when the lay off occurs;

b) have been laid off for the whole of his working hours on a day he is normally required to work;

c) not have unreasonably refused an offer of alternative employment which was suitable in all the circumstances;

d) have complied with any reasonable requirements imposed by the employer with a view to ensuring that his services are available;

e) not have been laid off because of a strike, lock out or other industrial action involving any employee of the employer or of any associated employer; and

f) have been available for employment on that day.

An employee who is entitled to a guarantee payment is entitled to be paid at the guaranteed hourly rate, subject to a maximum limit for one day. There is a maximum entitlement of five guarantee payments in any period of three months.

Suspension from work on medical grounds

For the legislation governing suspension from work on medical grounds, ss 19-22 of the 1978 Act as amended by the Employment Act 1982 and see Protection (medical suspension) Order 1985 (these were consolidated by the Employment Rights Act 1996 and s 64 now deals)
The above Act provides that an employee who is suspended from work is entitled to be paid by his employer if that suspension is in consequence of a requirement imposed under certain statutory provisions or a recommendation made in a Code of Practice issued or approved under s 16 of the Health and safety at Work Act 1974. There are certain eligibility criteria concerning length of employment etc. An employee is entitled to be paid for up to twenty six weeks of such suspension.

Maternity pay and leave

Apart from important protection from unfair dismissal because of pregnancy, the Employment Rights Act 1996 provides four further protections in relation to pregnancy - the right to maternity leave, the right to return to work after maternity leave, the right to time off for ante-natal care and the right to maternity pay.

Right to maternity leave

Section 71 implements the EC Pregnancy Directive (Council Directive 92/85/EEC). The section gives all pregnant employees a general right to maternity leave. It gives the right to the benefit of all the terms of her contract excluding pay. The period of the leave is 14 weeks. The employer must be informed at least 21 days before leave commences that she intends to exercise her rights, and of the date her absence will commence and must be in writing if the employer requires. The employer can request a certificate of proof of pregnancy and expected date of birth.

If the employee has already a contractual right to maternity pay/leave, she may exercise her right to the more favourable. If there is a redundancy situation during the leave period and it is not practicable because of the redundancy for the employer to continue to employ her under her existing contract, she is entitled to be offered a suitable vacancy before her employment ends. If a woman intends to return to work before the end of maternity leave, seven days notice must be given.

Right to return

By s 79 a woman who has been continuously employed by her employer for two years by the eleventh week before her expected date of confinement is entitled to up to 40 weeks maternity leave and the right to return to work after the birth. The 40 weeks comprises 11 weeks before birth and 29 after.

To exercise her right to return, the employee must comply with strict notice provisions contained within s 80 of the 1996 Act.

Time off for ante-natal care

To qualify for this right the employee must have made an appointment for ante-natal care on the advice of a doctor, midwife or health visitor. The employer may not refuse time off for the first visit, but for further appointments, the employer may ask for a certificate or appointment card or other evidence.

Statutory maternity pay

The Social Security Act of 1996 and the Statutory Maternity Pay regulations of the same year entitle certain employees to statutory maternity pay. If the employee has been working for the employer for 26 weeks by the 15th week before the expected week of confinement, she is entitled to SMP for 18 weeks. She is entitled to nine tenths of her pay for the first six weeks of the 18 and the Higher rate of Statutory Sick Pay for the further 18.

Insolvency of employer

For the legislation governing the insolvency of an employer, the Employment Rights Act 1996 applies. See also s 175 and schedule 6 of the Insolvency Act 1986.

If an employer becomes insolvent an employee acquires certain rights.

a) He becomes a preferential creditor in respect of up to four months unpaid wages or a maximum set by the Secretary of State. Certain other payments are also deemed to be preferential debts including guarantee payments, payment for time off for trade union activities and payment for ante -natal care. The employee is entitled to claim payments of certain amounts due to him from his employer from the Secretary of State who will pay them out of the redundancy fund. The classes of debt for which payment may be made include arrears of wages (up to a maximum of 8 weeks) holiday pay (6 weeks) and wages during the statutory minimum notice period.

6. TRADE UNIONS

The statutory definition of a trade union is now found in s1 (a) of the Trade Union and Labour relations (Consolidation) Act 1992 which provides that a trade union means:
'an organisation (whether temporary or permanent) which consists wholly or mainly of workers of one or more descriptions and whose principle purposes includes the regulations of relations between workers of that description or those descriptions and employers or employers associations'

The definition is wide and concentrates on the purpose of that body. Thus a body which had a subsidiary purpose of regulating relations between workers and employers would not be a trade union. In Midland Cold Storage v Turner, 1972, a shop stewards committee drawn from various trade unions was not a trade union within the definition since its purpose was to discuss whether industrial action should be taken and it did not engage in negotiation with employers.

Listing

The concept of maintaining some kind of voluntary listing of trade unions was introduced by the Trade Union Act 1871. Such a list continued with the compliance of the unions until the Industrial Relations Act 1971 which introduced a very different system of registration. Under that Act, only unions who registered were entitled to statutory immunity against certain industrial action. In addition, any unions who registered under the 1971 Act had to 'pay' for their immunity by subjecting their constitution, rules and accounts to outside scrutiny.

Union opposition to the Act demonstrated itself by a policy of non compliance and very few unions registered. Those that did were expelled from the TUC. The Trade Unions and Labour Relations Act 1974, which repealed the 1971 Act Reintroduced the concept of voluntary listing similar to that under the 1871 Act. The provisions are now in s 2 and 123 of the Trade Union and Labour Relations (Consolidation) Act 1992. These provide that the Certification Officer shall maintain a voluntary list of trade unions and employers associations.

Whilst there are few advantages to being listed, it is the first requisite to obtaining a certificate of independence. This certificate brings considerable advantages.

Independent Trade Unions

The Certification Officer can issue any union on the list with a certificate of independence. Such a certificate is conclusive evidence that a union is independent. An independent union is one which is not under the control of an employer or liable to interference from an employer arising out of financial, material or other support.

This definition was elaborated in the Court of Appeal and Squib UK Staff Association v Certification officer (1979).

Recognition of Trade Unions

The major purpose of any union is to protect and promote its members interests and the way it will do this is by collective bargaining. Recognised Trade Unions have certain rights. Recognised Trade Unions are entitled to information for collective bargaining purposes. Although there is now no formal way that a union can demand recognition from an employer, recognition procedures having been abolished by the Employment Act 1980, recognition is vitally important for it to perform its functions.

The above discussion raises a the question of when is a union recognised. The starting point is the statutory definition in s 178 (3) of the 1992 Act which defines recognition as 'recognition of the union by the employer....to any extent, for the purposes of collective bargaining.. However, this is vague and unhelpful and does not constitute formal recognition. Despite Article 15 of the European Social Charter which takes the position that collective bargaining should be promoted, it seems a long way off. The present Trade Union Reform and Employment Rights Act 1993 removes the statutory duty of ACAS to encourage the extension, development and reform of collective bargaining.

The Political Fund

The labour movement in the early years was reliant on a sympathetic Liberal Government to give it legal protection. While this partnership worked well, it soon became apparent that the movement required working class MPs who would fully understand the problems and provide true representation in Parliament. As such the movement decided to fund such MPs through union funds. This subsidy was declared illegal by the House of Lords and again a sympathetic liberal government came to the unions rescue with the passage of the Trade Unions Act 1913. Substantial amendments were made to the Act by the Trade Union Act 1984 although at the time the government renounced its intention of reintroducing the contracting in system but insisted that unions ballot their members every ten years to see if the members wished the political fund to be maintained.

The Trade Union Reform and Employment Rights Act 1993, however, introduced the contracting in system. Section 68 of the 1992 Act now provides that an employer shall not deduct union subscriptions from a workers wages unless the worker has authorised the deduction in writing within the past three years, the employer has notified the worker of any increases at least one month before the deduction is made and the employer has notified the employee of his right to withdraw the authorization at any time.

The 1993 Act also introduced stringent balloting procedures in relation to the maintenance of a political fund, requiring such ballots to be conducted in the same way as the ballot for the election of trade union officials.

The present law is contained in the 1992 Trade Union and Labour Relations (consolidation) Act 1992. Section 71(1) lays down that payment for political purposes whether made directly or indirectly can be made only from a separate political fund. Political Purposes are then defined in Section 72(1) as the expenditure of money:

a) on any contribution to the funds of, or on the payment of expenses incurred directly or indirectly, by a political party;

b) on the provisions of any service or property for use by or on behalf of any political party;

c) in connection with the registration of electors, the candidature of any person, the selection of any candidate or the holding of any ballot by the union in connection with any election to a political office;

d) on the maintenance of any holder of a political office;

e) on the holding of any conference by or on behalf of a political party or of any other meeting the purpose of which is the transaction of business in connection with a political party;

f) on the production, publication or distribution of any literature, document, film, sound recording or advertisement the main purpose of which is to persuade people to vote for a political party or candidate or persuade them not to vote for a political party or candidate.

The 1992 Act lays down conditions for the establishment and maintenance of a political fund. A political resolution must be passed by a majority of members voting on a ballot conducted according to the provisions of the act, that is, it must comply with the political ballot rules as approved by the certification officer. The Certification Officer cannot approve such rules unless they include the appointment of an independent scrutineer, entitlement of all the members to vote and the rules provide for a scrutineers report.

The Rule Book

The rules of a trade union form the terms of a contract between it and its members. They become part of a contract in the same way that collective agreements become part of the individuals employment contract between the employer and the employee. Apart from contract, other areas of law impact on the union rule book. Statute has now impacted in a variety of ways. By s 69 of the Trade Union and Labour Relations (Consolidation) Act 1992, for example, there is a rule in all union rule books allowing a member to terminate his membership on the giving of reasonable notice. In addition, both the Sex Discrimination Act 1975 and the Race Relations Act 1976 render it unlawful to discriminate on the grounds of race or sex, in relation to membership.

The Right to Information

The Employment Protection Act 1975 recognised that to be able to collectively bargain effectively, unions needed certain information from the employer and as such the Act introduced a right to receive certain information. This right has been retained and the provisions are now ss 181-5 of the Trade union and Labour Relations (Consolidation) Act 1992.

The employer only has to disclose information in relation to those matters for which the union is recognised for collective bargaining.

ACAS has produced a code of practice (ACAS Code of Practice 2: Disclosure of information to Trade Unions for Collective Bargaining Purposes) which in paragraph 11 lists the type of information it would be good industrial relations practice to disclose. This includes pay and befits, conditions of service, manpower, performance and financial information. Section 182 of the Act provides restrictions on information that the employer does not have to disclose, such as information in the interests of national security. Section 183 provides a remedy for a trade union where the employer has failed to provide information. The remedy is complaint to the Central Arbitration Committee (CAC). Sections 184-185 further strengthen the complaints procedure.

The closed Shop

There was no legal control over the closed shop until the Industrial Relations Act 1971. This Act introduced the concept of unfair dismissal. In 1988, the Employment Act 1988 rendered any dismissal for union or non union membership unfair in any circumstances (now s 152 of the Trade Union and Labour Relations (consolidation) Act 1992. As such, while post entry closed shops can still exist, no one can be legally compelled to join a union.

The legislation of 1988 however, did nothing to prevent pre-entry closed shops operating, pre entry meaning insistence on membership of a union before being offered employment. The Employment Act 1990 finally destroyed any protection which existed for the pre entry closed shop by rendering it illegal to discriminate on the grounds of membership of a union prior to employment. This is now ss 137-1243 of the Trade Union and Labour Relations (Consolidation) Act 1992.

57

7.THE RIGHTS OF TRADE UNION MEMBERS

Enforcement of the Rule Book

While there is a special statutory protection for union members in relation to rules relating to discipline and exclusion and expulsion a member must rely on the common law to enforce any other rule in the rule book. Although the rule book forms the contract of membership between the individual member and union, this will not always provide him with a remedy. Rather, the trade union member is treated in a similar way to a shareholder in a company and as such his remedies against the union are similar to those imposed against incorporated associations.

The simple proposition is that as a union as an entity only exists as a creation of statute, its legal capacity to act comes from its rules and to some extent from statute. As such, if the rules or statute lay down when a union can act then should the union act without fulfilling the requirements it has no capacity to do so and as such its actions are ultra vires.

Exclusion and Expulsion

We have already seen that essentially a trade union cannot legally enforce a closed shop and therefore it may appear that any discussion on exclusion and expulsion may be redundant. Closed shops still exist, however, in certain industries and whereas the employee may have a remedy against the employer for refusing to employ him because he is not a trade union member, that will not help him if the reason he is not such a member is that the union do not want him or have expelled him.

Discipline of union members

Although expulsion from the union may be imposed as a disciplinary sanction, it is not the only form of sanction imposed by a union on its members. The courts insist however, that the union must comply with the natural rules of justice when exercising sanctions against a member. These are:

1. Notice. A person must be given adequate notice of the charge against him and the potential penalty so that he has an opportunity to answer it. In Annamunthodo v Oilfield Workers Union (1961) the plaintiff knew that he was being charged with making allegations against the union presidents and knew he could be fined. He did not know that such conduct was treated as prejudicial to the union and that he could be expelled. It was held that his subsequent expulsion was void.

2. Opportunity to put his case. A person must be given the opportunity to put his side of the case and answer any charges against him.

3. Unbiased hearing. The hearing should be unbiased.

4. Representation. The rules do not specifically state that a person should be allowed legal representation and it appears from Enderby Town Football Club v Football Association (1971) that such representation can be specifically excluded by the rules as long as some kind of representative is allowed.

Commissioner for the Rights of Trade Union Members

The above office was created by the Employment Act 1988 and the provisions are now in the 1992 Act. The Commissioner may give assistance to individuals in the following Matters:

a) failure to hold a ballot before industrial action;

b) failure to permit members to inspect union accounts;

c) unlawful application of union property by trustees

d) failure to maintain a register of members

e) failure to comply with balloting provisions in relation to the political fund;

f) failure to bring or continue proceedings to recover property used to unlawfully indemnify an individual;

g) failure to comply with the balloting provisions in relation to the trade union elections;

h) application of union funds for unlawful political purposes;

i) alleged breaches of union rules in relation to appointment to any office, disciplinary proceedings, authorization or endorsement of industrial action, balloting, the application of the unions funds or property, the imposition or collection of levies for industrial action purposes and the constitution or proceedings of any committee, conference or body of the union.

Action Short of Dismissal

The law affords a certain amount of protection against an employer. The law protects an employee who is dismissed for trade union membership or non membership or for taking part in trade union activities at the appropriate time. Protection against dismissal is complemented by protection against action short of dismissal for one of the above grounds and is now found in s 146 of the Trade Union and Labour Relations (Consolidation) Act 1992. Should a tribunal find a complaint well founded it can make a declaration to that effect and award compensation to offset any loss caused by the action. In addition, either the complainant or the employer may join the union as a co-respondent if it was union pressure which induced the action and the tribunal can order that some or all of the compensation be paid by the union.

Refusal to grant a benefit on these grounds is action short of dismissal for the purposes of protection. In NCB v Ridgeway (1987) it was held that refusal to giver a pay rise negotiated with the UDM to NUM Members was unlawful action short of dismissal. In other words it is sufficient if the employer discriminates against members of a particular union and it is not necessary to show discrimination against union members as a whole.

8.INDUSTRIAL ACTION

The present law on industrial action has had a chequered history. For many years the law was, to a large extent, non interventionist in this area. The main piece of legislation governing industrial action was the Trade Disputes Act 1906 which created the basic immunities.

Change came with the Conservative Government in the early 70's.. The Industrial Relations Act of 1971. The Act introduced a system of registration for trade unions and attacked the closed shop. Since 1979, there have been a number of reforms, ten pieces of legislation in all. Employment legislation overall is part of broader economic policy, that of the encouragement of market forces. Reduce the power of the unions and you remove the obstacles to competitiveness. The 1993 Labour Relations Act is the latest in a long line of legislation designed to weaken unions.

Industrial Action and the Contract of Employment

Virtually all forms of industrial action will constitute a breach of contract on the part of the employee. There are a number of forms, or types of industrial action.

Go Slow

A go slow is a breach of an implied term to work at a reasonable pace in the absence of justifying circumstances.

Work to rule

The leading case of **Secretary of State for Employment v Aslef (1972)** decided that such an action could constitute a breach of contract, as the employees were following a rule book set out by the employer which did not constitute a contract.

Overtime ban

Whether this action constitutes a breach of contract depends on whether the overtime is compulsory or voluntary and involves looking at the terms of the contract itself.

Blacking

This may take a variety of forms. If a reasonable order is given by the employer however, and the employee refuses to undertake the work then this can be seen as breach of contract. Another form of blacking may constitute refusing to work with ones fellow employees. In Bowes and Partners v Press (1894) miners refused an order to go down in a cage with a non unionist. It was held that their action was a breach of contract.

Strike without notice

A strike is a situation where an individual withdraws his labour and refuses to work. As such, he is in breach of contract by refusing to work.

Strike with notice

This area is complicated and a number of court cases have tried to determine whether a strike with notice is in fact breach of contract or resignation of the employee. One leading case is that of Miles v Wakefield Metropolitan District Council (1987) House of Lords where it was held that all industrial action is a repudiatory breach of contract since there is an intention to harm the employers business which goes fundamentally against the duty of loyalty and co-operation which the employee owes to the employer. If this view is correct and the intention behind the action is one of legality, it would suggest that any strike notice, whether of correct length or not is notice of a breach of contract and it will only be construed as notice to terminate if it is expressed to be so.

Trade Dispute

In terms of legal liabilities, it is of the utmost significance whether an act is done in contemplation or furtherance of a trade dispute' since the statutory immunities discussed below only apply in certain circumstances. If an act falls outside of a trade dispute, the immunities cease to operate and the full rigour of the law applies.

A trade dispute is defined as '... a dispute between workers and their employer which relates wholly or mainly to one or more of the following, that is to say:

a) terms and conditions of employment, or the physical condition in which any workers are required to work;

b) engagement or non engagement or termination or suspension or the duties of employment, of one or more workers;

c) allocation of work or the duties of employment as between workers or groups of workers;

d) matters of discipline

e) the membership or non membership of a trade union on the part of a worker;

f) facilities for officials of a trade union and

g) machinery for negotiation or consultation and other procedures, relating to any of the foregoing matters, including the recognition by employers or employers associations of the right of a trade union to represent workers in any such negotiations or consultation or ion the carrying out of such procedures'.

The above definition was introduced in 1982 and the present definition is narrower in two broad respects:

a) it extends only to disputes between workers and their employers. It does not embrace disputes between workers and workers.

b) the dispute must relate wholly or mainly to one of the matters mentioned in the 1993 Act.

Industrial action and the economic torts

Inducement of a breach of contract

Since the passage of the Employment Act 1982, trade unions are no longer immune from suit in tort. If a person induces a party to break that contract, the injured party may sue the inducer in tort for inducement of a breach of contract. However, in order to be liable, the defendant must have induced an unlawful act. If the unlawful act is a breach of contract, the contract must exist and be valid in law at the time of inducement. (Long v Smithson) 1918.Knowledge and intention are also necessary requisites for an unlawful act.

Further, the concept of inducement is important here. The word inducement implies pressure being put on an unwilling party, but what amount of inducement doers the law require. The key fact seems to be the intention of the person communicating, or the speaker and if that person intends that the contract be broken then there is an inducement even if the speaker is merely communicating a set of facts to the recipient of the information.

Intimidation

The basis of this tort is the use of unlawful threats to induce a party to commit a lawful act which causes injury, classically, threatening industrial action which causes the employer to lawfully terminate an employees contract. The requirements of the tort are unlawful threats, intention to harm, causation and loss to the plaintiff.

Conspiracy

This tort consists of two forms, the first simple conspiracy to injure and the second to use unlawful means. The existence of a simple conspiracy was recognised in Mogul Steamship v Mcgregor and Co (1892) when the House of Lords stated that the tort had three elements: a combination of at least two persons; intentionally causing loss; and the predominant purpose is not to further a legitimate interest. In addition, there must be an agreement to injure, not just a co-incidental action. This is different to criminal conspiracy where the intention to cause loss forms the basis of the offence even if no loss occurs.

Interference with a trade or business by unlawful means

This tort was declared to exist by the Court of Appeal in Hadmor Productions Limited v Hamilton (1981). In Hadmor it was alleged that ACCT officials threatened to persuade their members to refuse to transmit television programmes produced by Hadmor. Thames Television had acquired a licence to transmit the programmes but was under no contractual obligation to do so. Therefore, Hadmor had no contract to breach in this case. It was held, however, that a tort existed. Although the essence of a tort is unlawful means an intention to harm a plaintiff can also be a tort.

Economic duress

All industrial action is intended to put pressure on the employer. In contact law, economic pressure can amount to duress and, if proved, the contract can be avoided and any money paid under it recovered. Normally this argument is not used against unions as they have no contract with the employer. However, in Universe Tankships of Monrovia v International Transport Workers Federation (1983) such a contract did exist. The Federation, as part of its campaign against flags of convenience, insisted that employers pay a sum into the unions welfare fund as the price for lifting the blacking of a ship. As soon as the blacking was lifted the employers sought to recover the money they had paid, arguing the payment had been made under duress and therefore was avoidable. The House of Lords said that if the action had been protected by the immunities, that is, if it was in contemplation or furtherance of a trade dispute, the employer could not circumvent the protection by bringing an action for duress. However, since payment into a welfare fund is not a recognised trade dispute, there was no such protection and the employers action succeeded.

Statutory Immunities

It can be seen from the above that unions can commit a great number of economic torts when they take industrial action, but we have also seen that in some circumstances there will be statutory immunity from liability for the commission of certain torts. The immunity is now contained in s 219 of the Trade Union and Labour Relations (consolidation) Act 1992 which states:
"An act done by a person in contemplation or furtherance of a trade dispute is not actionable in tort on the ground only -

a) that it induces another person to break a contract or interferes or induces another person to interfere with its performance or

b) that it consists in his threatening that a contract (whether one to which he is a party or not) will be broken or its performance interfered with, or that he will induce another person to break a contract or interfere with its performance.

It will be sen therefore that protection is not afforded against the commission of any tort and that such torts as libel and slander, trespass, breach of statutory duty and so on have no immunity.

Trade dispute

The definition of a trade dispute is to be found in s 244(1) of the 1992 Act. This provides that the trade dispute is:

"a dispute between workers and their employer which relates wholly or mainly to....... terms and conditions of employment, or physical conditions, engagement or non engagement, or termination or suspension of employment, allocation of work, matters of discipline, membership or otherwise of a trade union, facilities for officials of trade unions and machinery for negotiation"

Trade union liability

The 1906 Trade Disputes Act introduced immunity from tortious liability for trade unions. This blanket immunity was removed by the Employment Act 1082 and now a union has the same immunity as its individual members. There is a statutory limit on the damages that can be awarded against a union, first introduced in 1982 and now contained in s 22 of the 1992 Consolidation Act. The amount of damages depends on the number of members the trade union has. If there are less than 5,000 the maximum is £10,000. Between 5,000 and 25,000 the maximum is £50,000. Between 25,000 and 50,000 the maximum is £125,000 and over 100,000 the limit is £250,000. Each separate action may result in the maximum being imposed. Therefore, if more than one employer takes action against the union then the limit can be imposed separately for each employer. Furthermore, the limit only applies to damages and not for fines for contempt. Thus in the NGA dispute against the Stockport messenger in 1984 the union was fined £675,000 for contempt.

Loss of trade union immunity

Trade Union Immunity depends on the protected torts being committed and the balloting and notice requirements being complied with. Breach of any of these conditions will render the union liable for any tortious wrongs committed.

A ballot is required in respect of any act done by a trade union, that is, in respect of any action authorised or endorsed by the union. Entitlement to vote must be accorded to all members of the union who will be induced to take part in the action and the ballot will be ineffective if this provision is not complied with.

Picketing

Picketing is a method by which a trade union can strengthen a strike. It can prevent workers from entering the workplace and so increase the disruption to the employer. The problem with picketing from a legal point of view is that it involves a consideration of both the civil and criminal law. The criminal law becomes involved because the fact that picketing involves a group of people standing around can create criminal liability. In addition, pickets will normally interfere with contracts, be committing a trespass and often be committing a private nuisance, so rendering them potentially liable in tort. As such it is necessary to consider all the potential liability and look at the immunity.

Criminal liability, for example may be committing the offence of obstructing the highway, obstructing a police officer during the course of his duty or causing a public nuisance generally.

Civil liability might be that of committing a private nuisance, which is unlawful interference with an individuals enjoyment of his land, trespass to the highway or general economic torts such as breach of contract of employment.

Immunity for pickets is contained in s 220 of the 1992 Act. This renders it lawful for a person, in contemplation or furtherance of a trade dispute, to attend at or near his own place of work for the purpose of peacefully obtaining or communicating information, or peacefully persuading a person to work or not to work. In addition, a trade union official may peacefully picket at or near the place of work of a member of the union whom he is accompanying or whom he represents Unemployed employees are allowed to picket their former place of work if their employment was terminated in connection with the trade dispute or the dismissal gave rise to the trade dispute.

Remedies

Obviously, although the individual member commits the tort, it is more beneficial for an employer to sue the union, hence the removal of blanket union immunity in 1982. The majority of employers, however, do not want damages but rather want to prevent the action from commencing or to stop it as soon as possible. The most common remedy sought is that of injunctive relief. If the union fails to comply with an injunction the two methods of enforcement are committal for contempt and sequestration of the union assets. The court may imprison for contempt, fine or order security for good behaviour.

9. DISCRIMINATION IN EMPLOYMENT

In this chapter a number of Acts of Parliament are considered. The earlier enactments have been subject to considerable amendment by subsequent legislation and it is important to refer to the amended rather than original legislation.

The enactments which will be considered are the Equal Pay Act 1970, as amended by the sex discrimination Act 1975 and the Equal pay (amendment) regulations 1983, the sex discrimination Act 1975 (as amended by the Sex Discrimination Act 1986) and the Race Relations Act 1976. We will also look at the Disability Discrimination Act 1996.

Equal Pay

In broad terms, the Equal Pay Act 1970 is concerned with less favourable treatment of one person relative to another in respect of matters governed by the contract under which a person is employed whereas the Sex Discrimination act 1975 deals with less favourable treatment in matters not governed by the contract, on grounds of sex and/or marital status.

The Equal Pay Act 1970 has been influenced by the treaty of Rome and the effect of certain European Community Directives have been considerable in this area and have significant practical consequences for any applicant contemplating bringing an action alleging breach of the 1970 Act.

Article 119 of the Treaty of Rome provides that: "each member state shall maintain the application of the principle that men and women should receive equal pay for equal work. For the purpose of this article, pay means the ordinary basic or minimum wage or salary and any other consideration, whether in cash or kind, which the worker receives, directly or indirectly in respect of his employment from his employer. The

Article is directly enforceable by individuals in the courts of member states of the EEC.

Sex Discrimination Act 1975

In relation to employment, the Sex Discrimination Act is intended to render discrimination on the grounds of sex and/or the fact that a person is married unlawful as regards those areas of employment not dealt with by the terms of the contract. The Act renders discrimination on the above grounds unlawful except in the following cases.

a) Discrimination by way of special treatment afforded to women in connection with pregnancy or childbirth.

b) Where in the previous year there were no or few members of one sex doing a particular job, ceratin discrimination in favour of members of that sex is allowed.

c) Discrimination in the selection, promotion or training of a person is permissible where being a man or woman is a genuine occupational qualification.

d) There are special rules relating to the police, prison officers and ministers of religion.

e) There are special rules relating to death or retirement. The position here has been much influenced by community law which in turn led to the amendment of the Sex Discrimination Act 1986. Under Community law it is quite clear that the domestic legislation of a member state may fix discriminatory retirement ages.

Section 6 of the Act provides that the following areas of employment are within the scope of the act:

a) Arrangements for selecting of employees and making offers of employment.

b) The terms upon which employment is offered but not the terms themselves when employment has been obtained, this latter matter being within the scope of the Equal Pay ct.

c) Access to promotion, training, transfer or any other benefit, facilities or services.

d) Dismissal or the subjecting of a person to any other detriment, eg, suspension from work.

It is unlawful to publish, or cause to be published an advertisement which indicates, or might reasonably indicate, an intention to do an act which is contrary to the Act.

The meaning of discrimination. The Act embodies three kinds of discrimination, direct discrimination (unfavourable treatment on grounds of race, sex etc. Indirect discrimination-this is where the complainant must demonstrate that the employer applies a requirement or condition which he applies or would apply to members of the other sex/single persons. That it is to the complainants detriment because he or she cannot comply with it.

An example of the operation of this provision would be where an employer requires all his employees to be over six feet tall. This could only be justified if the employer could demonstrate that the job demanded it.

One important case in this area is Price v Civil Service Commission (1978) Held: a civil service condition that candidates for certain posts should be no more than 28 years of age was indirect discrimination because women in their late twenties were frequently occupied in having and rearing children.

Discrimination by victimisation. S 4, this deals with discrimination against a person who has brought proceedings, given evidence, information, alleged a contravention etc under the Sex Discrimination Act or Equal Pay Act. Such a person must not be treated less favourably by the alleged discriminator than another person in those circumstances was or would be treated.

In relation to discrimination on grounds of sex (as opposed to discrimination against married persons) s7 provides that ceratin kinds of employment are excluded from the operation of the Act, namely where being a member of one sex is a "genuine occupational qualification" for the job. Two general points should be noted:

a) These provisions do not apply to the terms upon which employment is offered, dismissal or subjecting a person to any other detriment.

b) These provisions do not apply to the filling of a vacancy where the employer already has male (or female) employees capable of filling it and whom it would be reasonable to employ on those duties and whose numbers are sufficient to meet the employers likely requirements without undue inconvenience.

Being a man or woman is a genuine occupational qualification for a job where the essential nature of the job calls for a man for reasons of physiology or authenticity eg actors, models etc. In addition where the job needs to be held by a man to preserve decency or privacy or the job is likely to involve the holder doing work or living in a private home and needs to be held by a same sex person because objections might be raised to a member of the opposite sex in attendance.

Also, the nature or the location of the establishment effectively requires the employee to live in and in the absence of separate sleeping accommodation and sanitary facilities, it is not reasonable to expect the employer to provide such things. In addition, the nature of the establishment where the work is done, ie, a hospital or prison requires that the job be done by a man.

Race Relations Act 1976

The 1976 Act is concerned with discrimination on grounds of colour, race, nationality, or ethnic or national origin. Some difficulty has been experienced over the question of the meaning of ethnic origin and in particular its relationship with race. An important defining case in this respect was Mandla v Lee (1983). The House of Lords resolved the matter. The question was whether Sikhs are a group of persons defined by ethnic origin so as to fall within the protection of the Act. It was held that Sikhs did constitute an ethnic group. "Ethnic" was used in the Act in a sense much wider than that of "race" and an ethnic group can be identified by some or all of such essential factors as a long history, cultural tradition, common geographical origin, common language and a common religion.

It should be noted that a racial group cannot be defined by the factor of language alone.

The 1976 Act is concerned not only with employment but covers also such things as the provision of services, housing etc.

There are a number of exceptions to the 1976 Act including where being of a certain race etc is deemed to be a genuine occupational qualification, such as specific providers of services to defined communities.

The Act may be enforced by individuals but the Commission for Racial Equality has wide powers. The Commission for Racial Equality is empowered to issue codes of practice on ceratin matters.

Discrimination on the grounds of disability

In 1995 the Disability Discrimination Act was passed. In relation to employment, it makes all employers of over 20 employees or more legally liable for discrimination against disabled people. Part 11 of the Act, relating to employment, came into force at the end of 1996 at which time there will be a code of practice in force to help on interpretation.

To be protected against discrimination an individual must be a person who has a disability or had a disability. Disability is defined as physical or mental impairment, which has a substantial and long term effect on the persons ability to carry out day to day activities.

In relation to employment the individual is protected against discrimination. It should be noted that the Act only mentions discrimination on the grounds of disability and thus, unlike the Race Relations Act and Sex Discrimination Act will allow an employer to positively discriminate in the case of a person with a disability.

The Act, in s 4 outlines acts of discrimination. These principally cover the arrangements for appointing employees, the terms on which employment is offered and refusal of employment. It is also unlawful to discriminate in the terms of employment, in the opportunities offered for training, promotion, transfer or any other benefit or to dismiss a person because of disability.

Section 11 provides for limited protection in relation to advertisements. Monitoring of the legislation will be by the National Disability Council.

10. TERMINATION OF EMPLOYMENT

There are a number of ways in which a contract of employment may come to an end. At common law, a contract of employment can be validly terminated by an employer giving notice to an employee in accordance with the terms of the contract or, in the absence of such a term, by giving reasonable notice. If sufficient notice was given, the employee had no further rights and this meant that dismissal could be entirely arbitrary. However, in recent times provisions have been introduced whereby an employee may be entitled to compensation for loss of job despite the fact that he was given notice. It should be noted that once notice has been given, it can only effectively be withdrawn with the consent of the other party.

Dismissal with notice

The length of notice which must be given by an employer to an employee is determined by reference to the following criteria to be applied in the following order:

a) Express terms of the contract. if the contract of employment expressly provides for a period of notice, this must be observed unless that period is less than the statutory minimum to which that particular employee is entitled under d) below.

b) In the absence of an express term it may be impossible to imply a term into the contract, for example, by custom. Again, such a period may not be less than the statutory custom.

c) If there is no express or implied term of the contract, the courts may rely on a reasonable period. What is "reasonable" depends upon such factors as the status of the employee, salary, length of employment with that employer, age etc. The "reasonable" period cannot be less than the statutory minimum.

d) Statutory minimum. In the absence of any of the above criteria, or where they produce a period less than the following, the statutory minimum in s 86 of the 1996 Act must be applied in respect of those employees covered by that section. Section 86 provides that for an employee continuously employed for between one month and two years, the notice period is one week; for an employee employed for more than two years, he is entitled to one week for each year of continuous employment subject to a maximum of twelve weeks notice after twelve years of employment.

These rights do not apply to a contract for the performance of a specific task which is not expected to last for more than three months.

Summary dismissal

Summary dismissal is where an employer dismisses an employee without giving the employee the amount of notice to which that individual is entitled. If there is no justification, such dismissal is wrongful and an action can be brought.

The remedy for wrongful dismissal is damages representing the loss of wages during the period of notice that ought to have been given. In addition, wrongful dismissal may also be unfair dismissal within the meaning of the 1978 Act.

Circumstances which justify summary dismissal

The question of what justifies summary dismissal is not one that can be answered with a simple rule since each case must be decided according to the particular circumstances. However, a general principle has emerged that summary dismissal is justified if the conduct of the employee is such that it prevents further satisfactory continuance of the relationship. This was the finding in Sinclair v Neighbour. (1967)

The status of the employee in question is a relevant consideration as is the fact that the employee has a history of misconduct as opposed to an isolated incident.

Dismissals Procedure

If the contract states that dismissal is to be according to an established pattern (e.g. that there will be two warnings before dismissal occurs) it is a breach of contract if the procedure is not observed. (Tomlinson v L.M.S Rly (1944). If the contract states that the dismissal may only occur for certain specified reasons, a dismissal is wrongful if the reason for the dismissal is other than specified in the contract.

Waiver of rights

If an employee"s conduct justified a summary dismissal, the right must have been exercised within a reasonable time of the conduct which allegedly justified the action since delay may amount to a waiver of the breach of contract.

Employee leaving

An employee is entitled to terminate employment at any time by giving the amount of notice required by the contract. If the employee is deemed to have been entitled to terminate employment by reason of the employers conduct, that may constitute a "constructive dismissal and the fact that he gave notice makes no difference.

If an employers attitude causes an employee to terminate his contract without notice, this may well constitute constructive dismissal and the employee may act accordingly.

Termination by agreement

The parties to a contract of employment as with any other contract, may terminate their relationship by agreement at any time upon such terms as they may agree, e.g. payment of money as a golden handshake. It should be noted that a termination by agreement is not a dismissal for the purposes of the redundancy and unfair dismissals provisions of the 1996 Act. However, the tribunals are concerned to ensure that any alleged agreement to terminate a contract of employment is real and not merely a result of pressure imposed on an employee who is unaware of the significance of agreeing to terminate the contract and who faces dismissal as an alternative to so agreeing.

Termination by frustration

Frustration occurs whenever the law recognises that without default of either party a contractual obligation has become incapable of being performed because the circumstance in which performance would be called for would render it a thing different from that which was undertaken by the contract. Lord Radcliffe in Davis Contractors v Fareham UDC (1956).

In the context of a contract of employment, the term frustration means that circumstances have arisen, without the fault of either party, that make it impossible for the contract to be performed in the way that may be reasonably expected and the contract automatically terminates without the need for notice to be given. Frustration of the contract is not deemed to be dismissal for legislative purposes.

Examples of frustration may be: sickness In Notcutt v Universal

Equipment Co (1986), a worker with 27 years service, who was two years from retirement suffered a permanently incapacitating heart attack. The court decided that this rendered performance of the contract impossible and therefore the contract was frustrated as he was unable to perform his obligation to work. The employee was therefore not entitled to sick pay during his period of notice.

Imprisonment is another example, however this has caused problems. Recently, however, the Court of Appeal has allowed a four year apprenticeship contract to be frustrated by a six months borstal sentence: FC Shepherd Ltd v Jerrom (1986). In this case court held that such a period of imprisonment made the performance of the contract impossible.

As with the sickness, the courts will tend to look at each case on its own merits without applying hard and fast rules.

Action for wrongful dismissal

An employee who has been wrongfully dismissed may bring an action for damages against his former employer representing the amount of wages owed to him in respect of work already done and in respect of wages that the employee would have earned had he been given the amount of notice to which he was entitled. the amount of wages lost is determined by the ordinary principles of common law and includes all sums connected with the job, such as loss of tips etc.

Damages for wrongful dismissal cannot normally include compensation for injured feelings or pride or the fact that future earnings may be affected. The object of damages is to compensate the injured party for what he actually lost, not to punish the party in breach of contract, and therefore the courts have developed principles to ensure that the employee who has been wrongfully dismissed receives compensation only for his actual loss.

Damages against employee

Where an employee fails to give sufficient notice to his employer, the employer may sue the employee for damages representing the loss which follows from the breach of contract. In practice, such actions are infrequent because the loss is often minimal.

Specific performance

Specific performance is an order from the court directing that the parties to a contract perform their contractual obligations. It is a fundamental principle of labour law that specific performance is newer granted to compel performance of a contract of employment and this principle is now embodied in s 235 of the Trade Union and Labour Relations (Consolidation) Act 1992.

Injunction

An injunction is an order from a court forbidding certain conduct, e.g. the breaking of a term of the contract of employment. Hence it may be used to prevent a breach of a covenant restraining an employee from taking employment with a rival of his former employer. The courts usually refuse to grant an injunction if it compels performance. By virtue of the Trade Union and Labour Relations Act 1992, no court may issue an injunction if the effect of such an order would be to compel an employee to do any work or to attend any place to work.

However, where the injunction compelling performance is to the benefit of the employee, the court may be prepared to grant such an order. In Hill v CA Parsons Ltd (1972) the defendant employers wished to enter into an agreement with an organisation of workers whereby it was agreed that all employers in ceratin sections, including the plaintiff, would be obliged to join that organisation. This arrangement was legal at the time but under the Industrial Relations Act 1971 it would have been invalid. The plaintiff did not wish to join the organisation and he was dismissed with four weeks notice. The Court of Appeal held that he was wrongfully dismissed since he was entitled to at least six months notice and furthermore an injunction was awarded which prevented the employee from being dismissed until that time elapsed by which time he would have a remedy under the 1971 Act.

Declaration

A declaration is an order from the court which simply determines the rights of the parties in the case. It has no binding force in itself and is not available to all employees being restricted to those persons whose employment is derived from statute.

Written statement of reasons for dismissal

An employee who has been continuously employed for at least two years and who has been dismissed is entitled to receive, upon request, a written statement of the reasons for his dismissal.

A claim may be presented to an industrial tribunal by an employee that his employer has "unreasonably" refused to provide a written statement of the reasons for dismissal or that it is inadequate or untrue. The right to a written statement only arises where the employee has been dismissed by his employer.

Suspension

In accordance with the general principle that an employer fulfils his contractual obligations by paying wages in accordance with the contract of employment, he may suspend an employee on full wages without breach of contract. An employer may only suspend an employee without pay if the contract expressly or impliedly provided for this. If the contract does not so provide, it is a breach of contract. Therefore, an employee who is suspended without contractual authority may treat himself as dismissed and claim accordingly.

11. UNFAIR DISMISSAL

The present law relating to unfair dismissal is to be found in the Employment Rights Act 1996.

The significance of the concept of unfair dismissal is that it represents a further, and most important, step towards recognising the property right which an employee has in his job. Additionally, it is no longer possible for an employer to end a contract by simply giving notice and thereby totally discharging his responsibilities. The threat of dismissal is no longer quite so important since the employee has a remedy if the threat is implemented.

The 1996 Act provides that, subject to certain specified exceptions, every employee has the right not to be unfairly dismissed. It should be noted that a complaint of unfair dismissal does not depend upon the employer having acted in breach of contract but simply that the employer has terminated the contract in circumstances which are unfair.

Certain categories of employees are excluded: employees who, at the effective date of termination of the contract have been continuously employed for less than two years, persons over retiring age, persons employed in the police service, share fishermen, employees who ordinarily work outside Great Britain, employees employed on fixed term contracts and persons covered by a designated dismissals procedure agreement.

Dismissal

If an action for unfair dismissal is to succeed, the employee must first establish that he was dismissed within the meaning of the Act The employee must establish constructive dismissal if alleged. The Act provides that:

"an employee shall be treated as dismissed by his employer if the contract under which he is employed by the employer is terminated by the employer whether it is so terminated by notice or without notice or where under that contract he is employed for a fixed term, that term expires without being renewed under the same contract or the employee terminates that contract, with or without notice, in circumstances such that he is entitled to terminate it without notice by reason of the employers conduct".

The Act refers to the concept of so-called "constructive; dismissal. If an employee leaves employment entirely voluntarily, there is no dismissal but if he leaves because of the employers conduct then it may be deemed "constructive"

The courts and tribunals have been concerned to define the circumstances in which an employee is entitled to regard himself as having been constructively dismissed. In Western Excavating Ltd v Sharp (1978) the tribunals found that sufficiently unreasonable behaviour on the part of the employer entitled an employee to leave his job and claim constructive dismissal. However, the Court of Appeal rejected the unreasonableness test and established that the correct test is one based on strict contractual principles. Accordingly, an employee is only able successfully to argue constructive dismissal where the employer has breached the contract in such a way as to justify the employee in treating himself as discharged from further performance. The action of an employer may involve breach of an express or implied term.

When is dismissal unfair

The expression "unfair dismissal" is in no sense a commonsense expression capable of being understood by the person in the street. Whether a dismissal is unfair is affected, but not conclusively determined, by whether one or both parties has broken the terms of the contract of employment. The employer cannot, in seeking to show that a dismissal was not unfair rely on alleged misconduct not known to him at the time of the dismissal. An otherwise fair dismissal is not automatically rendered unfair by a failure to give proper notice.

Reasonableness. It is for the employer to establish the reason for the dismissal. The tribunal must then satisfy itself as to whether the employer acted reasonably or unreasonably. The EAT laid down the following general principles in Iceland Frozen Foods v Jones (1982):

a) In applying the provisions of the 1996 Act a tribunal must consider the reasonableness of the employers conduct and not simply whether they (the members of the tribunal) consider the dismissal unfair.

b) In judging the reasonableness of the employers conduct a tribunal must not substitute its own decision as to what was the right course to adopt for that of the employer.

c) In many cases there is a band of reasonable responses to the employees conduct within which one employer might take one view and another quite reasonably another.

d) The function of the tribunal is to determine whether in the particular circumstances the decision to dismiss fell within the band of reasonable responses which a reasonable employer might have adopted. If the dismissal falls within the band it is fair. If it falls outside the band it is unfair.

In deciding whether an employer acted reasonably, the industrial tribunal is required to have regard to the provisions of the ACAS Code of Practice ;Disciplinary Code of Practice and Procedures in Employment. In broad terms, this provides that the disciplinary rules and procedures ought to have been made known to each employee and that a disciplinary procedure ought to contain certain essential procedures.

Reasons for dismissal

There are five categories of reasons which, if one is established by the employer, may make the dismissal fair provided that the tribunal is satisfied that the employer acted reasonably. These are as follows:

a) Capability or qualification

b) Conduct

c) Redundancy

d) Illegality of continued employment

e) Some other substantial reason.

In addition, an employer in certain circumstances, can dismiss an employee for reasons connected to pregnancy. Usually, it is automatically unfair to do so unless the employer can establish that at the effective date of termination, because of her pregnancy, she:

a) is or will have become incapable of adequately doing the work she is employed to do or: or

b) cannot or will not be able to do the work she is employed to do without a contravention (either by her or her employer) of a duty of restriction imposed by law.

In Brown v Stockton on Tees Borough Council (1988) the House of Lords held that if a woman was selected for redundancy because she is pregnant, such a dismissal is automatically unfair. Indeed, Lord Griffiths stated that "it surely cannot have been intended that an employer should be entitled to take advantage of a redundancy situation to weed out his pregnant employer".

However, even where the circumstances of a and b above apply, the dismissal is still unfair if the employer has a suitable vacancy, i.e. appropriate for a pregnant woman to do and not substantially less favourable than her existing employment in relation to the nature, terms and place of employment, which he fails to offer her.

Dismissal for trade union reasons

References in this section are to the Trade Union and Labour Relations (Consolidation) Act 1992.

Trade Union membership or activities. Except in exceptional cases, a dismissal is automatically unfair if the employee can establish that the principal reason for it was that the employer was, or proposed to become, a member of an independent trade union, or that the employee had taken or proposed to take part in the activities of an independent trade union at any appropriate time or that the employee was not a member of any or a particular trade union, or had refused or proposed to refuse to become or remain a member.

Other reasons for dismissal

An industrial tribunal cannot determine whether a dismissal was fair or unfair if it is known that at the date of dismissal the employer was conducting or instituting a lock out or the complainant was taking part in a strike or other industrial action, unless it is shown:

a) that one or more relevant employees of the same employer have not been dismissed: or

b) that any such employee has, before the expiry of the period of three months beginning with the employee"s date of dismissal, been offered re-engagement and that the complainant has not been offered re-engagement.

National security

If an employee has shown to have been dismissed on grounds of national security, as evidenced by a certificate signed by or on behalf of a minister of the Crown, the tribunal must dismiss the complaint. In Council of Civil Service Unions v Minister for the Civil Service (1985) (the GCHQ case), the court held that the requirements of national security outweighed those of fairness when the minister decided to ban trade unions at GCHQ, without consultation with the trade unions. Workers who refused to give up their trade union membership were subsequently fairly dismissed.

Procedure

An employee who considers that he has been unfairly dismissed may present a complain to the Central Office of Industrial Tribunals within three months of the effective date of termination or within such further period as the tribunal considers reasonable in a case where it is satisfied that it was not reasonably practicable for the complaint to be presented within a time period of three months.

Where the dismissal is unfair (failure to offer re-engagement where the dismissal is connected with a lockout or strike) the time limit is six months from the date of dismissal.

A copy of the application is sent to the employer as respondent. If the employer wishes to contest any aspect of the complaint, he must enter a "notice of appearance" within 14 days, although tribunals have a wide discretion to grant an extension of time. Once this has happened, a date is set down for the hearing of the case by an industrial tribunal.

Conciliation

A copy of the application is also sent to a conciliation officer. He is under a statutory duty, either at the request of the parties or on his own initiative, to endeavour to promote a voluntary settlement of the issue, either by way of an agreement to reinstate or re-engage the complainant or an agreement as to the payment of compensation in respect of the dismissal. there is no legal duty upon the parties to co-operate with the conciliation officer.

Pre-hearing Assessments

Under the Industrial Tribunals Regulations (S! 1985/16) provision is made for a pre-hearing assessment of the case to be made at the request of either of the parties or on the notion of the tribunal itself. At the tribunal, it is for the complainant to establish that he was dismissed (unless dismissal is conceded). It is then for the tribunal to satisfy itself as to whether the dismissal was fair or unfair in accordance with the principles stated above. If the dismissal is found to be unfair, the tribunal will consider the remedies which may be awarded. An appeal, on a point of law only, lies from an industrial tribunal to the Employment Appeal Tribunal.

Remedies

Reinstatement and re-engagement orders. If the tribunal finds the dismissal unfair, it must explain to the complainant the remedies available and ask if he wishes to be reinstated or re-engaged. If the employee indicates that this is his wish then the tribunal must consider whether it is practicable for the employer to comply with such an order. If the employer complies, but not fully, with a reinstatement or re-engagement order then, unless the tribunal is satisfied that it was not practicable to comply with the order, an additional award of compensation must be made.

If a reinstatement or re-engagement order is made but not complied with at all or if no such order is made, the tribunal must make an award of compensation on the basis of the following:

a) basic award, amount of which is calculated in line with redundancy payments;

b) compensatory award, being an amount that the tribunal considers just and equitable in all the circumstances having regard to the loss suffered by the complainant in consequence of the dismissal in so far as the loss is attributable to action taken by the employer subject to a maximum limit.

12. REDUNDANCY

Compensation for redundancy was one of the first employment protection rights introduced into our law. The first piece if legislation was the Redundancy Payments Act 1965 and the law is now contained in the main in the Employment Rights Act 1996.

In order to claim a redundancy payment an employee must have two years continuous service and be dismissed for reasons of redundancy. The definition of dismissal for redundancy purposes is contained within s 136 of the Employment Rights Act 196. These situations are the same as unfair dismissal that is, employer termination with or without notice, a fixed term contract expiring and constructive dismissal In addition, by s 139(4), if the employment is terminated by the death, dissolution or liquidation of the employer, or the appointment of a receiver, there is dismissal for reasons of redundancy.

The definition of redundancy is found in s 139(1) of the Act. This states that a redundancy has occurred if the dismissal is wholly or mainly attributable to:

a) the fact that his employer has ceased or intends to cease, to carry on the business for the purposes for which the employee was employed by him, or has ceased, or intends to cease, to carry on that business in the place where the employee was so employed or

b) the fact that the requirements of that business for employees to carry out work of a particular kind, or for employees to carry out work of a particular kind in the place where he was so employed, have ceased or diminished or are expected to cease or diminish.

This means that the redundancy occurs in three situations - the employer increasing business the employee moving his place of business or the employer reducing his labour force.

Misconduct and redundancy

Section 140(1) of the Employment Rights Act 1996 provides that in certain situations the employee will be disentitled to a redundancy payment. This occurs when the employee terminates the contract where:

a) the employee commits an act of misconduct and the employer dismisses without notice or

b) the employee commits an act of misconduct and the employer dismisses with shorter notice than the redundancy notice or

c) the employer, when the redundancy notice expires, gives the employee a statement in writing that the employer is entitled, by virtue of the employees conduct, to dismiss without notice.

There are two exceptions to this. By s 140 (2) where an employee, while under notice of redundancy, takes part in a strike or other industrial action to protest against the redundancies. If however, an employee who is on strike is selected for redundancy, the tribunal will have no jurisdiction to hear the case unless there are selective dismissals (Simmons v Hoover (1977)). By S 143 the employer can extend the redundancy notice period and require the employees to work in order to make up the days lost by the industrial action and if the employees lose they disentitle themselves to a redundancy payment.

Suitable alternative employment

If the employer offers the employee his old job back or a different job which is suitable alternative employment, the new contact starts on the termination of the old or within four weeks of the old contract expiring and the employee unreasonably refuses the offer he is disentitled to a redundancy payment by virtue of sections 141(2) and (3). The section therefore means that two questions must be asked: is the offer suitable alternative employment and is the employees refusal of that offer reasonable.

Trial period in new employment

If the terms of the new contract differ (wholly or in part) from the old contract, then by s 138 the employee is entitled to a trial period. By subsection (3) the statutory trial period is four weeks., but this can be extended by the employees contract as long as the period is in writing and specified precisely. If the employee is dismissed during the trial period, he is treated as being dismissed for the reason his original contract ended, that is, redundancy, and ion the date his original contract ended, so entitling him to claim a redundancy payment. If the employee resigns, he is treated as dismissed for redundancy, unless his resignation was unreasonable.

Lay off and short time working

In order to prevent redundancies, the employer may temporarily lay off his workers to put them on short time. By s 147 a lay off is where no work or pay is provided by the employer. Short time working is where less than half a weeks pay is earned. By s 148 where the lay off or short time has lasted for more than four consecutive weeks or six weeks in any thirteen, the employee can give notice to his employer that he intends to claim a redundancy payment. He must give the notice in writing. The employer has a defence if he can show that he reasonably expects to provide full time work for the next thirteen weeks and he raises this defence in written counter notice served within seven days of receipt of the employees intention to claim.

Redundancy compensation

A redundancy payment is calculated in the same way as the basic award for unfair dismissal and is therefore based on age and years of service. However, unlike the basic award, periods of employment below the age of 18 do not count and the employees period of continuity is deemed to start at his 18th birthday. (Employment Rights Act 1996 s 211(2). Again, unlike the basic award there is no deduction for contributory conduct, but like the basic award, there will be no reduction for each month the employee works in the year before he attains the normal retirement age for the job, so that on reaching the age, or 65, whichever is lower, entitlement to a redundancy payment ceases.

If the redundancy is caused by the employers insolvency, the employee may make a claim for a redundancy payment to the Department of Employment under s 166 of the Employment Rights Act 1996. While the Employee ranks as a preferential creditor in his employers insolvency, this will not be much use if the employer has no assets and therefore additionally the Department can pay certain sums to the employee from the National Insurance Fund. This can be up to eight weeks wages, up to six weeks holiday pay, a basic award and other payments.

Consultation

Failure to consult the employee about his redundancy may render the dismissal unfair. Unions must be consulted too. Where the employer has broken his statutory duty to consult, the union or employee representatives can apply to a tribunal for a protective award which is payable to those employees in respect of whom the representatives should have been consulted. Similar provisions relate to consultation where there is a transfer of an undertaking under the Transfer of Undertakings Regulations 1981. Where such a transfer takes place, Regulation 10 creates a duty on both the transferor and the transferee to inform the representatives.

The remedy for failure to comply with the consultation provisions under the regulations is found in Regulation 11. The employer can raise the defence of special; circumstances. The maximum award which can be made under the Regulations is four weeks pay. This is set off against any protective award given to the employee. Since 1993, the duty on the tribunal to offset this payment against wages or payment in lieu of notice is removed.

13. HEALTH AND SAFETY

The Health and Safety at Work Act 1974.

Although not seen as implied duties in the contract of employment, it would be incomplete to talk about the employers liability in relation to the safety of his employees without a brief overview of the statutory provisions.

The 1974 Act was introduced as a result of the Robens Committee report of 1972. The Committee found that the law on health and safety was piecemeal and badly structured, with eleven pieces of major legislation supplemented by over 500 supplementary statutory provisions. The majority of the law based liability on occupation of premises. The Committee proposed a unification of the law, basing liability on employment not occupation of premises.

The Committees findings were embodied in the Health and Safety at work Act 1974. The aim of the Act is twofold - to lay down general duties across the whole area of employment, and to provide a unified system of enforcement under the control of the Health and Safety Executive and local authorities. General duties are imposed upon various types of people, for example employers, suppliers and manufacturers, with the aim of ensuring a safe working environment.

Section 2(1) lays down the general duty on employers: it "It shall be the duty of every employer to ensure, so far as is reasonably practicable, the health, safety and welfare of all his employees. This is further specified by subsection (2). The phrase to which all these duties are subject is "so far as is reasonably practicable". The basis of the duties under s 2(2) is that of employment - it covers duties owed by n employer to his employees; the duties, however, extend beyond the employment relationship. Section 3(1) provides that employers should conduct their business in such a way, "in so far as is reasonably practicable to protect persons other than their own employees from risks to their health and safety.

Liability is imposed not only on those who physically occupy premises but also on those who are responsible for the maintenance of such premises, or the access to and exit from the premises. In addition, liability is imposed against those responsible for safety and absence of risk concerning plant or substances used on the premises.

Protection of those other than employees is continued in s 5. This imposes a duty on those who control work premises to use the best means practicable to prevent the emission of offensive or noxious substances and to render harmless any such substances which are so emitted. This general duty overlaps with the more specific duties laid down in the Control of Pollution Act 1974.

The Act attempts to increase protection by imposing duties on designers, manufacturers, importers and suppliers. A chain of responsibility is therefore imposed from the design and manufacture of an article to its installation, use and maintenance. It can be seen, however, that the duties under the Act overlap and this demonstrates the stated aim of the legislation of accident prevention.

The duty owed to employees in that by s 2 of the Act, if the Employer employs five or more persons he should have a general policy on health and safety and bring this policy to the notice of his employees. The policy should identify who is responsible for health and safety and should point out particular health and safety problems and arrangements for dealing with them. The policy should also cover such matters as training and supervision, inspection procedures, safety precautions and consultative arrangements. In addition, it must tell the employee how he can complain about any health and safety risk to which he feels he is being exposed.

While the common law imposes no duty on the employee to look after his own health and safety, failure to do so could mean that any damages could be wiped out by the employer raising the defence of contributory negligence. given that the aim of the statutory duty is not to provide compensation, the Act places a duty on the individual employee to have regard to his own safety and that of those around him. Often, employers will make breach of health and safety regulations a disciplinary offence and in some case it may be fair to dismiss an employee for such a breach. In Rogers v Wicks and Wilson COIT 90/97 wilful breach of a no smoking policy imposed for safety reasons was held to be a justifiable reason for dismissal.

INDEX

A

ACAS 10

Action short of dismissal 62

Action for wrongful dismissal 82

Ante - Natal 50

Apprentices 24

Arbitration 11

Armed forces 25

B

Blacking 64

C

Central Arbitration Committee 11

Certification Officer 11

Closed shop 57

Codes of Practice 10

Commissioner:

(For Protection against Unlawful Industrial Action) 16
(For Rights of Trade Union Members) 61

Commission for Racial Equality 15

Continuous Employment 22

Collective agreements 31

Consultation 97

Contract of employment 17

Covenants (in restraint of trade) 38

D

Damages 83

Declaration 84

Definition (of contract) 17

Directors 24

Disability (Discrimination Act) 76

Discipline 60

Dismissal (for trade union reasons) 90 (Unfair) 86

E

Economic Duress 68

Employment Appeal Tribunal (EAT) 9

Enforcement (of rule book) 59

Equal Opportunities Commission 14

Equal Pay 72

Exclusion 59

Expulsion 59

Express Statements 30

European Courts 13

F

Fixed term contract 37

Form of contract 20

G

Go Slow 63

Government Training Schemes 28

Guarantee payments 45

H

Health and Safety

(At Work Act) 99
(Commission) 15
(Executive) 15

I

Inducement of Breach of Contract 66

Independent Trade Unions 53

Industrial action 63-72

Industrial Tribunals 7

Injunctions 83

Interference 67

L

Lay off 96

Liability 69

Listing 52

Loss (of immunity) 70

M

Maternity (leave) 49
     (pay)   49

Member (Trade Union) 59

Minors 26

Minimum Terms Orders 30
     (Statutory Standards) 30
Misconduct (and redundancy) 95

N

National Security Council 91

O

Overtime (ban) 64

P

Partners 24

Payments 45

Patents 42

Picketing 70

Political Fund 54

Police 25

Pre - Hearing 92

Probationary Employees 27

Public sector employees 25

R

Race Relations Act 75

Reasons (for dismissal) 89

Renumeration 46

Recognition (of Trade Unions) 53

Redundancy 94

Rehabilitation of Offenders Act 1974 22

Right (to return) 43
    (to information) 56

Rule Book 56

S

Secretary of State 11

Selection (of employees) 21

Sex Discrimination Act 1975 73

Sex Discrimination 73

Significance (of contract) 29

Sources (of terms of contract) 29

Specific Performance 83

Strike (with notice) 64
        (without notice) 64

Suitable alternative employment 95

Summary dismissal 79

Suspension 84

T

Termination (by agreement) 81
        (by frustration) 81
        (of employment) 78

Temporary employees 27

Torts 66

Trade disputes 65

Trial period 96

Trade Unions 52-71

Trade Union Liability 69

Transfer of Undertakings 23

U

Unlawful industrial action 63

W

Wages Act 1986 46

Wages Council 46

Work to rule 64

THE KEEPER

WORLD OF THE VISCEREBUS BOOK 1

OZ MARI G.

ACKNOWLEDGMENTS

The Keeper is my attempt at telling a sweet love story set in a fantastical world. It is also my first YA novel. The book contains elements that I truly love. But it would have ended up as boring were it not for the following people.

My eternal gratitude to:

My best friend for life, Maricar J, for the unwavering support and encouragement, for being always open to read a first draft and point out what my stories lacked.

And the rest of the beta readers who gave me objective feedback.

I dedicate this book to:
My son, Joshua, the inspiration for everything I do.
Finally, to my two cats, iO and Laki, who journeyed with me
with little complaint.

PROLOGUE

It has been told that Prometheus, the creator of all creatures on earth, gave life to two types of being in the likeness of the gods.

The first was the humans who he moulded from clay and earth. He gave them fire as a gift. This generosity infuriated Zeus. He bound Prometheus at Mount Caucasus where the latter's punishment was to have his liver eaten every day by a giant eagle, another titan named Aetos. The liver would regrow every night, and the torturous cycle was to be for thirty thousand years.

Prometheus, legend said, created a pair of second beings as his companions during his suffering. They were not just made in the image of the gods, but from its true essence.

Prometheus added a piece of his liver to the soil and rocks he used to fashion the new creatures, thus bestowing them with superhuman strength, speed, slow aging, and super senses. He also gave them the power to shape shift into animals to enable them to hide from Zeus.

However, he was unaware that the saliva of Aetos tainted a

portion of the liver. And his second creation inherited the need to consume viscera.

He called them Viscerebus, or viscera-eaters.

Once Prometheus was free, he bid the Viscerebus to live among humans. Thus, begun the conflict between the two.

The Viscerebus hunted the humans for their viscera, and the humans hunted them back for survival.

For decades, they were locked in a fierce battle for supremacy. The Viscerebus were stronger, faster, and more powerful, but the humans had centuries of head start in population. They outnumbered the Viscerebus, and it shifted the balance of power.

To protect their own, the Viscerebi formed a Tribunal and engineered a system that ensured the survival of their kind.

They set up a process of procuring fresh viscera without the need to kill humans; the distribution of the victus to their kind to stop them from hunting humans; and the campaign to convince the humans that the Viscerebi were creatures of lore.

They perfected the strategy for millennia, and the Viscerebi thrived, hidden in plain sight among human societies all over the world.

Their success hinged on keeping the Veil of Secrecy intact —the hiding of their existence from the humans at all costs.

But like air, secrets could only be contained through insulation. And like all insulation, it would never be permanent.

When two different beings coexist, their imperfections could create either conflict or cohesion.

1 ASWANG, ERDIA AND HUMAN

Veren stood in the middle of the forest. He breathed deep, trying to pick up the scent of the wild boar he heard foraging. The thick foliage overhead filtered the remaining sunlight, making the forest darker but not dark enough to trigger his night vision.

A breeze blew by him. It carried the smell of the trees, the rotting leaves, the decaying fruits on the forest floor, and the musky odour of the boar. He scanned the direction of the scent until he saw movement two hundred meters away. The animal was digging for something by the roots of the banyan trees.

Veren looked around to see if any of his fellow cadets were close to his location. He centred his senses, listening for human voices, and smelling for them. He could not detect any. With his gun slung behind him to keep his hands free, he lowered his centre of gravity and sprinted towards the unsuspecting boar; the wind whizzed past his ears, the wet squish of the leaves on the ground muffling the sound of his feet.

His speed was too much for the boar. It was a mere split second before the animal realised he was coming. It lifted its

head from the ground just before it found itself raised by the hind legs. He swung the boar against the tree trunk, crushing its skull with the force of the blow.

He crouched down and inspected his kill.

Oh, damn... I shattered one tusk.

With a sigh, he took out his handgun and shot the dead boar in the head where the tree had done the most damage. It would be hard to explain to his superior the true cause of its death otherwise. It required tremendous strength to shatter a pig's cranium. A gunshot would be the easiest way to avoid questions.

Inherent caution coloured all of his interactions with humans, just as it did with every single one of his kind. By nature, his kind avoid any potential exposure to their existence. There was no need to alarm the humans and create suspicion.

As he walked back to their camp in the woods, the dead boar slung over his shoulder, he encountered some human hunters along the way. He avoided crossing paths with them. It was easy enough, as he could hear them and their heavy treads on the forest floor. He found himself replying to their conversation in his head.

"I think we should hunt close to that military encampment," one human male said to his companions. There were three of them.

"Why? There are no bandits in these woods."

"Yeah, maybe not, but I heard there are Aswangs."

Yes. There is. Me, he thought.

"Well, we have guns."

"I am not sure if guns can kill Aswangs ..."

Sure they can, if you pump enough bullets in us and we bleed to death before our ability to heal and regenerate catches up.

4

"Well, what do you think those military men carry as weapons? Guns. And I'm sure they don't use silver bullets."

It was funny how humans had melded one tale of legend into another. For most people, their legends were part of old beliefs, stories passed on through generations and told to scare children. Not one of those tales was accurate.

"I can't believe you still believe in Aswangs ... In this day and age, we would have heard of attacks on humans. We all know what they're after."

To hide their existence, and their need for human viscera, the *Tribunal* had perfected a system of securing much-needed organs without having to kill any humans. Veren believed that it was pure genius to operate most of the funeral parlours, morgues, and mortuaries all over the world. It gave Aswangs access to fresh viscera without the humans' knowledge. The process became seamless over centuries of experience.

"Yeah, not to mention that our military would definitely go after them if they attacked humans. They like nothing better but a reason to kill."

Yes, I agree. And it would be catastrophic to our kind.

Thinking about what the *Tribunal* did for him, how they took care of him, never failed to make his heart swell with gratitude, Veren's vow to serve the community that nurtured him remained his driving goal. And his path to that goal was to become an *Iztari*.

Nothing could be nobler than protecting his kind from the peril that surrounded them all within the human communities. It was a necessity to be in proximity to them, as their need for human viscera was critical to their daily survival.

Military academies all over the world were the natural training grounds for people like him who desired to belong to their elite law enforcement. There were always a few of his kind who graduated every year. Several staffs in the Academy

were *Aswangs,* including the Commandant, who took care of supplying them with raw human viscera every three days.

"It's creepy enough in these woods. Stop your horror stories or we'll be too scared to hunt later."

The words of the hunters faded into the distance.

As he walked back to rejoin his troop, his thoughts replayed the discussion other *Aswangs* in the Academy were engaged in last night. There was no one in his class to discuss his opinions with. He was the only *Aswang* there, and he was not close with anyone in the lower and upper classes.

Some of his kind favoured surfacing and showing their might and ruling over the humans. In his opinion, to play on the humans' fear of *Aswangs,* scare them into submission, offered limited value. Fear could be a powerful deterrent, but it tended to wane in potency given enough time. History was littered with toppled governments through revolutions orchestrated by terrified people.

The *Viscerebus* might be stronger, faster, and superior to the humans, but at the odds of thirty to one, even their superior traits could not survive an attack, whether in retaliation or fear. Humans had the numbers and weapons to kill them.

They were safer if they remained hidden in plain sight, unnoticed by the humans and thought of only as a relic of a superstitious past.

Humans were less likely to attack an enemy they did not believe to exist.

Manila, same time, same day.

Anza watched her classmates giggle over selfies with the boys they met at the mall during the weekend. They were on their midday break, waiting for the next class to start. The

thought of the boys waiting in the parking lot later excited the three girls. They talked about hanging out with them at the Cosy Café located across the street from the main gate of their school.

The tall and slim Elyse, half-Filipino and half-German, led the girls. The other two were attractive and stylish: Rizzi with her mixed Arabian blood, and Summer's half Chinese heritage. All three were popular and fit the mould of archetypal it-girls. But what really made them unique was they were not mean, hurtful, or selfish, as one might assume.

On the surface, Anza fit the group well. She was petite, slim, and had been told multiple times that she was attractive. She preferred to think these girls wanted her in their group because she tried to match their kindness whenever she could, to compensate for every time she rejected their invitation to go out, and not for her looks.

She wanted to be friends with them, but her father and the laws of the *Viscerebus Tribunal* would not allow it.

"Anza, come with us. They will bring their friend with them. He's interested in meeting you," Elyse prodded her. "He's also into music and photography," she added with a smile.

"Interested in me? How does he know about me?" She had been very careful not to get her pictures on any social media.

"I posted our year-end class photos on my Instagram. He saw it and asked Kirk for an introduction to you," Elyse replied casually.

For her classmates, this was commonplace. Nothing to worry about. For her kind, it was always a concern. It was a footprint to be erased, a snapshot of time that could come back to haunt a slow-ageing *Aswang*. It shouldn't have been an issue for her, because she would age just like a normal human, but

she grew up trained in the same rules as her family. It became a habit for her.

"I'm not sure ... My dad won't like it." Her usual alibi was a hundred per cent true.

"Well, they're arriving twenty minutes early, so come with us and chat with them," Elyse implored. "You can leave once your father arrives. Please ..."

All three girls begged her to say yes. It would be embarrassing to say no, and the temptation to give in was strong.

"Okay," she said with a nod.

"Great!" Elyse jumped up from her seat and gave her a quick hug.

She must like that Kirk guy a lot for her to be that excited to make me say yes.

As she watched the three girls chat about their weekend activities, a sense of envy pierced her heart. She wanted to join them. Just once. They asked her every time, and she kept saying no. It was a wonder that they hadn't given up on being nice to her.

Maybe being seatmates helped. She sat behind Elyse, and whenever the trio chatted with each other, she was within hearing range. It was convenient and natural for Elyse to include her in the conversation. As Elyse was the leader of the three, Rizzi and Summer accepted and followed her example.

Two hours later, as she put her things away, she debated whether to tell her father about the early class dismissal today. This meant she wouldn't have to talk to the guy, but Elyse interrupted her thoughts.

"Are you nervous, Anza?" Her smile was gentle and concerned.

She nodded. "A little."

"Why? You're very pretty." Elyse sounded surprised as she looked her over from head to foot.

"It's not my looks that worry me," she began, but Rizzi interjected.

"Anza, with your baby-doll looks, just bat those lashes and you'll have the poor guy eating out of your hand." Rizzi giggled at her own statement.

"Or, you can jam with him. We heard he's a sucker for girls who can sing," Summer added.

Elyse and Rizzi smiled in agreement.

Her classmates misunderstood the source of her reluctance. They didn't know that meeting the boy, no matter how much she liked him after, would never lead to anything. It would be a pointless exercise.

And apart from being forbidden to tell them the truth, they would not believe her even if she broke the *Veil of Secrecy*. They would think her crazy if she told them her entire family was *Aswang*.

That afternoon, for forty minutes, she had a sample of the life she would lead if she inhabited her human heritage. The boy, Mark, was good-looking, charming, and endearingly nervous.

The girls flirted with the boys, laughed at jokes, shared some drinks, and assured that they would see each other again during the coming weekends—the simple joys of connecting with people her age. It was fun, enriching ... and in principle, harmless.

She left them reluctantly. She wanted to stay longer. Not so much because of Mark, but she felt greedy for the moments shared with humans. She had seen what her life could be if her parents allowed her to live the life that her humanity could afford her. She didn't have the long life her parents enjoyed, but they didn't seem to realise this.

Her family was due for *Transit* soon. This meant they would move somewhere far away and new. She would have to

go to a new school, meet new people, but couldn't make friends with any of them. And that would repeat in another twenty-five years.

Her life with her family was destined to be limited and lonely, with no one but her parents, uncles, aunts, and cousins as contributors to her experience. She would never fulfil her full potential. She could never have her photos published, her songs sung in airwaves, her poetry read. Just like the contents of her social media, it would just be for her own eyes, like a digital diary.

And this grieved her—the premature death of her potential, the wasting of her life.

Manuu Soledad, the head of his household, came home from a meeting with the *Matriarch* and the *Patriarch* of their *Gentem's Tribunal.*

They discussed the logistics of the *Transit* of Manuu's family, which comprised his daughter and wife.

Normally, this would be a simple arrangement if it just involved his immediate family. But his wife's family, whom they had gotten very close to during the past twelve years, wanted to join them. That required a more extensive logistical setup.

One small family moving into a new community would be unnoticed, but three moving to the same place at the same time would attract attention. The local *Tribunal* decided they could all move to Auckland together, provided they would not live in the same community. Their homes would have to be at least four kilometres apart. At least for the first five years.

For the *Viscerebus,* a *Transit* was a normal part of existence. It was a requirement that they go through every twenty to

thirty years, to hide their slow-ageing and longevity. The humans would notice, otherwise.

He was glad the rest of the family would *Transit* with them for the sake of his only daughter, Anza. This was to be her first, and it would be difficult for a teenager like her to cut ties from all her human friends and classmates, to leave behind everything connected to her life in the Philippines.

To have someone close to her age, like her cousin Xandrei, who was so fond of her, would make the process easier on his beloved daughter. She had been quiet and withdrawn for the past few months, especially since the day he did not permit her to attend her school fair. He knew then that she was missing the company of young people.

As his car passed along the coastal road, he thought of the house that he bought in Auckland Bay. His Anza would love it. It offered plenty of photo-worthy scenes. His daughter's poetic soul would appreciate the scenery and the view.

At least, Anza would not have to get used to a new name and identity. He kept their current one. Next year, after Anza finished Year 12, they would fly to their new *Gentem*, to start their *Transit*.

The whole of New Zealand was picturesque. No doubt Anza would enjoy taking photos and writing songs in their new home country.

2 AWAY FROM HOME

Veren slung his duffel bag over his shoulder. They had called him to the *Iztari* head office for a quick briefing. He was planning to take his bag home first, but it was no hardship to pass by the office before going home.

They instructed him to go straight to the office of the *Chief Iztari*, which was on the third floor. He walked into his mentor's corner office with a thrill of anticipation.

Edrigu Orzabal was waiting for him, a smile of satisfaction on his face. Edrigu gave him a tight hug and a thump on the back.

"Congratulations, Veren! Papa told me you graduated top of your class," Edrigu said.

"Thank you, Sir! It was the least I can do," he replied.

He couldn't help but to grin back. It flattered him that his achievement pleased his mentor and Don Lorenzo Ibarra, his sponsor. He thought he owed it to them to do well. They were his only family in this world.

"So, how long do you have before they give you your first deployment?" Edrigu asked.

"I don't know, but we have about a month-long break before we report back to camp for more training," he replied.

"Okay. What do you plan to do with your month?"

"Can I spend it here at the office?" He was hopeful Edrigu would say yes.

"You do not have to. You're allowed to take a break, you know," Edrigu said. He got up and walked to the corner of his office, where a small bar was installed. He pulled out two bottles of cold beer and handed him one.

This surprised him. He didn't realise they could drink in the *Iztari* office. He hesitated.

Edrigu chuckled. "It's allowed during special occasions, and today qualifies," he said in a manner of explanation.

"Thank you, Sir." He accepted the beer.

They clinked their bottles together and toasted to his graduation from the Military Academy. They had spent few companionable moments together.

Veren's heart swelled as he gazed at his mentor, and around the room they were in. The entire building felt like home to him since the first time he stepped into the premises sixteen years ago.

"I prefer to spend my summer break here," Veren said after a moment. "I've always wanted to become an *Iztari*. So, if it's okay with you, Sir, I would love to do this."

Edrigu looked at him, his expression paternal. At least Veren would like to think that was how a father would look at a son—indulgent, patient, and caring. His mentor also seemed to read deeper into him than he cared to think about himself, much less reveal to anyone. Only self-discipline stopped him from looking away.

"Don't you want to spend your summer doing carefree things, like being with people your age, partying, meeting young women, getting a girlfriend, and all those sorts of

things?" Edrigu asked. "The opportunities to do that once your work begins will be slim."

"No, Sir. I've spent all my life with people my age. I'm not interested in parties, and while I don't mind meeting girls for a laugh or two, I think it would be unfair to any potential girlfriend of mine to be in a relationship with a man like me, who has no plans of getting serious," he said, and he meant it.

"Okay, if that's what you prefer," Edrigu said, then nodded. "I will train you myself. Come here in the morning at eight a.m. For now, go home and rest. You deserve it." His mentor patted him on the shoulder and gave him a shove toward the door.

"Thank you, Sir. I'll see you tomorrow," he said, giving Edrigu an *Iztari* salute. He took his leave, his duffel bag slung over his shoulders once more.

———

Edrigu watched his protege walk out. It was a pity the boy was too young for his granddaughter, Yuana, and that she was already deeply involved with a human. Otherwise, he would set them up. Veren was the type of man that any grandfather would want their granddaughter to meet. Smart, intelligent, driven, and with his heart in the right place.

And as he was an *Aswang*, everything would be easier for his granddaughter.

———

ONE YEAR LATER.

Anza wasn't looking forward to today's itinerary. Her father and stepmother, the entire extended family, would go on their quarterly holiday to their mountain lodge. It would be a very

long drive, and she had nothing to be excited about for when they would get to their destination.

They would leave her alone in the cabin when they all went out, giving vent to their natural inclination to transform and be themselves.

She couldn't take part in the activities they all looked forward to, which were all geared towards a demonstration of supernatural skills that she didn't have: super strength, super speed, super senses, and shape-shifting. She was the only one in their midst, an *Erdia*, a half-Aswang who shared their blood-line, but none of their powers.

The only thing of value she had for her father's kind was that her viscera could power them better than a human's. At times, she fantasised about incidents where they would need her to give them her liver to save their lives.

But the reality was, the scenario would never happen, and if it did, her father would never allow it.

She was her father's princess, and he treated her like one to a fault. Her parents loved her, and that blinded them to the fact that she was not like them. They treated her like a *Viscerebus*, and raised her to follow the laws and the codes of their world, including the *Veil of Secrecy*.

When they went for their *Transit*, they would expect her to go with them. They would have to move to an unfamiliar country where no one knew who they were. It would be a complete severing of connection with any humans from their previous life.

They seemed to have forgotten the fact that she was as human as her late mother and most of the people in her school. She would age like the humans. And eventually, she would look older than her parents, and she would die long before her parents were halfway through their lifetime.

In the meantime, she would live the Viscerebus life. With

no permanent roots, with no longtime friendships or relationships with any non-*Viscerebus*.

She sighed and got into the car beside her Momstie. She leaned back and closed her eyes, the plush leather comforting, the floral scent of the air freshener familiar. Her parents chatted quietly about the *Transit*. That suited her. She was not in the mood for conversation.

It would be a few hours before they arrived at their destination. A convoy of their families' cars followed theirs. Memories of how she felt as she listened to her classmates talk about going to the movies during the weekend, and of their sleepover tonight, were still fresh. The piercing sense of envy and longing hurt. They invited her, but she had to decline. Her father never allowed her to hang out with her human classmates.

She understood her father's reasoning, always followed his dictates, never doubted that he only meant well, and she used to agree with him. She wasn't so sure anymore.

Four hours later, their car entered the gated compound of their mountain lodge. A thick growth of trees surrounded the property like a wall closing in. The sounds of the forest—the crickets, the birds, the wind that rustled the leaves—were unusually loud. Anza found the familiar fragrance of the wilderness cloying. Everything about it made her uncomfortable. It highlighted the feeling that she didn't want to be here.

Her room in the lodge was unchanged. The caretakers had cleaned it, as expected. The bed and the linens were fresh. They had aired it, for it did not have the musty smell of a room long unused. They would have done all this within a day. Their *Erdia* caretakers lived in the lodge year-round and went on holiday during their visits, leaving them to their privacy when-

ever they'd come. It was a neat arrangement her family preferred.

With a deep sigh, she looked around her room, her sight landing on her bag. She couldn't be bothered to unpack, so she left it alone. There was nothing much in it, anyway, just the essentials for a three-day break.

She could hear the cacophony of her family outside. They were all in high spirits. Her step-uncle's booming voice dominated as he said something funny. A chorus of laughter followed it. Momsie would be in the kitchen now, supervising the supplies they brought for the weekend - the food, the wine, and everything they would need to spend a memorable family event.

Like before. Like always.

An unwelcome knock pounded on her door. She trudged towards it. It was her cousin, or more correctly, her step-cousin, Xandrei.

"Anz, we'll set up the barbecue outside. Would you like to join us?" The smile on his face was wide and cajoling.

She nodded and followed him out to the verandah.

Xandrei looked down at her, one arm rested against the door as he regarded her. Despite the two-year gap between them and the difference in interests, they were close. Or, as close as she allowed herself to be with him. Xandrei was always attentive to her. He had a depth to him that most people would never know. They bonded over their common love for poetry, which seemed incongruous as Xandrei looked every bit the jock.

And they were both unhappy with their *Viscerebus* trait. In her case, the lack of it. For Xandrei, he found his inability to use his full strength and speed in the sports that he loved, frustrating. There was nothing he could do, because it would violate the *Veil of Secrecy* if he did.

Xandrei compared it to fighting one-handed: it was fun in the beginning, but it became less and less so. Their shared exasperation on this impediment was another reason they had gotten closer in the last five years.

The grill sat on the uncovered portion of the long verandah that wrapped around the lodge. Its position allowed the smoke to waft out into the air once they started cooking. Beside it was a small table laden with raw steaks, marinated chicken breasts and drumsticks, prawns on skewers, corn on the cobs, pineapples, plantains, and pre-baked potatoes wrapped in foil, all ready for the grilling.

Xandrei fired up the grill, while Anza hung back and waited for it to heat. She could see his surreptitious glances. He seemed to sense her disquiet, but he would not ask her directly. He would wait for her to open up. That was Xandrei's way.

He may have to wait for a long time, though, because she didn't know what was wrong with herself, or the source of her unhappiness and dissatisfaction. Her heart was heavy with a combination of grief and anger, a sense of injustice that grew bigger every day.

She was like a keg of gunpowder awaiting contact with a lit fuse that was crawling ever closer.

Anza watched as her cousins horsed around in the gated backyard of their lodge. The ancient trees that surrounded the area seemed bigger and lusher. It added security to the walls that fenced their property. Laughter came louder as the older ones teased the younger ones to the point of annoyance. Immature tempers flared and her younger cousins shifted into their *Animus* out of frustration.

Her fourteen-year-old cousin, a rascal named Caleb, had

been making fun of his sister's crush with Caleb's human friend. The twelve-year-old got so fed up with the antics of her older brother that she, Shelagh, transformed into a hyena. She snarled, growled, and snapped at her older brother. The elders laughed it off. However, their father intervened when Shelagh clamped her jaws on Caleb's calf muscle. He cried out in pain, unable to shake her off.

"Enough, Caleb! Shelagh, stop! You're drawing blood!"

Her uncle's stern voice arrested Shelagh's fury. She let go of her brother's leg and shifted back into her human form. She was teary-eyed out of wrath and frustration. Her brother's blood rimmed her lips.

Caleb glared at his sister. His hand pressed against the bleeding calf muscle that was almost torn off. The bite looked deep, but it would take less than an hour to heal. Her uncle gave Caleb a handkerchief to bind the wound. Shelagh stood with a sullen pout over her brother as she wiped her mouth on the neckline of her pink T-shirt dress and left a streak of a bloodstain on it. Her mother shrieked in exasperation. Blood was hard to remove from cotton fabric.

It's funny that what this household considers commonplace is probably horrific to a human.

Tomorrow, her family would venture into the woods, then shape-shift into a land-based predatory animal to hunt or merely to run around. And by habit, they would leave her alone in the house. It was like being the permanent designated driver when your family and friends went out to get wasted. She was the only one sober, and not by choice.

In the past, she didn't mind. The solitude afforded her time to write songs or poetry, read a book, or take photos. This time, the prospect of being left behind was distressing. She felt... excluded.

She didn't realise the pasted smile on her face had faltered

and that she was fidgeting, until Xandrei nudged her side with his elbow.

"Should I hunt him down, Anza?" Xandrei asked, his expression calm. But his eyes bored into hers.

"Who?" She looked up at him, startled.

"Whoever it was who put such a grim frown on your face," he said. Xandrei touched her forehead and stroked the lines away.

"No one did this to me. I was just … preoccupied."

She walked away and sat in one of the six rattan chairs that lined the verandah. She didn't want to talk about her restlessness, but Xandrei followed and sat beside her.

"Something is bothering you. And if I would hazard a guess, it's your 'otherness,' as you call it. You're back to thinking you're out of place, again," he said, his eyes on her intently.

The truth in his words stabbed at her heart. He read her right. Her discontent had bubbled over the surface. The desire to understand became overwhelming. "How does it feel, Xandrei?"

"Feel what?" Xandrei looked at her, a frown on his forehead.

"To shape-shift. But more to the point, why do you want to?"

It took Xandrei a long moment to respond. His eyes narrowed as he examined his own thoughts. "It's hard to articulate, Anz, but it's like a growing constriction. At first, you hardly notice it, but as the days go, you become uncomfortably trapped, until it becomes a driving need. So, when opportunities to let loose are available, we view it with full enthusiasm."

"Like removing your socks at the end of a long, hot day?" Her lame attempt at analogy made him laugh.

"Yes, actually." Xandrei was still laughing and shaking his head, "It's a very precise analogy, if I may say so."

In a strange way, she could relate to what he described. It was how she felt exactly—trapped. And she wanted to be free. Being unable to do so was driving her to the point of rebellion. Xandrei could remove his proverbial socks, while she could not.

"So, what's bothering you, Anza?" Xandrei's question was serious this time.

"I'm just tired, Xandrei." She avoided his gaze and picked on the loose rattan weave on the chair instead.

"Tired of being the only *Erdia* in a family of Aswangs?"

"I guess ..." It was the closest to admission she could give to him.

To reveal more might give him an idea of what had been brewing in her mind for months now. She wasn't ready to have anyone find out about it, as her plans had not crystallised yet.

Her reticence should have made it clear to Xandrei she was not ready to discuss what was in her heart, but he continued to stare at her with watchful intensity. Her cousin was worried. She patted his hand in reassurance, got up, and went inside to help her stepmother in the kitchen. She needed to go somewhere in which she wouldn't be the discussion or the focus of intense scrutiny.

Her Momstie was preparing the family's *sustenance* for tonight. It was a raw human liver. Her father kept her stepmother company and was gazing at her with soft, loving eyes. She took a seat beside her father, and together they watched Momstie portion the liver in neat, even slices.

Everyone would have a slice, except her. She had seen her parents and her extended family eat raw human viscera countless times, and she was used to the scene. It never bothered her before, but now, her 'otherness' intensified.

She absentmindedly picked up a napkin, twisted it into a thin strip, and fed it into the flame of the lighted

cinnamon candle. The napkin burned in slow degrees; its cinnamon scent took on a burnt smell. The rising smoke mesmerised her and took her out of her own mind. It calmed the chaos in her. The curling smoke unravelled into nothingness. She wished the path to her decision would solidify in contrast.

On impulse, her stepmother's soft hands reached out and stopped her. Momstie never liked this habit. She considered it a nervous tick. Her father didn't mind it. He looked at it as a self-soothing habit. Her dad intuitively connected her tendency to set little things alight when she needed to sort out something in her mind.

With a sigh, she dropped the half-burned material at the base of the candle holder.

"Are you okay, Anza?" Her father's gaze was intent. "You're kindling again."

She nodded and said, "I'm okay, Dad. Just bored." She smiled at them both. She didn't want them to probe. Her stepmother had always associated smiles with a positive frame of mind. Hopefully, her Momstie could influence her father. But even she seemed unconvinced.

The voices of their family floated into the kitchen. Everyone was back and had congregated in the living room. It was *sustenance* time. Her Momstie walked off with the bowl of the human liver to where the family waited.

Her father kept looking at her, assessing her. He was wavering between asking her and waiting for her to open up to him. Half of her wanted him to press her, but her other half knew that his response would remain the same. He would, with a gentle and firm voice, tell her she was too young to know her own mind.

Her stepmother popped her head in through the door a moment later. "Anza, the ice delivery guy is coming tomorrow

morning. Can you handle it while we're away?" It broke the tension in the air.

"Yes, Momstie," she replied, her tone cheerful.

She didn't mind the errand. It was something to do in a day full of nothing.

———————

That night, in one corner of the living room, the male adults were playing cards while the females were engaged in gossip in the kitchen. The younger ones busied themselves with a board game in the breakfast lounge with more passion than could be expected from the game. Her teenage cousins were, like her, occupied with their gadgets.

Her rambunctious Uncle Heydar, a burly man whose clean-cut look was a complete opposite to his personality, went around the room singing in a deep baritone. The lyrics annoyed the women, but it entertained the young ones.

Her family filled the house with chatter, laughter, and activities. They kept each other entertained with their own antics and stories. Her family was content being themselves. They were complete.

It was beyond her to pretend to be upbeat. She kept to herself, with her headphones on. Music floated in her ears and drowned the hum of noise surrounding her. It helped as everyone was in full volume.

She sat at the corner chair and put up a pretence of chatting with her friends on the phone, looking at social media posts, scrolling past photos and articles, and watching videos. She was the picture of engrossed.

In reality, she was drowning in misery.

"You need not feel like an outsider, Anz. Don't set yourself apart. Choose to belong," Xandrei murmured on her forehead

as he dropped an affectionate kiss on it. He left her to her own company and proceeded to his room.

His words made her sit up. It drove the clouds of melancholy from her mind. It sparked an idea of how she could end her inner turmoil.

Choose to belong. Of course!

I have always had a choice, but I never thought about taking the step to claim it.

And I might just have the perfect opportunity tomorrow.

Then, she took in her first freeing breath in months.

Early the following day, the sun was just rising, but their kitchen was already abuzz with activities. Every single one of her family members was preparing for their day out. They would spend the better part of it running in the woods in their *Animus,* hunting for deer, wild boar, or whatever took their fancy.

She would have preferred to stay in bed, to pretend that she was still asleep, so she wouldn't have to see them off. She didn't want to be discouraged from her plan. A knock on her door forced her to get up, to open it and engage with whoever was outside.

It was Xandrei.

"Your mom is calling for you. I think she wants to leave a few instructions."

She knew he didn't miss the signs that she barely slept, but was wise enough to keep his opinion to himself. Her cousin was the soul of diplomacy and tact.

She followed him out to the living room. Everyone was waiting and raring to go. Each one wore a tracksuit and a snapped-on bag strapped diagonally around one shoulder. The

bag would keep their clothes and shoes while they were in their animal form, so it would be within easy reach when they'd return to their human forms.

"Anza, the payment for the ice is on the kitchen table. Have them put the twelve bags of ice cubes in the big freezer and the big block in the smaller one," her stepmother said.

"Yes, Momstie," she said.

Her heart had been picking up its beat as the seconds bled away. A plan had crystallised in her head last night, and being left alone was crucial to its execution. She noticed Xandrei had hung back. He didn't seem ready to leave like the rest. He could ruin her plan or remove her time advantage if he stayed.

"Are you not running out with everyone?" she asked.

"Are you okay being alone here, Anza?" He ignored her question, a frown on his face. "I don't want to leave you here by yourself."

"Oh, don't be silly," she said. She pushed him toward the rest. "I'll be fine." She added a lilt in her tone to reassure him.

"No, truly, Anz. I don't mind staying in today," he said.

He stared at her, trying to assess her sincerity. But she heard the reluctance in his voice. Xandrei loved running in the woods in his *Animus* since he never got to do it in the city.

"No, I won't let you pass up this chance to unleash your *Animus*. Don't worry. I'm okay," she insisted.

"Are you sure?" Xandrei's uncertainty was fading.

"Yes," she said, her tone emphatic. "I'll lock up behind you, so I'll be safe. Find me some wild guavas and we're even." She offered him her most reassuring smile. "Go and take off the proverbial socks."

He grinned at the quip, a touch of relief on his face. He dropped a kiss on her forehead, snapped on his own leather bag under his right arm and around his left shoulder, then headed out after the others.

Soon, everyone ran full tilt to the woods. They disappeared behind the thick cover of trees, their shouts of goodbye fading. She rushed to Xandrei's room to get his backpack. She would borrow it without his permission, as it was much better for travelling than her own. It would keep her hands free.

She found it on the chair by the bed, opened but still full. Her cousin, like herself, didn't bother to unpack. She dumped his stuff into a drawer in his wardrobe and slid it shut. A quick search of the many pockets of the bag ensured that she had taken out everything that belonged to him.

She took the backpack into her room and loaded the contents of her own bag into it: extra jeans, two t-shirts, a bath and face towel, toiletries. As an afterthought, she took one of Xandrei's t-shirts from his wardrobe. She would use that as her nightclothes, as she didn't bring her own during this trip. She was in a hurry to finish this before the iceman arrived. With house keys in hand, she took the backpack to the kitchen to wait for the ice delivery.

She had enough time to write her parents two notes. The longer one explained her plan. That should lessen their worry. But she placed it in her father's wallet, where he wouldn't find it as soon as they had returned.

She needed as much time as she could get to cover more distance before they looked for her. Her second, shorter note was a decoy—it said she went to the nearby creek to take some photos. This one she left on the kitchen table, propped against the coffee maker.

She had just finished having breakfast when she heard the approaching truck. Her heart pounded like a giant woodpecker. She stuffed the two water bottles and the sandwiches she packed into a plastic container into her bag.

Ten minutes later, the ice was loaded and stored in the freezer. She paid the men and asked them for a ride to the city.

She told them she needed to buy something, and the old driver obliged. When asked how she was going to come back, she told them her father was going to pick her up.

With the house locked up and a last look around, she hurried out and got into the front with the driver and his assistant for a ride to the city. She wanted to cry, but held herself in check. She had chosen her path, and she needed to follow it. This was where she belonged—with the humans.

And she needed to learn to live as they do.

———

It surprised Veren when he picked up his phone to find it was Edrigu calling him. He just got home from the *Iztari* office. There must have been something he had forgotten to do.

"Hello, Sir?"

"Veren, can you come back to the office? I have a case for you." Edrigu's voice was even, but there was a sense of urgency in it.

"Yes, Sir. I'll be there in twenty minutes," he replied. He grabbed the backpack he had dropped on his bed just a minute ago.

Sixteen minutes later, he walked back into Edrigu's office. He was on a video call with a worried-looking gentleman.

"Take a seat, Veren," Edrigu said, then turned back to the gentleman on the screen. "Manuu, this is Veren. I think he is the perfect person to find your daughter. As we agreed, we will have more success in getting to her and convincing her to come back home if she doesn't feel threatened by the *Iztaris*."

The man on the screen looked at him closely. He seemed unconvinced. "He looks so young, Drig."

"Veren is twenty-three, well-trained, capable, and he has my complete trust, Manuu. The office will use both approaches

so we can recover her in the quickest time possible. But I think Veren will be more successful at this," Edrigu said. "I will send a second team to cover other areas."

Edrigu's trust and open endorsement warmed his heart. But Veren kept his face impassive, his posture erect. He listened and kept all questions to himself. He wanted to receive the full instruction from his mentor before he asked them.

"Okay, I trust your judgment. You know best how to do this," Manuu said, his fatherly concern palpable. "But please hurry, Drig. She's only sixteen and an *Erdia*. She cannot protect herself."

"Don't worry, Manuu. We will get her back. She cannot have gotten that far. Now, send me a copy of her letter to you," Edrigu said. The man nodded and hung up.

Edrigu turned to him. "As you heard, I'm assigning you to this case. Manuu is a good friend of my father-in-law, and his daughter, an *Erdia*, ran away. We need to find her ASAP."

Veren nodded. "She ran away with her boyfriend?" he asked. Such cases were common.

Edrigu shook his head. "No, Manuu does not think so. According to him, Anza has been despondent for the past few months. She didn't seem to want to go in *Transit*. Her cousin said that she was feeling like she doesn't belong with them. She is the only *Erdia* in their closely knit family." Edrigu pushed a copy of the printed picture of the missing girl to him.

He picked up the photo and inspected her image. She was pretty. Long black hair, enormous eyes, innocent-looking face. Almost no makeup. Slim and petite. Around five foot three, at most. She looked younger than her sixteen years suggested.

Could this be an old photo?

She might look different now. Most sixteen year-olds he had met looked far older than their age because of how they dressed and all the makeup they would wear.

"Is the picture recent, Sir?"

"Yes, that was taken a month ago, on her sixteenth birthday," Edrigu replied. He printed the attachment that he'd just received from the email. It was the letter from the runaway girl to her father.

Edrigu read it aloud.

"Dear Daddy, please do not be angry. Do not worry. I went to live with the humankind where I belong. I love you and Momstie with all my heart, but I am not like you and the rest of the family. Time will separate us anyway since I do not have your long lives. Let me establish a root here this early. Allow me to find a family that will be like me, mortal and human, while I have the time to do so. This is not forever. When you leave for your Transit, keep our post office box open. Send me a letter there so I know where I can get in touch with you. I will write to you to let you know how I am doing, that I am well. I love you and you will always be in my heart, Anza."

The antics of the runaway girl annoyed Veren. It was too bratty of her to leave her family on a whim, just because she was feeling insecure about being an *Erdia*.

To make her parents worry like that was just petty and inconsiderate. This girl did not know how it was to be an orphan, to be at the mercy of other people's generosity and kindness. She had no idea what it meant to be truly alone.

"How can she be the only *Erdia* in her family, Sir? Her mother should be like her, at least, right?" he asked.

Edrigu shook his head. "No. Her biological mother was human and died of complications during childbirth. She was referring to her stepmother, an *Aswang* who married her father when she was three."

"Okay. So, what do you want me to do, Sir? From what I understood, you want me to find her. Why me and not the *Iztaris*?"

He wanted to get the full picture, the objectives for this case, and what Edrigu expected him to achieve.

"The simple aim is to find her and bring her back. I believe she could relate to you better than my other *Iztaris* because Anza is closer to your age. We don't know for how long she has planned this. Her father said she's smart and organised, just a tad emotional. No doubt because she's still a teenager," Edrigu speculated. "So, if she had planned this well, she would be harder to find. She would factor in our presence and the possibility that the *Iztaris* will try to recover her. She might have prepared for that." His brows knitted in concentration.

"So, does it mean that when I find her, I must bring her back without telling her the *Iztari* office sent me?" he asked.

Edrigu smiled. "Without telling her that an *Iztari* found her."

His eyes widened with disbelief in what he heard, "*Iztari*? Am I one now?"

Edrigu's smile widened. "Yes, this is your first official case. You are the youngest *Iztari* in the history of this office."

"And if I don't find her? If I fail to bring her back?" He still couldn't believe it.

"Don't say that. And you won't fail. But even if you do, the outcome will not affect your appointment. When you return, you will begin your Iztari fight training. Welcome to the team." Edrigu held out his hand to shake his.

He clasped it tight. In his gratitude, he shook his mentor's hand with vigour. "I will not let you down, Sir," he said, too excited to say more.

Edrigu laughed. "I'm convinced you won't. So off you go. I gave you access to her file. Learn about her tonight, and you will be off to the area where she was last seen—Tuguegarao City. From there, you will figure out where she could have gone to hide."

"Okay, thank you, Sir. I appreciate this opportunity," he said, giddy and fired up at the same time.

With a quick *Iztari* salute, Veren left the office. He had to stop himself from jumping with joy. His blood was afire with excitement, ready to begin the preparation for the case.

He was confident he would find her and bring her home no matter what. Even if he had to sedate her the whole way back.

3 A NEW MISSION

Veren sat in a local coffee shop in Tuguegarao City. He didn't expect it to be so dense with low-rise buildings and people. The streets were typical of small cities: tight four lanes of concrete with almost no sidewalk. Old homes made of wood and stone and semi-new buildings made of glass and cement stood side by side along the road. Cars, jeepneys, and tricycles roamed the roads in a noisy parade, but there wasn't much traffic. Their pace was slow, but steady.

He was waiting for the man who delivered ice to the household of Anza Soledad, the last person who saw her. According to Manuu Soledad, the man gave Anza a ride to the city and dropped her off across the street. Then, he drove away. Still, Veren wanted to interview the man himself to see if he could pick more clues that the Soledads missed.

While he waited, he reviewed the digital file of his subject, everything about her on record and whatever else he had learned from her family. Aetheranza Soledad, or Anza, as her parents Manuu and Leire Soledad called her.

Interesting name.

If there was one dead giveaway for an *Aswang* parentage, it was their name. Their kind had a penchant for very ancient and unusual names for their children.

He was glad that his target had social media. As an *Erdia*, she had an advantage over *Aswangs* like himself—their Tribunal allowed her the leeway to create a social media account, for as long as there was no exposure of her *Aswang* relatives in it.

The photos of her showed a well-dressed young girl, fashionable even. Her social media was as extensive as any average human teenager. She filled it with pictures of her travels, the books she read, movies she watched, places she dined in. There were brief clips of her singing songs she wrote herself. Her voice was sweet and clear, almost angelic.

The contents of her pages were engaging. She could easily be a popular influencer, if not for one specific thing—she did not have followers. It was like she designed her social media to be a journal; it was private and exclusive to herself. A record of the moments of her life, to be reviewed later in old age.

That struck a chord in him.

Her family said that she was good at school. She was passionate and strong-willed, but otherwise a dutiful daughter. Her father and stepmother gave him differing opinions on her personality.

According to Manuu Soledad, she was a book-loving, introverted girl. Reserved, observant, and content to be by herself.

Her stepmother disagreed—she claimed Anza loved poetry and music, but she craved affection and social interaction. It would seem her stepmother was correct in that aspect.

He thought about the other information provided to him by her family. He knew she carried little, as she came to the lodge with a small bag. And she borrowed her cousin's backpack. This meant that more than likely, she saw an opportunity

to leave, that this was impulsive rather than a pre-planned action.

"Mr. Albareda?"

An older man stood by his table. He looked to be in his mid-fifties, with sun-browned skin and thinning hair. He smelled of the sun, sweat and a tinge of coolant. The man had one arm darker than the other, which told Veren that he drove with the said arm propped on the window of the truck.

He nodded in acknowledgement, "Mang Andong?"

Veren stood up and offered his hand to the man, who shook it after a moment of hesitation. The older man's grip was limp and weak; the hand was dusty.

Mang Andong took the seat he offered, and after their order of coffee arrived, the man asked him, "What can I do for you, Mr. Albareda?"

"Our family asked me to look for my cousin, Anza. I believe you gave her a ride from the lodge and dropped her off here?"

This was the practised spiel he agreed on with the Soledad family.

"Yes. I told them that already," the man said with a nod.

As Manuu Soledad told him, Mang Andong seemed very open and cooperative. Veren's tablet was open and ready to note what Mang Andong would say. He was also taping their conversation, so he could review it later.

"Yes, Sir. My uncle told me you did. Did you notice anything about her? Did she say or ask you about anything during the ride? Was she carrying anything with her?"

Mang Andong was quiet for a moment as he dredged his memory.

"No, I don't think so. She just said thank you when she first got into the truck and thank you when she got off. She saw this coffee shop and asked to be let off here. That's where I dropped

her off." He pointed to the open space across from the coffee shop.

Veren looked out at it. There was nothing of note on that side of the road.

"Did she ask to be dropped off at this coffee shop in particular?"

"No ... not really ... I guess I just assumed. It was early morning, and this coffee shop is popular with the local teenagers. I thought she needed breakfast," he said.

Veren looked around and realised that Mang Andong was right. It was now getting filled with young people, coming in small groups of two or three.

"Did you see her go into the shop?" He wanted that clarified.

"No, but I looked at the side mirror and I saw her cross the street. That was it." The man took a careful sip from his styrofoam cup. "I hope you find her. She's so young," Mang Andong said, his face serious, his tone touched with concern.

"I hope so, too, Sir," he said. "Thank you for your help." He shook the kind gentleman's hand for the second time.

When Mang Andong left, Veren got out to the front of the coffee shop and surveyed the area. There was nothing of note until he realised there was a small travel agency three doors away. It was closed at the moment, but it could be worth looking into later.

When he got back to his table, the manager of the coffee shop hovered near it. He had requested to speak to her earlier, but she was not in yet. She was here now.

"My staff said that you were looking for me?"

A human female in her mid-thirties asked this with a slight frown on her face. She smelled of cinnamon, baked bread, and the coffee powder that dusted her right-hand sleeve. She must have ground some coffee beans and transferred them to a jar.

He nodded.

"Yes, I just want to ask some questions about my missing cousin. We believe she may have stopped here two days ago." He handed her the picture of Anza. "She looks like this."

The woman looked at it, trying to recall. "I'm sure I didn't encounter her—I'm good with faces. Approximately, what time do you think she might have come in here?"

"Around eight to eight-thirty a.m."

"My assistant may have come across her. I was on the afternoon shift two days ago. He won't be here until after lunch, around one p.m. You can come back to ask him later," she suggested.

"Thank you, I'll do that," he said, nodding.

"Anything else I can help you with?" she asked. Her unremarkable facial features changed into something pleasant as she smiled.

"Ah ... What time does that travel agency next door open?" he asked.

"Oh, you mean the Travel Bug? That office has been closed for a few months now. They transferred near the City Hall," she replied.

"Oh, okay. I'll check them out." He stowed his work tablet into his backpack, zipped it close, then slung it over his shoulder. "I will return here at one-thirty p.m., if that's okay."

"Sure. See you later," the manager said.

He left the shop and walked to the nearby Travel Bug to examine it. Faded stickers of airline logos and posters of tourist sites and destinations covered the dirty glass doors. There was a sign on the wall that said, 'WE TRANSFERRED TO OUR NEW LOCATION.' A map of the new address was included. He snapped a photo. This was where he was going next.

If Anza came here, she must have looked at the window display. He noticed the most prominently displayed picture

was Batanes island, and remembered the destination shots she had posted on her social media.

The island might appeal to her poetic soul.

He had a gut feel about it, and was convinced she went to Batanes, but his mind told him not to jump to the conclusion. He didn't know her very well. Batanes Island might not meet her standards. She grew up in comfort and luxury. The island's rustic reputation might have dissuaded her.

He walked to the travel agency's new location, a mere four blocks away from their old one. Their new office was cramped, with mismatched tables and chairs, set back-to-back with each other. Two old metal file cabinets were set against the far wall. It had the usual chaos of phone ringing, a pair of dusty computers, and plastic inbox trays piled high with various documents. Though the staff accommodated his questions, the interview yielded nothing. Anza didn't go there at all.

He spent that morning walking around the area. He noted the structures he passed by: small stores, and some middle-sized houses in between commercial spaces. Anza would not take up residence here, he thought. It was too close to their mountain lodge. If she had wanted to disappear as she stated in her letter, she would go somewhere else. The city would only be her jump-off point.

He asked some locals who he encountered along the street where the bus station was, and they directed him to it. It was another couple of blocks away. He found a big, covered area with greasy, gravelled ground. The air stank of petrol and burnt tires. There were about ten buses parked. He noted the various destinations the bus company covered, and his spirit sank a little.

If she took one of the buses from here, she could be anywhere.

He interviewed the ticket officer, a man in a grimy brown shirt and a paunch. While the man was sure he had never

encountered Anza, he was kind enough to call in the bus drivers and their assistants to ask if they saw her on any of their trips. No one had seen her. Of course, it was possible they just didn't remember seeing her.

"Maybe she went to Batanes," the ticket officer said out of the blue.

It made Veren's heart jump. "How do you get to the island from here?" he asked.

"You fly. There's no other way." The ticket officer shrugged. The man turned to the line of ticket buyers that accumulated behind him during their discussion.

Veren walked back to the coffee shop to have lunch and waited for the assistant manager. His thoughts were full of the possibilities of Batanes. He would need consent from Anza's parents to secure her flight information if she flew there. The airlines would never give it to him otherwise.

The coffee shop was full of diners when he arrived. A smiling manager welcomed him as he entered.

"You're back. My assistant will be here in half an hour. Will you have lunch while you wait?" she asked, her smile turned expectant.

"Yeah, that's the plan," he said, and smiled back in response.

"Good. Thank you for contributing to the local economy."

She looked around for a second and found him a seat in the shop's corner. He ordered coffee and meat pie.

Forty-five minutes later, the manager brought the assistant over and introduced him. He was a younger man, though older than him, with a pleasant, round face.

"Mr. Albareda, this is my assistant. Clyde, Mr. Albareda here wanted to talk to you about his cousin. He's looking for her and was wondering if she came here during your shift two days ago," she said in a manner of introduction.

He shook the man's hand, and they both sat down together at his table. He showed Clyde the picture of Anza, who looked at it, his brows knitted together.

"I think she came in here and bought a drink," he drawled.

The information raised his hopes.

"Did she say anything? Mention anything at all?" he asked, mentally crossing his fingers.

"Not to me. But she spoke to the guard briefly before she left. I think she was asking for direction," Clyde said.

"Can I speak to your guard?" Impatience rode him.

"Sure, let me call him." Clyde raised his hand and beckoned the guard over, who approached them.

"Yes, Sir?" The guard inclined his head to Clyde.

"Manong, do you remember this girl?" Clyde showed him the picture of Anza. "She was here two days ago."

"Oh yes, I remember." The guard's face brightened in recognition. "She asked me where the airport was, and how to get there," he replied.

Veren's heart jumped in excitement at his words. That was a solid lead.

"Did she say anything else, Sir?" he asked, wanting to make sure.

The guard shook his head.

With a thank you, he left them and hurried to the airport. He knew where it was. Half an hour later, he was in a queue at the ticketing office. As expected, the airline staff would not divulge details of Anza's flight. He expected it, but it was still frustrating. He would lose some time to secure the required affidavit.

With one last effort, he tried to get the cooperation of the counter staff. A female human who, he realised, was flirting with him. He gave her his best smile as he pleaded his case. She shook her head regretfully.

"I really can't—it's company policy. Besides, Mr. Albareda, she would have needed a written consent form from an adult to book her flight. She's a minor."

That information made him sit up.

"Is there any other way that she could have gotten a seat without the consent form?" He was so sure in his gut that Anza took this route. She would not travel by bus anywhere.

"Hmm, well, if she booked through a travel agency, then we can only check her in. And the only thing we would require during check-in is her ID," she said.

"Where is the closest travel agency?" he asked her, his own smile conspiratorial. Hers widened.

"There are three in the building next door," she replied. "Try the first one on the left," she added.

He took her hand and clasped it tightly in gratitude. "I will look for you when I check-in," he said.

She looped her hair behind her ear, looking up at him from behind her lashes. For a moment, he was thankful for the genes he inherited from his parents, whoever they were. To be decent-looking had definite benefits.

Veren rushed to the building next door and went to the one the ticket officer hinted at. He got lucky. He encountered the woman who handled Anza's airline reservation and ticket. She confirmed his hunch. Anza flew to Batanes Island that same day. She was lucky to have caught that day's flight by chance.

Veren booked himself for the following day. He was fortunate the low season made it possible for him to secure a seat, as flights to the island were only three times a week. The travel agent said that during peak periods, the seats would be booked to capacity weeks in advance.

With a satisfied sigh, he contacted Anza's father to inform him where he was going. It took him a few minutes to pacify Manuu Soledad and convince him not to fly to Batanes, as they

do not know exactly where she was, and she might just bolt again if spooked.

He took a room in an inn close to the airport and to spend the rest of the day researching about the island Anza disappeared to and reviewing her files.

Batanes Island's population was too small to support an Aswang, much less a community. No viable source for *victus*, or fresh human viscera that he needed to stabilise his human form. With his consumption of *sustenance* yesterday, he would have five days to find and bring Anza home before he would need to fly back to the mainland to secure his *victus*.

It was best to focus on his target.

He needed all the information he could find out about Anza. His mission required him to approach her incognito. Her father didn't want her to be returned by force or by guile to the family, he wanted Anza to come home voluntarily. Manuu Soledad was afraid that if forced, she might run away again, never to be found.

She could not know that he was an *Iztari*. Based on what he found out about her, she could be wilful. This meant he needed to be as cunning as he could be to convince this girl to come home on her own accord. Sedating her into unconsciousness was not an option.

It's a pity... That would be easier.

Anza looked around at her rented room. The room was neat, with pastel-coloured walls, floral curtains and bedspread. Everything about it appealed to her, especially the beautiful garden view and the cosy verandah. The breeze that wafted from the open door brought the fragrance of jasmine, which covered the garden below.

She really liked it here. It made her feel safe and at home, but she would have to leave this place to find cheaper accommodation and a job.

When I find a stable job, I will come back to this room and rent it for a day as a reward. Hopefully, it won't take long.

She needed to find a job before she ran out of cash. The money she had withdrawn from the ATM two days ago would not go very far. She would have taken more if there was no maximum limit, and she didn't want to make another withdrawal here, as that would pinpoint her location. Her father would trace her through her credit card and ATM use. Paying in cash was the way to go for her.

She missed her father and stepmother. And she was guilt ridden for ruining their holiday. By now, her parents would be frantic. And for sure, they had already deployed the *Iztaris* after her. Hopefully, she had covered her tracks well enough. She hoped that when they'd find her, she would be settled and have a good job to convince her father that they could leave her behind to live on her own and be independent.

With a heavy heart, she picked up her backpack. Another day of looking for a job. A glance in the mirror startled her, her look still unfamiliar. She had her hair dyed a lighter brown, cut shorter just past her shoulders from its usual waist length. She styled it in a more sophisticated way.

The negative feedback from the jobs she applied to was mostly because of her age. No one wanted to accept her because she looked too young. Today, with her new hairstyle and the full make-up, she looked older. Hopefully, this would also help hide her from the *Iztaris*.

On her itinerary today: quick breakfast first, then an entire day of job hunting.

Four hours later, she was unsuccessful, tired, and demoralised. She didn't have any experience and couldn't provide any references from any of the locals. They gave her pitying looks, advice to go home and focus on her studies, and sent her off. No one wanted to hire a strange girl who looked like she had never done a day's work in her life.

Her footsteps were as leaden as her heart as she sat down on a plastic chair outside a small, local eatery. She was hungry, thirsty, and close to tears. A prepubescent girl approached her with a laminated menu.

"Miss, what would you like to order?" she asked, without glancing at her, her focus on the small pad of paper in her hand, pen poised to write.

Anza took a deep breath to steady her emotions and glanced at the menu. She had scrambled eggs and toast for breakfast, which was not adequate fuel for all the walking she did this morning. She ordered noodles and a boiled egg for protein. She must learn to live and eat simply until she could afford it.

Her food arrived, served hot by the same girl. The server also placed a cold, light brown beverage on the old, Formica-covered table.

"I didn't order this ..." she began. She wanted to keep to her budget, to stretch her cash as far as she could.

"It's free with every order. It's house iced tea." The girl informed her, her tone dispassionate, and then left her to usher in a couple who just arrived.

Anza mumbled her thanks to the girl's departing back. She felt overwhelmed by a stroke of good fortune, and a wave of self-pity followed in its wake. Her chest tightened as she tried to control the expanding pain that bloomed in her heart. Hot tears pricked at the back of her eyes. She breathed deep and tucked into her noodles to stem the desire to cry.

But she couldn't stop the tears from running down her cheeks. She was truly alone, in a situation she made for herself, one she still believed was necessary for her future.

It was hard to chew when her jaw was taut with the effort to keep her sobs in. She was thankful that the noodles, aided by the broth, just slid down her throat. The hot broth warmed her stomach and soothed even her throbbing heart.

It fortified her.

She took a deep, shuddering breath. Crying would not help her situation. She wiped the tears on her face, resolved to continue her search for a job. She forced herself to finish her noodles and the egg. Her appetite left her two spoonfuls ago, but she needed to eat and didn't want to waste food. She had the rest of the afternoon to accomplish her immediate goal. She needed fuel.

With renewed faith in herself, she considered what her new strategy would be. This time she needed to find a reference, and she had an idea who she would approach. A glance in her hand mirror told her she needed to fix her face. Her mascara smudged when she wiped her hand across her eyes, and her tears created tracks on her cheeks. She didn't know how to fix her makeup without her kit.

She got up and proceeded to the ladies' room.

Ten minutes later, fresh-faced and determined, she went back to her inn. She needed her landlord's help. Hopefully, Mrs. Bassig would be generous enough to extend her a helping hand.

Veren wanted something to perk him up. His flight was an unpleasant experience. It was delayed and the voyage itself was bumpy. He was hungry, and he lost time. Anger borne out of

frustration tightened his chest, but it was useless to fume about the wasted morning.

He would have to make up lost ground in the afternoon.

The outdoor seating in the coffee shop provided an ambience that suited the area and his need for a calming influence. It reflected the spirit of the island—quaint, cosy, and relaxed. The wide cream and brown awning overhead softened the sun's glare, and the breeze that ruffled his hair was lukewarm.

He sat outside to drink his coffee and was savouring the first sip when he noticed a young woman across the street. He watched her walk to the local eatery, her shoulders slumped, head bowed—her posture telegraphed defeat and misery.

Seeing a familiar emotion in another person called out to some part of him.

He averted his eyes to shake away the sentiment that resurfaced in him, because he had no time to feel sorry for a stranger. He had a job to do, and he needed to focus. To find his target might take more than the time he had on his hands, and he did not want to fail.

But he found himself drawn to the woman. He could see how upset she was. Her shoulder-length hair could not hide the tautness in her jaw as she fought against her pain, or the movement in her throat as she swallowed down her emotions. Tears glistened on her cheeks as she hunched over her bowl of noodles. He noticed the struggle in her as she tried to control her shoulders from shaking.

And his heart contracted in sympathy.

Then her spine straightened, her chest expanded as she drew a breath. Fascinated, he saw her pull herself together and wipe the tears with the back of her hand like a child. He heard the deep indrawn breath as she fortified her courage. And he could not help but admire the way she recovered so fast from

whatever devastation she had suffered earlier. She looked less like a child and more a woman at that moment.

He wished, for an instant, that his quarry, Anza Soledad, was as evocative as this unknown woman across the street.

She continued eating with the grim determination of a soldier who decided to plough into battle. Her fighting spirit showed clearly in the straightened line of her back and the stubborn jut of her jaw. Then she stood up and went inside the local eatery, presumably to fix herself. He waited with anticipation for her to come out again. For a second, he thought he lost her through a backdoor and was disappointed, but when she came out, his heart stopped.

Her face wiped clean, her hair tied in a ponytail, he recognised who his crying lady was—Anza Soledad.

His target.

I found her.

A thrill of satisfaction ran through him.

Veren jumped up and followed her as she crossed the street. He kept a decent distance between them, making sure that she was always within sight.

Her eventual destination was an inn that looked like a renovated ancestral home. She walked into the lobby with purpose and familiarity. She approached the counter. The staff seemed to recognise her, their manner familiar, their smiles welcoming. He saw her sit on the couch. She looked like she was waiting for someone.

He didn't want to book a room until he was sure that she was staying here. He took a brochure, chose a seat close to her, and pretended to peruse the material. Then an idea struck him. He turned to her with a slight smile.

"Miss, are you staying here?" he asked. "How are the rooms?" He kept his tone and facial expression neutral and mild, so as not to alarm her.

"It's nice here. Clean, secure, and the staff are friendly," she replied, her expression polite, but not inviting any further exchange. Natural restraint ruled her interaction with strangers.

Her parents trained her well. She didn't confirm if she was staying here.

A buxom older woman, her grey-tinged hair set in a loose bun, came out from behind the reception counter and drew Anza's attention. The front office staff pointed at Anza. The woman smiled from a distance and beckoned Anza over.

Anza stood up and hastened towards her. He followed on the pretext of inquiring for a room. Their conversation reached his ears clearly.

"Anza, what can I do for you?" The older woman asked, her gaze soft.

"I have a favour to ask, Mrs. Bassig," Anza replied. Her tone was hesitant, almost shy.

The older woman looked surprised, but smiled just the same. She invited Anza into her office. Anza complied and followed Mrs. Bassig to the room behind the reception desk. The door closed on his ability to eavesdrop.

He trusted his instinct and booked himself a room. The only way for the manager to know Anza, and for Anza to have enough confidence to ask for a favour from the older woman, was because she was staying here.

He took his time filling up the registration form. And when he got his key and Anza had not come out yet from the office, he asked the front desk staff for tourist site suggestions. With the tourism brochures in hand, he stood by the counter and made a show of studying them with careful intent.

A few minutes later, Anza came out of the office with a bright smile and sparkling eyes. She looked both relieved and excited. She thanked Mrs. Bassig profusely.

"So, when do you want to start, Anza?" the older woman asked.

"It's up to you, Mrs. Bassig, but I'm ready to start anytime."

"Why don't you check out the place that I recommended to you first? Get yourself settled and then we can start your training on Monday. Iza, the one you will replace, will not be available to train you till then," Mrs. Bassig said.

"Okay, Mrs. Bassig. I'm very grateful. I don't know how to thank you," Anza said. There was a slight tremble in her voice.

"Do your best, Anza—that will be the thank you I want," Mrs. Bassig said, and with an affectionate pat on her shoulder, the older woman left Anza, who stood teary-eyed as if she still could not believe her luck.

"Congratulations!" Veren said in a soft tone, startling her.

"Excuse me?" she asked, blinking her tears away. "It looks like you got the job," he said, pointing back towards the reception area. At her silence, he added, "Sorry, I can't help but overhear. I was checking in."

"Oh … Yes. I did," she replied. Her earlier relief coloured her voice and tinted her smile.

"Well, I took your recommendation and got a room here. So, thank you," he said.

"You're welcome. How long are you staying?" Her response was automatic, out of politeness rather than from genuine interest.

"I don't know yet." He shrugged. It was the truth.

"Long holiday?" she asked. Her question, this time, carried a tinge of curiosity.

"Yes, maybe," he replied. "How about you?" He wanted to keep his lies to her to a minimum. Perhaps he could pick up some more information about her.

She just gave him a sad, brief smile. A spark of fear and

determination glowed in her eyes. The flash of pride and protectiveness rose in him, and it took him by surprise.

"So, I'll see you around?" she asked, but her tone carried no expectation. She was being polite once again.

"Yes, definitely. Hopefully this afternoon?" He turned on the charm now, his smile friendly and harmless. Now that he found her, she was in his keeping, and would remain under his protection until she returned home.

"This afternoon?" she asked, a slight frown appeared on her brow.

"Yes, I would like to invite you for coffee. For helping me find good accommodation," he said with a deeper smile.

"Ah ... I'm not sure." Her rejection sounded like an automatic reaction. "Um ... I need to check out a place that Mrs. Bassig recommended to me," she said, reluctant and regretful at the same time. Her smile dimmed.

"Can I come with you?" he asked. "I have nothing else to do ..." When she didn't respond, he said, "I would like to explore the area, mingle with the locals, and I don't want to look like a loser by walking alone ...".

She hesitated for a while, regarding him with careful intent. He kept his expression benign and waited for her reply. Finally, she gave him a shy smile and nodded. "Okay."

He couldn't hide his obvious delight at her response. "So, what time are we leaving?"

"I was thinking of doing that now," she said.

"Well then, let's go," he said, and held her elbow.

She threw him a speculative glance. He could see her prudent side warred with her desire to socialise, to connect with another human being. He gave her another reassuring, friendly look, to tip the balance in his favour.

She returned it, and walked towards her destination. He took a relaxed step beside her, pleased with this minor success.

4 CROSSING OF PATHS

Anza was very aware of the man walking beside her. She watched him through her peripheral vision. He was lithe and fit, like an athlete. If she was to guess, he would be a swimmer, based on the width of his shoulders. And he was tall; her head came up to the middle of his chest. His skin had a slight tan, a sign that he enjoyed spending time outdoors. And while he seemed relaxed in his manner, he moved with a certain controlled gait that reminded her of soldiers.

"My name is Veren—Veren Albareda," he said.

He offered his right hand to her. She stopped, looked up at him, then grasped his offered hand. His grip was warm, his hand big enough to envelop both of hers. Manual tasks had roughened his palm.

"I'm Anza," she replied.

Her voice faltered as she took a full look at his face. His eyes were almond-shaped, their colour an odd light brown with amber flecks, framed by straight brows that almost didn't taper at the ends. There was a slight, natural bump on his nose. His lean cheeks and square jaw reminded her of her father. There

was nothing remarkable in the individual features of his face, but combined, the result was striking.

It was hard to guess how old he was. He seemed both young and mature, but if she would warrant a guess, he would be in his early twenties.

"Do you have a last name, Anza?" he asked. His lips curved in a crooked smile.

The sight of it made her retract her earlier description of his facial features. His lips were remarkable. They were full, yet masculine. Most of the men in her family had a thin upper lip.

"Sol ... Soledad," she replied. She was uncertain if it was a good idea to tell him her last name. She glanced at him again, gauging her own instinct about him. He looked too young to be an *Iztari*.

"I'm very pleased to meet you, Anza Soledad," he said. He seemed pleased with her response.

"Likewise," she replied.

He covered her hand he still held with the other, and shook it once again. She pulled her hand away—his warm grasp made her fingers tingle. She resumed their walk to mask her nervousness. He fell beside her with effortless grace, shortening his gait to match hers.

"So, are you from this region?" he asked.

She shook her head. "No, I'm from the ... south," she replied. She didn't want to reveal more information about herself.

"South, like Batangas? Or like Cebu?" Veren's eyebrow raised in inquiry.

"Not as far south as Cebu. Closer to Batangas," she replied. She braced herself for more questions, but Veren surprised her by dropping the topic.

"So, where are we going?" he asked instead.

"Ah, it's a bed space place. Mrs. Bassig recommended it," she replied.

"Bed space? You're no longer staying at Mrs. Bassig's?" He seemed alarmed at the thought.

"I can't afford to stay there. My future salary will not be enough to cover my cost of living." It was painful to accept that she was no longer the Anza Soledad who never had to worry about basic survival needs like food and shelter.

Veren touched her elbow, halting her step. He stared at her, as if trying to understand why she needed to work.

"Are you in trouble, Anza?"

His question startled her.

She shook her head. "No," she replied. She didn't know what else to say.

"Okay, but if you are, let me know. I'm your bodyguard, after all," Veren said, his tone light, almost joking, but she could detect an underlying seriousness in his statement.

She didn't know what to think, so she walked on. They found the house exactly where and how it was described by Mrs. Bassig. It was a medium-sized structure, made of stone and wood, old but well maintained, with a colourful garden in front and surrounded by a white wooden fence made of driftwood.

Low, thick bushes with tiny red and white flowers rein-forced the fence. There were clucking chickens roaming and pecking around the garden, and a small triangular roof-like structure on the ground with a rooster perched on top of it. The wooden gate was low, with a number 32 painted on it.

The thin, elderly owner named Teresa ushered them into her living room. The windows to the house were all open, the short flowery curtains that swayed with the breeze providing privacy to the residents. The house smelled of fried bananas

and ginger tea. Her furniture was made of similar driftwood material, upholstered in green floral fabric.

"Hija, I have no available bed space today. The next available one would be on Tuesday. I can reserve that for you if you want to wait," she said after she set the ginger tea and bananas covered in crispy batter in front of them.

Her heart sank. A week away. That would mean she would have to spend more of her money on her accommodation, something she would rather not do.

Could there be other options?

"Do you know of any other bed spaces here?" At least a temporary one until Tuesday.

"My brother operates one. It's in the next barangay, so it's quite a walk from your workplace. Plus, he accepts male bedspacers, too, so you might not feel comfortable with that." The elderly woman glanced at Veren beside her; she seemed to gauge what their relationship was.

Veren's gaze was intent on her. His face was impassive, but Anza sensed that he didn't like the idea of her sleeping in proximity with strange men. She didn't like it either. However, the landlady was looking at her expectantly, waiting for her response, and she didn't know what to say.

"Manang Teresa, can you give us the phone number of your brother? And yours as well. Anza needs to think about it," Veren suggested. The old lady nodded and wrote the numbers down on a piece of paper, then handed it to him.

They took their leave and strolled back to their inn. Her mind juggled her options. A week's stay at her current accommodation could cover five months of rent in the bed space place.

Maybe I could stay at the other bed space for a week and then move to Manang Teresa's after?

She was so preoccupied with her own thoughts that she didn't notice when Veren pulled her to a small cafe. At her puzzled look, he pointed at the sign and said, "Coffee, remember? I owe you one."

"Okay." She allowed herself to be pushed gently to a chair.

"What would you like?"

"Mocha or latte," she replied.

He nodded and approached the counter.

Moments later, Veren came back with two lattes. They sipped their respective cups in silence. Out of habit, she pulled out a paper napkin from the holder, twisted it into a thin strip, and fed it into the flame of the lit candle on the table. Calm settled in her as she watched the smoke spiral upwards. With it, the earlier dismay for the situation.

Veren set his cup down. It startled her out of her reverie and made her drop the napkin on the table. She looked up to find his eyes on her.

"Anza. I hope I don't appear a presumptuous prick to you ... Granted, we just met, and I still fall in the category of a stranger, but ..." His statement faded, and an awkward silence followed.

"But?" She wasn't sure what he wanted to say.

"I'm not comfortable with you sleeping in a house where there are strange men. It sounds dangerous," he said, face serious.

She didn't know what to say to that, given that she had the same concern. "It doesn't seem so different from having a room in an Airbnb like Mrs. Bassig's." Her defence to justify the plan was half-hearted.

"It's different. You get your own room in Mrs. Bassig's. In a bed space, you'll end up sharing a room with others. Hopefully, all women, but you might be unlucky enough to bunk in with a man. How will you be able to sleep when you have valuables to guard?"

To hear him say it made her feel worse that she had even considered staying there for a week.

"Veren, an extra week at Mrs. Bassig's is equivalent to five months of rent at Manang Teresa's. I think I can handle a—a week." Her voice faltered at the look of alarm on Veren's face.

After a moment, he said, "I have a suggestion."

"What is it?"

"If I hire you as my tour guide for a week at the cost of what you pay for your current room at Mrs. Bassig's, would you do it?" he asked.

"What? I'm not qualified to be a tour guide ... I'm also a visitor here. I just arrived and I don't know the area at all." She said this weakly—his offer had her heart pounding with hope.

"Okay, as a travel companion then," he suggested.

His offer was perplexing, and his persistence baffled her. "But ... why? Why are you helping me?"

"Why not?" He shrugged. "To travel with friends is always better than travelling alone," he reasoned.

She looked at him, trying to find a reason to say no. His offer was so tempting as a much-needed lifeline.

"But I can't afford the cost of travelling with you. The transportation, the food, the entrance fees ..." The reality of her financial status dampened her hope.

"I'll take care of all that. So, don't worry," Veren said, confidence reassuring.

"It seems... unfair to you. Taking me with you as you go around would double your cost, then add what you would pay me every day. It sounds excessive." She was unwilling to take advantage of him, even if his offer was god-sent.

Veren considered what she said for a moment, thinking.

"Okay then, while we're travelling together, would you consider telling me about you? I'll pay for your stories and that would cover the cost of the travel. Your daily fee will be for the

companionship." The matter-of-fact way he explained this made it sound like a fair trade.

"What happens if you tire of my company, or I bore you with my stories?"

"That's a risk I am willing to take ... So, is that a deal?"

There was no reason to decline his offer. It would solve her problem, and she had another week of staying in relative comfort. As much as she wanted to ignore it, he had been pleasant so far, and he intrigued her.

She took a deep breath and decided to trust him. She offered her hand, and they shook on it.

"When do we start?" she asked.

"Today is good," he said. There was a crooked smile on his lips and a twinkle in his eyes.

"No, it's almost the end of the day. You won't get your days' worth. Why don't we officially start tomorrow?"

"Well, I'm already enjoying your company now, so I'd be the one taking advantage of you if we don't count today," he said.

"Take today as an activity between friends. It costs you nothing." It was the least that she could give him.

"So, can we spend dinner as friends as well?" he asked.

She felt the full blast of his charm, and a frisson of thrill went through her. In her panic, she nodded. Her throat was a little constricted for words.

Veren felt pleased with himself. He secured Anza's safety and gained her trust. Now, he found a way to get to know her and discover the best way to convince her to go back home to her parents.

He debated whether he should tell her father that he had

located Anza. But Manuu Soledad might preempt his plans and ruin his chance of fulfilling his mission in full. However, he would have to say something to Mr. Soledad later, or the man might just fly in and show up unannounced. He settled on sending him a text message to inform him that he was still looking for her. He got lucky when he chanced upon her so quickly—he would take advantage of that.

Edrigu Orzabal was a different matter. He didn't want to lie to his mentor. Edrigu knew he was flying to Basco. His mentor would assume that he was still looking for her today, and if he didn't call, Edrigu would assume there was nothing yet to report. Veren had a few hours before he needed to call him.

For now, he had to shower and change. He would meet Anza at six p.m., which gave him two hours to prepare for even-tualities. While he had consumed enough human viscera to last him a week, it didn't hurt to cover all the bases. He must convince Anza before the week was out, because he would need to be back on the mainland to get his *sustenance*.

He sat down with his tablet to record the details of the day, his observations and what he learned about her so far. Anza was not what he expected. He assumed she would be bratty, and half-expected her to give up and go home before he could find her.

It was the foremost reason he was in a hurry to beat her to it. To find her was not enough of an accomplishment. He wanted to be instrumental to her decision to go home, so there would be no doubt he did his job to its fullest extent. He wanted to earn the resolution of the case, rather than get it resolved by default.

Based on what he saw from her yesterday, before he realised it was her, he thought she had grit and the fighting spirit to continue. This girl would not give up, and if he hadn't

been lucky yesterday to have been in the right place at the right time, he probably would have run out of time looking for her.

Anza was still in a daze. She was breathless with the idea of having dinner with Veren. Her pulse hadn't slowed down even after she showered on autopilot. She wasn't even sure if she shampooed her hair. She relied on the texture of her tresses as she wriggled her fingers through, drying them upside down under the blast of the electric fan.

No boy, human or *Aswang,* had ever expressed this much interest in her before. And Veren was no longer a boy. She was unused to the attention shown to her by an attractive man, and it created this heady emotion.

Come to think of it, it's similar, although a little more intense than what I feel for Xandrei.

It was different because Veren was a stranger. He was just a decent guy who was sorry for her, and maybe she reminded him of his sister.

I don't even know if he has a sister.

With a sigh, she straightened up and flipped her hair back. The electric fan had dried it enough. The method gave her hair the body she wanted. She brushed it back into place, then secured the front pieces behind her head with a barrette. The baby hairs that grew around her face refused to be tamed without the aid of hairspray, so she gave up. This would have to do.

She couldn't behave around Veren like her giggly class-mates whenever they saw a boy. It would be humiliating. She would embarrass him and make their daily interactions awkward.

I must regard him as an older brother.

She would treat him like how she treated her cousin Xandrei, since there was nothing different in how Veren treated her from how her cousin did.

She spent the next couple of hours on an emotional seesaw between diverting herself from getting too excited about the dinner to imagining different scenarios, then chastising herself.

After a week, Veren could leave Basco, and she would have to focus on her goal to be independent. His friendship, the first-ever outside of her limited sphere, one formed naturally, was a good beginning to her new life. Hopefully, the memories that would come out of it would be worth remembering for the years to come.

She felt human already.

───────────

Veren was already waiting in the lobby when she arrived. It surprised her because she had left her room early. She was expecting to wait for him. He waved at her from the distance. A wide, delighted smile was on his face. He had changed into faded grey jeans and a dark blue T-shirt under a grey hoodie that was unzipped at the front. He looked carefree and young.

"Hungry?" he asked as she came closer.

She nodded in response. It was the best explanation for her being early. And it also explained why he was earlier than her. He must have been hungry, too.

He took her hand and pulled her with him. Like an older brother pulling his younger sister along. He walked her to a motorcycle parked at the side of the entrance and handed her a helmet.

She hesitated, unable to hide a slight alarm at the idea. A jolt of uncertainty struck her heart. She had never ridden a motorcycle before. It looked dangerous. She met Veren's gaze.

The helmet was still in his hand as he waited for her to accept it. His happy expression was both encouraging and challenging.

Take a chance, Anza. It's just a motorbike ride.

With a deep breath, she took the helmet and put it on under Veren's approving gaze. He fastened the strap under her chin. Her sense of bravery kicked up a notch, and the anticipation of the motorbike ride replaced some of her fears.

As she straddled the bike behind him, she didn't know where to attribute the added thrill that coursed through her, whether it was from the upcoming ride or the unfamiliar sensation of being pressed close to a male body—one that belonged to someone not related to her.

"Hold tight, Anza. And relax. Just lean on me. Don't worry, I'm an expert at motorbikes. I won't let you fall," Veren said over his shoulder.

He must have noticed my death grip around his middle.

"Ready?" he asked.

She nodded.

With a small jolt, they zoomed into the road towards the mystery destination of their dinner. She forgot to ask him where they were going.

Five minutes into the ride, she relaxed. Veren did not lie: he *was* an experienced rider. After the initial starting jolt, the drive smoothened into a fluid motion. The hum of the engine became noticeable to her, together with the feel of Veren's firm and warm back.

It was a brief ride, but with the newness of the experience, it felt drawn out yet fleeting. The surrounding sights went past in a blur of old houses, native vegetation, and people. Her focus was on the sensations rather than the view.

When they reached their destination, it came as a surprise.

She was expecting a simple neighbourhood eatery. Instead, the place looked like a must-go for tourists.

Perched atop a hill, the restaurant offered a stunning view of Vayang Rolling Hills. In the waning light, she could see the building was made of packed earth, bamboo, and wood. It had the thatched roof characteristic of the native Ivatan houses in the area. The flowering plants and green hedges that surrounded the restaurant compound gave it a homey yet magical quality.

The sea breeze that rolled from the ocean cooled the place. There was a small blackboard by the entrance that had the specials for the day: grilled flying fish served on Kabaya leaf, and coconut crabs cooked in coconut milk.

The wait staff ushered them to a table near the window. There were about eight tables in the restaurant, four already occupied. The air had a slight flavour of turmeric, coconut, banana leaves, and sea air.

"I don't know about you, but I find today's specials hard to resist. Do you like seafood?" Veren asked, his eyes gleaming.

"I love seafood. I've never had flying fish and coconut crab before," she said, unable to curb her own excitement.

"Okay, let's get those, and ... some Luñis," he said.

"What's a Luñis?" Everything on this island cuisine-wise was new to her, but that couldn't have put her off, as nothing could be stranger than what her *Aswang* family partook in regularly.

"It's an indigenous dish of preserved pork, usually served fried, crispy, and paired with turmeric rice," he replied.

"How do you know all this?" It amazed her that he knew so much about the island in such a short time.

"Internet searches. I do them before I visit any place," he said, a smug look on his face. "Did you not do the same before you came here?"

"No. My decision to come here was ... an impulse."

"Why? What brought you here? It seems such a long way away from where you were from—the south close to Batangas."

"I'll tell you tomorrow when I'm officially in your employ." She would avoid answering questions about her identity for as long as she could and evade it with every means she had.

He looked at her, eyes narrowed in speculation, then he shrugged his shoulders. "Fair enough."

He got back to perusing the menu. She did the same.

Veren was glad he had already chosen what he wanted to eat when he saw the blackboard earlier. He wasn't reading the menu—he was trying to sense Anza's mood. She came out relaxed, fresh-faced and every bit the sixteen year-old that she was. There was something about her that appealed to him—a mixture of vulnerability and fire. She made him want to tease her, challenge her to take chances, and keep her safe and take care of her in equal measure.

She was reluctant to get on the motorbike earlier. He expected her reaction. It was not the safest form of transportation for most people, and she was a sheltered young woman who was used to the chauffeured, four-wheel kind. He liked bikes but would have rented a car for her if there was one available. It was the spark of courage he saw in her earlier that made him goad her. He had a feeling she would accept his challenge.

And he was right.

He was glad to have chosen this restaurant. Anza did not expect it. He smiled to himself when he recalled her expression. She liked this place. He noticed that his efforts to develop her trust in him had kept her off-balanced and it was proving effective. She needed to reach the point where his words would

have enough sway in her decisions. She needed to heed his advice to come home voluntarily.

"Are you ready to order?" he asked.

She said she was hungry earlier. She only had noodles for lunch, and because she was upset then, she might not have eaten well. As far as he knew, she only had a cup of coffee aside from that. She smiled and nodded at him, putting her menu down. He beckoned the server over and ordered both the coconut crab and the flying fish, plus an order of Luñis.

"What would you like to drink?" he asked.

She didn't respond. Instead, her eyes were full of speculation.

"Will you order a beer?" she asked.

"For you? No, you're too young." He wasn't about to corrupt her with bad habits.

"Not for me, for you," she said, her upper lip curled in mild annoyance.

That made him smile. That one action displayed sparks of her inner fire.

"Well, yeah, I am having a beer ..."

"I'd like to take a sip out of yours ... Just for the experience." Her tone was hopeful, like a little girl asking for ice cream, but the gleam of naughtiness in her eyes was adult.

"Ah, I guess that's okay. I'll give you a sip. But what would you like to drink?"

He felt pleased and somewhat guilty for enabling Anza, for allowing himself to be used to test her new independence, to sharpen her claws. On the plus side, this would deepen her trust in him.

"I will have Kalamansi juice," she said after perusing the drink menu.

The server came with their drinks five minutes later. She was looking expectantly at his beer, which arrived ice cold. Her

glance flew to his face when he made no move to hand the bottle over. With a chuckle, he pushed it to her.

An excited giggle escaped her as she lifted the bottle to her lips too quickly. He didn't have time to warn her as she took a huge gulp and swallowed the icy liquid. She spluttered and snorted the beer out of her mouth and nose, her body wracked with coughs, her eyes watering.

He found it impossible not to laugh even as he patted her back gently and gave her his handkerchief. Anza glared at him through teary eyes. As her cough subsided, she took a sip of water from the glass he handed her. He held the bottom to control the amount that she could take. She didn't resist. That pleased him. Already, she trusted him more.

The server hovered with a rag to wipe the splatter of beer on the table, but he motioned him away. He wiped the table dry with the napkins himself. He didn't want Anza to be more embarrassed. Her cheeks were delightfully red as she looked across from him and saw the people on the next table watching her. The flush of colour spread to her face and neck.

"Are you alright?" he asked as she dabbed her cheeks and eyes with his handkerchief. Her coughing had stopped.

She nodded, looking mortified still. He grinned at her. He couldn't help it. She looked so adorable with her red-rimmed eyes, the flush of high colour on her face and neck, defiance in her jawline. She looked incandescent with life.

"What do you think of the beer?" He tried to keep his face straight.

"It was painful, especially up the nose." Her tone and expression went deadpan. Her lips quivered, and for a split second, he thought she would cry. His gaze flew to her eyes in alarm. Mirth sparkled in her eyes as she tried to stop herself. Their eyes met, and they both burst out laughing.

"You weren't supposed to snort the beer, Anza," he said after he calmed down, in a tone reminiscent of a professor.

"The beer had a mind of its own. I wanted it to go down my throat, but it travelled up instead," she said. The humour of the incident lingered in her gaze.

As he looked at her face, the inner fire he saw in her seemed to have set her alight from within. She glowed. At that moment, he had a glimpse of what she could look like when she had grown into her womanhood. And it kindled something in him that expanded in his chest.

He felt glad that he was here, with her, tonight.

Their server arrived with their food, breaking the electrified moment. The aroma of the grilled flying fish came with the fragrance of heated banana leaves and a hint of citrus. Their crabs looked deliciously rich, the orange shells bathed in coconut cream. The golden-brown pork dish looked crunchy and mouthwatering.

They tucked into their food in relative silence. Anza was hungry as he watched her eat with complete absorption and enjoyment. She savoured a new dish with singularity—she would put it in her mouth, close her eyes, inhale deep, then hum under her breath as if she was engaging all her senses in one go. Her eating habits entranced him.

She didn't just eat her food, she experienced it.

This revealed more than words ever could as to why she rebelled and ran away. Her thirst to experience life to the fullest was deep, and her family, without conscious thought, hindered it.

It amused him to see her suck the flesh out of the crab claws. Her delight in it was so contagious that he ended up copying her. It became a game of who slurped the loudest. This was the first time a meal transcended into an event. It etched itself into his memory.

The sparkle in her eyes told him all was right in her world at that moment. She was happy. It sent a glad note to his heart and with it a sliver of apprehension. She might get used to this human life and that would make it hard for him to convince her to come home to her parents, to their kind, their world, and its veiled existence.

With their bellies full of food and in their hearts, merriment, they capped the night with coffee and enjoyed it over at the lookout point. The rhythmic sound of the waves crashing on the shore, the slight chill in the air paired well with the hot coffee. The result was very calming.

"That was a wonderful dinner," Anza said, glancing up at him. "Thank you."

Her hair was down from its earlier ponytail. The elastic seemed unable to hold it in place. The wind whipped it about her face, making it a challenge for her to drink her coffee in peace. He couldn't resist lifting the strands off of her cheeks and mouth and tucking them behind her ears.

She handed her cup to him as she self-consciously gathered her hair back in a low ponytail. She tucked the shorter baby hairs that grew around her face behind her ears. In that instance, she looked like the sixteen year-old that she was, and he felt a twinge of regret. She was still a baby. And the object of his mission. It was unseemly for him to develop a crush on a high-school student.

This must be how a crush works—the object of your interest seems to blossom right before your eyes, making her more beautiful, more compelling every second.

"What was your favourite dish?" he asked, to keep his mind off its present preoccupation.

She paused, her head tilted, eyes narrowed. "Hmm ... I can't decide. I like them all."

"If you can order only one dish when we dine next time,

which among the three would you reorder?" He was unsure why he wanted to find out her answer to his question, but it felt essential.

"I think ... the crab," she replied with a smile.

He was reminded of their slurping game and smiled back. "Yes, me too. It's a pity that it's an endangered species and we can't eat them regularly." They had tried to reorder another, but the restaurant limited each table to one order.

"Yes, that's sad. But I heartily support that rule. It's for the good of the coconut crab population," she replied.

"Are you a rule-breaker or a law-abiding citizen?" He now faced her as he handed her coffee back.

That gave her pause, although her stance was still relaxed. She took a sip from her cup and sighed. The sound was like a breeze on a scorching afternoon.

"I've never broken a law. I've always abided by it ... but ..."

He waited for her to continue. She seemed unable to.

"But not today?" he suggested. He kept his expression non-judgmental. He wanted her to open up.

She looked thoughtfully at him, as if gauging if she could take the step of trusting him with her secrets.

"Exactly—not today," she said.

His heart jolted a beat faster. "So, will you tell me why you came to be here? Why you're so far away from home?" he asked, staring at her.

She tucked the strand of hair the breeze had freed from behind her ear before she replied. "I ran away from home and came here to learn ... independence."

"What made you run away?" He needed to understand what drove someone like her to leave a family who seemed to love her, to put herself at risk in an environment she was unfamiliar with.

"I can't tell you," she whispered.

She spoke as if her heart was tight. He knew she was hoping he would accept her response and leave it at that.

"Is it something that can't be resolved?"

"I don't know," she replied.

The sigh that preceded the words was heartfelt. He wanted to probe, but he couldn't press her. Not yet. Then a dreadful idea dawned on him. There might be another reason she left home; one they did not consider.

He frowned. "Anza, were you getting hurt? Are you in any danger?" He prayed it wasn't so.

She looked touched by his concern. And he was glad when she shook her head.

"No, Veren. I'm not in any danger. And I wasn't getting abused at home. I ... just can't live the same way. I'm different from them, and I have to face that fact. Eventually, I'll have to leave them anyway. I just want to have an early start and not get too dependent on their presence. It's better to do it now while I'm young and able," she said.

He knew it was the most she could tell him. It was very difficult not to reassure her that he understood what she was going through. Silence reigned between them as he digested what she revealed. Her cousin and her mother were right about her and what made her run away from home.

Anza looked up and was struck by the expression on Veren's face. It was like he just saw her for the first time. And yet the way he angled his head as he fixed her with a penetrating stare made her feel like a revelation to him.

"Do you not think your parents will be anxious about you?" Veren asked. His frown was etched with concern.

"I had planned to send word to them that I'm okay. Hope-fully, it will suffice," she said.

"That wouldn't suffice. You're very young, and pardon me for saying so, but you don't strike me as someone who is used to this ... spartan kind of life," he said.

She couldn't contradict him. Mrs. Bassig made the same comment to her earlier, and it was her obvious naïvete that convinced Mrs. Bassig to offer her a trainee position as front desk and guest relations officer for the next six months.

"Is it that obvious that I'm inexperienced?"

"Hell, yeah! You look like a child, a sheltered child," he said. His voice had increased in intensity. He sounded annoyed, almost angry.

"I'm not a child. I'm already sixteen. Most people call me a young woman!"

Veren sighed, reaching out to take her icy hands between his. He shook his head as if he regretted having raised his voice earlier.

"Anza, for most parents, sixteen is still a child. And you look younger than sixteen." His tone was gentler.

"Well, I can't help that I have baby face genes in me..." She felt like stomping her feet, but that would just prove his point. Instead, she pulled her hand from his and turned away.

There was silence from Veren. She waited for his comment, but there was none. And when she glanced back at him, his lips quivered from the effort not to grin.

"I suppose declaring that I'm an adult, then throwing a tantrum to prove it, is counterproductive," she said.

Veren grinned.

Her own smile broke through her lips and spread to her heart.

5 THE DEVELOPMENT

He had been staring at his phone for almost an hour now since he returned from walking Anza to her room. He had been trying to decide what to report to Edrigu. Why he put himself up to the goal of convincing Anza to go home was beyond him.

A call-in for his progress for the day was due, and he didn't want to lie. If he told Edrigu that he found Anza already, he might wonder why he had not told Anza's father about it. He could use Manuu Soledad's own desire to have Anza come home at her own choice as the reason, but Edrigu might point out that Manuu would want to do the convincing himself. All he had to do was let Manuu know Anza's location.

With Manuu, he could pretend that he misunderstood his instruction, but with Edrigu, there wouldn't be any ambiguity. If his mentor gave him an order, he could not go against it.

Unless ...

An idea came to him. He dialled Edrigu's number, pulse picking up. His mentor answered in two rings.

"Good evening, Veren. How are you coming along in Basco?" Edrigu's voice was clear despite the distance.

"I'm good, Sir. I just called in to report on my progress." He kept his tone controlled to tamp down his own uneasiness at the minor deceit he would play on his mentor.

"Okay. Do you have solid leads about Manuu's daughter's location?" Edrigu asked.

"Yes, Sir. I found her this afternoon," he replied.

"Wow! That was fast. Have you told Manuu? What is the arrangement? When are you due back here?" Edrigu's questions made his heart race.

"I have not told Mr. Soledad that I found her. Ms. Soledad still does not know I am an *Iztari*, and I'm afraid if she finds out, she will disappear again. Her father wants her to come home willingly and telling him might not achieve that—he might show up here and spook her away." He hoped his voice wouldn't give away his exaggeration of the facts. "And, if she disappears this time, we may not find her again."

Edrigu was silent on the other line. He had the impression that his mentor knew what he was doing. With luck, Edrigu would consider the logic in his explanation.

"So, you want to convince her yourself?" Edrigu asked. The tone of clarification made Veren's heart skip a beat. His mentor read his intention with ease.

"Yes, I was hoping to do that, Sir." He held his breath as he waited for Edrigu's response.

"Okay. So, what kind of help do you need from me?" Edrigu asked.

Veren felt his relief like a loosening of a tight band on his chest.

"Help me reassure Mr. Soledad that he need not worry about his daughter, that I can convince her to come home voluntarily," he said.

"How much time do you need to accomplish this?"

"A week, hopefully, since I would need to go to the mainland for *sustenance* by then," he replied.

"Okay. I'll take care of Manuu. In the meantime, I will give a heads-up to the *Sustenance Supply* in the mainland to prepare for your needs," Edrigu said. "Just in case."

"Thank you, Sir. I truly appreciate it." His chest loosened with relief.

"You're welcome," Edrigu said, then hung up.

He was sure, at that moment, that his mentor knew exactly what he was up to and was giving him the latitude to do so. He felt better and guiltier by the end of that conversation. He fell asleep justifying to himself that he just wanted to complete the mission in its entirety.

Anza had been running through the night's events again and again in her head. The exhilaration she experienced tonight was all new to her. The mental back and forth of being hopeful and cautious, in giving meaning to each word and action that was part of this experience, had kept her unbalanced.

This must be what having a crush is like—being in constant awareness of his presence, his words, and actions.

Veren was the first male human she had spent this much time with. Her father's rules had prevented her from forming friendships, even with her classmates, limiting her to brief conversations and tepid, trivial pleasantries. The warnings of potential separation pain when they *Transit* was never far from her mind.

She blamed her own inexperience for her susceptibility to Veren's attention. But her father did not raise an airhead, so it would be an insult to him if she allowed a crush to sway her

within a few days of being independent. Veren may be human, but she was not about to exchange a dependency from one species to another.

Besides, depending on a man's affection as a source of joy would be counterproductive for her search for true happiness.

Tomorrow, I will look at all the actions and words of Veren to be nothing more than those from an older brother.

Or a good friend ...

No, an older brother ... Nothing could develop outside of a brother-sister relationship.

She walked into the lobby, expecting to see Veren, but he was nowhere. She was looking about for him when he came out of the gift shop at the corner. He was carrying a bottle of sunblock, which he handed to her.

"Are we going to the beach?" She looked at the bottle in her hand.

"We're going to a lighthouse. I don't know if the beach that comes with it is good for swimming, but I thought it best to be prepared," he said. "Do you want to get your swimsuit? Just in case it's possible to swim there?"

"I didn't bring one." There was a lake and a creek on their property, but like the previous trips, she was not expecting to swim, since her family always left her behind when they ventured into the woods.

Veren glanced at the gift shop, and she saw a rack of swimsuits inside. She stopped him before he turned back towards the shop.

"It's okay, I ... don't want to swim today. There will be other opportunities. We *are* on an island ..." She turned away and slid

the sunblock in her backpack to avoid any more conversation about the topic.

Veren's eyes narrowed. He looked like he wanted to insist, but she stopped him with a question. "Shall we go?"

"We're leaving in a while. I'm still waiting for something," he said, a small smile on his face.

She nodded and sat down on the couch. She was a tad hungry but didn't think she would have enough time to order a sandwich. Veren might be on a schedule, and she didn't want to cause a delay.

A coffee shop worker came out with a small picnic basket just as she was thinking to buy a bottle of water to tide her over. She handed the basket to Veren, who thanked her with a smile. The girl blushed and tittered.

"Shall we?" Veren inclined his head to her, and she followed him out to where he had parked his motorbike. He secured the basket at the back of the bike while she picked up the helmet she used the day before and put it on.

"Do you have a jacket?" Veren looked at her flimsy T-shirt.

She shook her head. Veren took off his own backpack and fished out a long-sleeved shirt.

"Put this on—the ride is long. You'll get cold," he said.

He helped her slide her backpack off, holding the cotton shirt as she pushed her arm through the sleeves. It was soft and well-worn. It carried his natural fragrance and something citrusy. The man smelled good ... and familiar. Yet, she couldn't identify it.

She was picking through the catalogue of scents in her memory when Veren grasped the front of the shirt and buttoned her up into it like a child. His action startled her into stillness, allowing him to do the task quickly.

The sleeves seemed a foot longer than her arms when she

held it up. Veren grinned and folded it back to allow her fingers to show.

"Shall we?" He nudged her chin with a knuckle. She nodded and followed, straddling the bike behind him.

I'm a little sister to him.

He's like the big brother I never had.

She repeated the words to herself as they zoomed along the country road, her arms wrapped around his waist, her thumbs hooked on his belt loops.

They drove through cliff-side roads that offered stunning views of the sea, and interior rural streets that oozed with quaintness. They zipped past towns humming with country life: women sweeping front lawns and hanging laundry; kids playing with sticks and well-used traditional toys; men walking with a purpose towards somewhere, and domestic animals and livestock meandering about.

It was such a simple, very human existence. She was both sad and glad to be in the middle of it. Life on this island contrasted sharply with her previous one. It was almost poetic that she had ended up here to start her new life as a human. It was a perfect representation of back to basic and starting from the bottom.

But if she was to start her life with this new beginning, she could not have chosen a more appropriate location. She was far safer here than if she had chosen the big city. A simpler life was easier to achieve among simple people and surroundings.

The ride took three hours. Her butt went numb, her throat dry, her stomach protested in hunger, yet she didn't ask for a break. She didn't want to inconvenience Veren. Her job was to be his companion, not a dependent. She was wondering how much longer the trip was going to take when they turned right into one of the country roads, and there it was: the Basco Lighthouse.

It gleamed white from the distance, standing solitary and imposing at the edge of a hill. It reminded her of the immobile Beefeater that guarded the Tower of London. Maybe because it appeared as dependable? This concrete guard looked like it watched and waited for passing ships in perfect patience for decades.

Their bike purred to a halt by the parking area in front of a building with a blue roof. It was a closed café. She hopped off to allow Veren to kick open the bike stand and secure it in place, then she removed her helmet to better view her surroundings. The sea, a deep aquamarine that blended into the intense blue of the sky. The hills were lush and emerald, like undulating pillows of vegetation.

And the air tasted of sea salt and adventure.

On impulse, she ran closer to the safety railing that protected the visitors from falling off the cliff. A wooden stairway with thick ropes for support snaked across the face of the hillside down to the beach.

The exceptional beauty and serenity of the scene drew her eyes in. The sound of the waves in a perpetual race to the shore, the bright blue sky that forced her to squint, and the light breeze that swept in from the sea soothed her ragged spirit. It seemed like the world had given her permission to dare. To live.

She looked back to check where Veren was. He had untied the basket from behind the bike and carried it with him as he approached her. He led her towards the lighthouse. They stopped by the grassy area in front of the circular tower. Veren unfolded a fabric she recognised to be a tablecloth from the coffee shop at their lobby. He knelt and unloaded the contents of the basket: bottled water, sandwiches, and packed garden salad.

"Let's eat first." He tugged at her hand to make her sit down. She slumped beside him, almost landing on his lap.

Veren chuckled and gave her a bottle of water, cap loosened. She drank it down to half and sighed in relief as the cool liquid soaked the parched tissues of her throat.

"I figured you were dehydrated," he said. Amusement glittered in his eyes.

"How could you tell?" She picked up a sandwich.

"Your lips were dry." He tapped the bow of her lips with a gentle finger.

Her gaze flew to his as her fingers covered her lips in defence. "It was a long ... and windy ride," she mumbled, focusing her gaze on the sandwich in her hands to will away the heat that bloomed on her cheeks.

It was a long roll that looked like a hotdog bun. She opened it to examine the filling. The scent of lemon and dill wafted from it. By the look of it, this was a lobster roll sandwich, the specialty of the coffee shop, but one she had yet to try.

"Eat. That looks delicious," Veren said. He was holding a big cheeseburger.

She took a bite and almost moaned—the chilled lobster meat was fresh and sweet, with a hint of mayonnaise, celery, lemon juice, and dill. The bread was soft and the combination of flavours sublime.

Veren shook his head at her, his expression a mixture of regret and amusement as he took a bite of his burger. She realised Veren might have ordered the lobster roll for himself, and she took what she wanted without care, without asking him.

"Oh, did you want this?" She felt guilty that she hadn't even asked Veren before she took the lobster roll.

He laughed. "It doesn't matter. It's just ... your appetite is contagious."

"No, truly, we can share. I *cannot* finish this." She set down

the bun to search for a knife to cut the roll in half. Veren stayed her movement, his cool hand on hers.

"No need to slice it. Eat and enjoy it. I'll finish the leftovers if there are any," he said.

"Won't that be off-putting ... to eat my leftovers?" she asked.

"You don't have rabies, so I'm not worried," he said. He stopped her protest by lifting her chin to close her mouth. "Stop arguing, little one. Just eat. I know you didn't have breakfast this morning."

Little one?

"How did you know?" She hoped she didn't look starved.

"I asked. They said you hadn't come down to breakfast."

"Oh ..."

She didn't know what to think about that. Veren had a mischievous twinkle in his eyes as he continued to eat. She followed his lead and finished her lobster roll.

Little one, really?

Like a puppy?

Veren watched Anza surreptitiously. She ate like a child, with full enjoyment. She was prim and proper when she was conscious of what she was doing, as if she had to stop herself from being too enthusiastic, from immersing herself in the moment. Yet, when she forgot herself, when the experience overcame her reserve, she soaked it all in, full senses deep.

It was stirring to behold.

Is this how she lived her life? Like a flame trapped in a glass jar, slowly suffocating at the lack of oxygen?

Anza reminded him of the young elephant he saw in Thailand a few years ago. It grew up tied to a metal pole, so it got accustomed to the limited movement of the length its leash

allowed. The animal was so used to being bound that it stayed within that range even though it had doubled in size and could uproot the pole if it so desired.

Anza was the elephant who walked beyond the range and uprooted the pole. However, the experience was so new to her that it scared her. She could still feel the imaginary leash of the *Vis* world and its restrictive power. She would never be free until the muscle memory of being reined in faded and left her completely. That would require exposure to the other side of her world, beyond her comfort zone and into unknown dangers.

In that moment, Veren could empathise with Manuu Soledad.

Anza roused something soft and intense in him, a sense of protectiveness that he had never felt for anyone before. She was like a kitten, all fluffy fur and claws; like a filly, ready to bolt anytime she got spooked. And Anza was a hair's breadth away from bolting deeper into a surrounding she was unfamiliar with.

Anza reclined on the picnic cloth, stretched her arms over-head, and arched her back. Her actions were almost feline. He realised she must have been sore from the ride. She was rigid that whole time, despite the relaxed hold she had around his waist. It disappointed him that she wasn't comfortable enough to lean on him. But then, they had only known each other for less than twenty-four hours. It would be odd if she lacked caution.

With her eyes closed, he could observe her face. She looked very young, a bud still far from full bloom. Her youthful features, her size, her physique, her vulnerability called to his masculine protective instinct. He understood why her father sheltered her the way he did.

Anza stirred as he was putting away the remnants of their lunch. She got up and collected the cloth, folded and placed it

into the basket. She was going to take it to the bike, but he took her by the hand and towed her toward the lighthouse. He placed the basket on a wooden bench by the circular stairs.

"Ready?" He smiled at her and pointed to the top of the tower.

"We can go up?" Her eyes rounded with undisguised excitement.

"Yes, we can. The view is best on the top."

She hesitated for a moment, gazing up. Her expression was a mixture of apprehension and thrill.

"Let's go." He tugged more firmly at her hand and made her choice easier.

With a giggle, she followed him up the narrow, winding stairs to the top. Their ascent was rushed. Halfway through, Anza stopped and gripped her sides, bent at the waist.

"Hang on," she gasped. Her face was flushed and glistening.

He gave her a couple of minutes' rest. Then, he pulled at her hand and said, "Hurry, while we have the lighthouse to ourselves. You can take pictures to your heart's content."

"How do you know I enjoy taking pictures," she asked, curious but without even not a tinge of suspicion.

Oops!

"Don't all teenagers?" He kept his tone neutral. Anza trusted him, and he needed to keep that trust. "Don't you have any social media?"

"Sure, I do, but it's private. Only for my consumption," she replied.

The familiar sadness flashed in her eyes.

"Don't you have followers?" he asked. He wanted to keep her talking. They were in the last five steps to the top.

She shook her head.

"Will you allow me to follow you online?" He made room

for her to step onto the platform, to the view. It unfolded before her, leaving her mouth agape, eyes wide.

"Wow!" she breathed out.

That drew a wide smile from Veren. Her delight gave him pleasure.

"Wow, indeed!" he said, following her gaze towards the horizon.

The sun was no longer overhead. The sky, where gaps between patches of thick clouds showed, was a clear blue, but he could sense an oncoming rain. He felt the change of pressure in the atmosphere and smelled it in the air. Anza had better take her photos soon.

A quiet sigh escaped Anza's lips, and regret flashed in her eyes. He realised that, since he met her, he had never seen her use her cell phone.

"Don't you want to take pictures?"

"No." She shook her head. There was a slight downturn at the corner of her lips. "It's all right. My social media isn't that important right now."

"You don't have to post it until you're ready." He wanted to capture this moment for her. "It may be a long time before we return here, so take the pictures now."

She looked even more crestfallen. "I don't want to turn my phone on," she said.

"Why?" He frowned.

"My father could be tracking my phone ..."

It surprised him that she knew about how cell phones worked. He didn't expect it. Also, she was right. The *Iztari* office was tracking the transmission from her phone. Once again, he felt chagrined at his quick misjudgment of her capabilities.

He took out his own phone and handed it to her.

"What's this for?" Her eyebrows quirked.

"Use mine. And click away," he said. "I'll transfer the photos to your phone later."

"Oh, thank you!" On impulse, she bounced on her feet and launched herself into his arms.

"You're welcome." He hugged her back. The jolt in his heart made him uncomfortable. "Now go, while the light is good. The clouds are rolling in ..." He pointed at the sky.

"Yes, boss!" She gave him a gleeful salute and a wide smile. Her face beamed with pure joy.

Anza spent the next fifteen minutes taking shot after shot. She deleted those that didn't meet her standards and showed him the images she liked. Her innate talent for photography was on full display.

"Are we going somewhere else after here?" she asked as she handed him his phone.

"No," he said, sliding the phone in his pocket. "Sunset is beautiful here. The locals highly recommend it."

"That would be awesome," she said, eyes lit up once again.

"Let's hope the rain doesn't come before that."

———

Luck was with them. The rain came as the sun sank across the horizon. Anza had just finished taking photos.

It started as a drizzle, then turned into a sudden downpour. The wind drove the rain towards them and forced them inside the lighthouse for shelter. They sat together on the floor by the glass window, as the dark columns of rain undulated with the wind and lashed against the transparent barrier.

Rainwater had soaked Anza's jeans, and the hem of the shirt he loaned her. Within minutes, she was shivering. The tremors that ran down her slim body travelled from her shoulders to his, where they touched.

"You're cold," he said, and pulled her closer to keep her warm. His arm curved around her.

Her discomfort was significant enough that she didn't resist. In fact, she gladly leaned into him, sighing as she did. He anchored her better, her head cradled in the crook of his arm and shoulder, her cheek pressed against his chest.

The hum of the wind and the hiss of the downpour was hypnotic. Mother nature expressed its raw power in the churning waters of the sea, by the vertical drive of the wind, and the darkening of the sky. Veren knew Anza had dozed off. Her weight had settled on him. He centred her body and head on his chest, to make her more comfortable.

The rain droned on for hours. With her limp, warm body nestled against his, both of his arms around her, a cocoon of contentment enveloped him. He was at peace. He held her to him, this delicate creature with the tensile strength of titanium now temporarily in his keeping.

Gladness seeped into his soul and lulled him to sleep.

Anza surfaced from her nap in slow degrees. Her awareness first centred on a familiar scent, then the warm, hard flesh under her cheek, and a steady beating of a heart. It took her a moment to realise she was half reclined on Veren, his arm curved around her.

He was still asleep. She was reluctant to leave the comfort of his arms, but she eased herself out, trying not to wake him. She sat up and looked around—they were on the floor, leaned against the concrete wall of the lighthouse.

The slow flash of the light overhead reminded her of the cameras of old. The glass window mirrored her image back at her in intermittent flashes. It showed her hair in disarray. She

pulled the hair tie off, then combed her fingers through her tresses, massaging her scalp.

The rain had stopped. The air smelled salty from the sea and tasted sweet from the wet grass. They should probably be heading home now. It was already dark, their ride was long, and she was hungry. Maybe she could ask Veren to stop by a convenience store for something to eat and drink. She gave Veren a gentle prod to rouse him.

"Hmm?" He blinked awake, looking up at her. He seemed disoriented and stared at her for a while.

"Shouldn't we go now? We have a long way to go," she whispered.

"Don't you want to wait for dawn? You can take photos of the sunrise to match your sunset shots," he murmured. Then he sat up and stretched his long limbs, a slight wince on his face.

"I would if I wasn't so hungry," she replied, and got up. Blood rushed to the numb places in her limbs, making her groan. "Pins and needles ..."

That made Veren smile.

"Do you think we can stop by somewhere for food?" She asked this to distract him from her embarrassment.

Veren's smile turned indulgent. He glanced at his watch. "I can do better. There's a cafe nearby." He jumped up and helped steady her on her feet.

"The blue and white building?" She gathered her hair back to tie it in a ponytail. "Isn't that closed?"

"It opens at 6 p.m.," he said, then stayed her hand. "Leave your hair down—it will help keep you warm." With a light touch, he smoothed the strands away from her face.

She found the affectionate gesture sweet.

Hand in hand, they walked down the circular stairs. They were the only two souls in the lighthouse. The weather discouraged tourists. The picnic basket was where they had left it, the

motorbike still at the front of the cafe that was now open. A white car was parked nearby. After securing their basket on the bike, they proceeded inside.

There were three people in the cafe, two boys and a girl. They all swivelled and gaped at Veren and her as they walked in. She felt self-conscious, as the two boys' interest was fixed at her. She glanced up at Veren. His face was impassive, but he was looking at the boys as well. A slight tension emanated from him. Veren seemed wary and on guard.

The server greeted and ushered them to a table at the other end of the room. Veren pulled the chair where she could see the three in her peripheral vision. The guys were still looking at her. Veren sat beside her with a direct vantage point to the other table. His relaxed pose was misleading.

She wanted to look at the other table, to see what had caused his stress, but she didn't want to be obvious about it. The menu proved to be a useful shield, as she peered at them from behind it. The boys were still throwing glances her way.

She then noticed the girl with them had her eyes on Veren. She was older than her, with waist-length, shiny, straight hair and a self-confidence that made her feel uneasy. Her interest in Veren was as obvious as the interest her companions directed at her.

A stirring of animosity against the woman rose in her. She glanced at Veren. He was busy reading the menu, uninterested in the woman's gaze from across the room.

"What would you like to have, little one?" Veren asked, his eyes still on the menu. "How starved are you?"

She was, earlier. At the moment, her annoyance had lessened her appetite. But she wouldn't let the other woman ruin her dinner.

"Very," she said, "I would like this one," She pointed to the chicken dish on her menu.

He lowered his menu and looked at what she pointed at. "Okay. Is that enough?" he asked. His gaze went back to his menu after a cursory glance at hers. "No soup or salad?"

"No. The chicken is enough." The bite of satisfaction lessened her growing irritation. Veren didn't even glance in the woman's direction.

Veren signalled the server over and placed their order. She kept her eyes on him as she thought of ways to keep Veren from exchanging looks with the woman ogling him. The odious girl was now waiting for a chance to catch his eye, a small, ready smile on her face.

"You look irate, little one," Veren said. He reached over and picked up a lock of her hair and tickled the side of her nose with it. "Is that hang-ger?" His tone was teasing.

"Hang-ger?" She frowned in confusion. "You mean hunger?"

"No. Hang-ger. Hunger-induced rage." His eyes twinkled in mischief.

"Oh ... No, I'm not ..." Anza began, her temper heated. She realised it was a better explanation for her attitude, "I guess I am." She smiled at him apologetically.

"A bit of patience, little one," Veren chuckled.

He reached out and playfully pinched her cheek. Pleased with their exchange, her brain scrambled for ways to keep him engaged. None of her previous experiences with her father or cousin Xandrei seemed applicable. She had never had to manipulate her father or cousin to keep their attention on her. Then she remembered their deal.

"Don't I owe you stories for the meals?" she asked.

"Oh, yeah." Veren's smile widened. He looked pleased to be reminded of it.

"So, what would you like to know?" She was thrilled her ploy worked.

"Tell me about your childhood." Veren scooted his chair closer, an encouraging smile on his face.

She hesitated for a bit as she thought how much she could divulge without giving too much, without revealing her true identity.

"I'm an only child. My mother died of birth complications. My dad raised me alone for the first three years of my life, and then he married my stepmom. I call her *Momstie*," she began. She paused as the server arrived with their drinks. She wanted no one else to hear of her life story.

"Momstie?" Veren asked as he unwrapped the straw and pushed it into his drink.

"Ah ... Momstie, short for stepmom ..."

Veren nodded. He seemed impressed with the nickname.

"How was your relationship with your parents? Your dad, in particular." He blew on his coffee.

"It's a great relationship. My dad doted on me, but he was ... overprotective." She stirred the straw in her iced tea.

"How so?"

She felt a twinge of guilt at the thought of talking about her father to a stranger. She sighed, "I'm not allowed to make friends, not even with my classmates."

"You have no friends of your own age?" Veren's focus was solely on her now.

"None ... Just my cousin, rather, my step-cousin Xandrei. He's eighteen. He's the only one I'm ... close to," she said.

"Did your cousin know?" he asked, his expression appraising. "Your plan to run away, I mean."

She shook her head. "No, he's overprotective as well. He would have told Momstie." She took a sip of the iced tea to loosen the knot in her chest, buying time should he ask for more details. As a compulsion, she reached out for the paper straw covering; the flame of the lit candle on their table beckoned.

"Okay." Veren seemed to understand. He reached out and covered her fidgeting fingers with his. "How about your step-mom? Do you get along with her?"

She nodded. "Yes—she treats me like her real daughter. Momstie is cool. Nothing bothers her. In short, we're very different."

Veren said nothing. He just continued to look at her and seemed to wait for her next words.

The arrival of their food interrupted their conversation. Veren's eyebrows knitted in a quick reaction, but his face became a pleasant mask when he turned to the server.

The tone of their dinner changed. Their interaction had always been lighthearted, but now there was a depth, an added layer to their relationship. It was almost tangible, the finest of threads, yet strong. She waited for him to ask questions, to cue her to return to their previous topic, but he kept their conversation friendly and casual.

Veren ordered grilled lobster for himself. It reminded her that she stole his lobster roll sandwich earlier.

"I'm sorry ..." She felt driven to apologise again.

Veren looked up in surprise. "For what?"

"I took your lobster roll this morning." She pointed to his dish.

He shrugged. "It's no big deal. Actually, after seeing you eat the roll, it made me crave lobster." He scooped a chunk from the shell, dipped it in the lemon butter sauce, and popped it into his mouth. "Oh ... that is good ..." His voice deepened in appreciation.

"So, you really bought the roll for me, and the burger for yourself?" she persisted, wanting reassurance.

Veren chewed and swallowed before he replied with, "I bought both for either of us. If you had chosen the burger, I

would have happily eaten the lobster. It was a simple matter of getting something I thought we would both like."

"Really? Are you—"

He cut her off. "Anza, eat your food. It's getting cold."

She smiled at him. In return, he gave the lock of her hair a slight tug and continued with his meal. There was a noticeable increase in the camaraderie between them during the rest of the dinner. They shared each other's food. She cut him a portion of her chicken and placed it on his plate. He reciprocated with his lobster but insisted she take a bite from his fork.

In her head, that last act could be sexy and romantic, just like in the movies.

Or platonic, like a big brother feeding his kid sister.

With her luck, it was probably the latter.

With two steaming cups of takeaway coffee, Veren drew Anza to her feet. The coffee shop would close soon. They would drink their coffee outside where they had lunch earlier. As Veren opened the door, a blast of frigid night air hit him. Behind him, Anza shivered.

He gave Anza the coffee cups to hold and pulled her into his jacket. Anza sighed, and it made him smile. They made their way back to the patch of grass in front of the lighthouse with a brief stop by their bike. He took the tablecloth from the picnic basket and tucked it under his jacket.

The downpour left the grounds wet. The tablecloth would not have offered protection. They ended up huddled on a dry patch atop a low boulder, their backs against the stone walls of the caretaker's house. The structure shielded them from the icy wind that swept inland from the sea.

"What brought you here in Batanes?" Anza asked as she blew on her hot coffee.

He took a sip before he answered. "Nothing in particular. Part of a bucket list ..." He wanted to avoid this topic. He didn't want to lie to her. It was a good thing she was too inexperienced to know how to probe for information.

Anza looked up from her cup and stared at him. "Will you tell me about your childhood?" she asked.

Fuck!

His heart leaped at the question. No one had asked him that question for years.

"Not much to tell. I was an orphan," he said. "My mentor took me under his wing when I was five, sent me to school, then gave me a job. He gave me everything a young person with no parents needs to survive and thrive." He adopted a relaxed posture to hide the fact that discussing his past was not a pleasant subject for him.

She didn't seem convinced by his facade. There was a frown on her face, but her eyes were devoid of her usual emotions. He couldn't tell what she was thinking. His little one had learned to mask her feelings.

Not good.

"It must have been hard," she said, her eyes never leaving him.

Darn!

He took a deep breath before responding. "Yes, I guess it was." Giving brief replies might discourage her from asking for more.

"So, what do you do now?" she asked, her head inclined to the side.

Holy Aquila! She's persistent.

He took a big gulp of his lukewarm coffee to buy time to plan his response.

"I'm in between jobs," he said. That was technically true. "I return to my new one in a month," he added.

"A month? Are you staying here for that long?" Anza was looking at her own cooling cup, her voice stilted.

"Maybe ... although it depends," he replied to the top of her head. He wished he could see her expression.

"On what? I thought this trip was part of your bucket list." Wish granted—she was looking at him again.

"Well, the items in my bucket list are not simple, one-layered things to be ticked off," he replied.

Anza's nod was slow, but whether she accepted and understood what he said was unclear. It seemed to be an automatic action she did when she was trying to make sense of the information she received.

They both turned towards some voices that were coming closer to them. The group of humans at the coffee shop were now going their way. Anza glanced at Veren with a frown. She couldn't make out what they were saying. Thanks to his superior hearing, the conversation of the incoming party was clear. The three were looking for them. The boys were keen on meeting Anza, and the girl was interested in him.

He sighed. They would have to deal with these juveniles unless they left the lighthouse. But he promised Anza the sunrise ...

"Oh ... do you think they're coming this way?" Anza asked, her nose wrinkled in disapproval.

"I'm afraid so, little one. You'll have to put effort into being sociable," he said.

She shook her head. He pulled her closer in a mock headlock.

"I don't know how to be sociable," she replied from beneath his arm, then untangled herself from his hold. He could almost imagine her pouting, except she wasn't the pouting kind.

"Then this is a good time to learn," he said, and released her.

Anza combed her hair back and twisted to face him. There was a worried crease on her brow and fear in her eyes.

"You did well with me. You weren't shy," he reminded her.

Her frown deepened. "You're different. You didn't give me time to think, and I forgot I didn't know how to be sociable," she said.

"Well, do what you did with me. Just answer their questions ... and don't frown." He touched her forehead to ease the creases. "And I'm here. I'll help you."

Three minutes later, the group caught up to them.

"Hi, guys! Are you waiting for the sunrise, too?" The only girl in the group was leading the pack. She wore a wide, friendly smile.

"Yes," he answered casually.

He surveyed the group standing ten feet away. She was carrying two bottled waters, one in each hand. The guy behind her was carrying an extra bottle. A quick look at the bottle caps told him that both were unopened.

"Can we join you?" she asked, then paused right in front of him. Her question was just for him, despite the word 'we'. She stood with a stance seemingly meant to emphasise her curvaceous hips. The girl apparently knew she possessed a splendid figure and was using it to her advantage.

Veren glanced at Anza to make sure she was okay. Her face showed no emotion, but he could feel the slight tension emanating from her. He almost said no.

"Sure, join us." He gestured toward the space in front of them. The soldier in him wanted them where he could see them.

"I'm Charisse," the girl said, waving with the bottle in her hand.

"I'm Veren."

"Hi—I'm Anza," Anza said. The tension in her shoulders increased, but her voice was calm.

"I'm Diego," the taller of the two boys said. He had short shorn hair at the back and the sides, but the front was longer and styled up. His smile revealed a pair of dimples and nice teeth.

"Hey—I'm Charlie," the other boy said. This one had longer, slicked-back hair. "Would you like some water?" Charlie asked, offering the bottle in his hand to Anza.

Veren intercepted it. He wanted to make sure it was safe. The bottle was chilled. He unscrewed the cap and handed it to Anza.

The boy's expression was telling. Charlie was unsure of how to react to Veren's protective gesture. Veren didn't care—he wanted this boy pre-warned that he was here to protect Anza.

"Thank you," Anza said, directing her remark to Charlie.

"Can we sit with you?" Charisse asked. She eyed the space in between Anza and him. She seemed to want him to scoot a little, to make room for her.

He nodded, but before Charisse could act on it, Anza moved nearer and covered that coveted gap. She took the option away and made her opinion about the situation clear.

Charisse, to her credit, was unfazed. She sat in front of him, cross-legged, her back to the view. The two boys copied her. The rock could only accommodate two-and-a-half people. Both Diego and Charlie positioned themselves right in front of Anza.

Time to do due diligence on the three. "So, where are you guys from?"

"We're from Baguio," Charisse replied with a disarming

full smile. "Diego and I are cousins. Charlie here is Diego's friend, frat brother, and my classmate."

"What brought you here?" Veren asked.

"We're on holiday," Charisse replied. Her free hand now played with her own hair, twirling it like most young women do when trying to be overtly feminine.

"Which school do you go to?" Anza's question sounded relaxed.

He glanced at her and noticed that her posture was rigid and almost defensive. Anza was asserting herself. His little one was flexing her confidence muscle.

"Oh, U.P. Baguio," Charisse said. She looked at Anza for the first time, her smile tight at the corners. The girl clearly saw Anza as competition.

"How about you, Anza? Which school do you go to?" Diego asked, his tone open and friendly.

"I don't know yet. I haven't decided where to go," Anza replied.

His little one was cool under pressure. When it came to hiding her background, Anza's years of practice as an *Erdia* showed.

"So, are you from here, or are you visiting like we are?" Charlie asked, glancing at Diego, a challenge in his gaze.

Veren could read the competition between the two boys. And he didn't like it. Their antics to win her regard might prove enough of an inducement for a young girl like Anza to want to stay with the humans longer.

"We're visiting." Anza's curt reply was guarded, not encouraging.

Veren inwardly smiled. So far, the boys hadn't enticed her. She was too inexperienced to use their attraction to her to her full advantage.

"How long are you here for?" Charisse asked. Her gentle touch on his knee ensured that he would look at her.

He turned to Charisse, who was smiling at him as she waited for his reply. Anza's interest in his reply to Charisse's question gleamed in her gaze, which had turned on him.

"For however long it takes to accomplish what we want to do here," he replied, answering for them both.

"Are you ... together?" Charisse's asked, her tone tentative, one eyebrow arched.

It was clear to him that she wanted to know her chances. The two boys were also keen to find out if Anza was available. He chose to misunderstand the question. He wasn't about to divulge the nature of their relationship.

"Yes. We came here together," he replied, and glanced at Anza.

Anza gave him a slow blink of annoyance. A quiet huff followed as she turned to Diego. He was unsure what caused her ire—he thought that she wouldn't want her circumstance known to strangers.

"So, Anza, are you going to University this coming school year?" Diego asked, outwardly glad to have her looking at him.

She shook her head. "11th grade."

"Oh, you're about ... 17?" Diego asked. "I'm 18, turning 19."

"I'm sixteen." Anza's admission came out reluctantly.

"Wow, you must have started school early," Charlie interjected, unwilling to stay in the background.

"No, I skipped first grade." Anza's response was automatic.

That was news to Veren. Her records didn't mention it.

"You must be smart, then." Charlie's comment had a hint of condescension.

Veren felt Anza's defensive barriers rise, annoyance in her eyes. His little one had claws and was preparing to use

them. Charlie was still smiling at her, unaware of the effects of his words. *This would be interesting to watch.*

"There are worse things than being smart," Anza said, her tone clipped.

Charlie's face fell as he realised his mistake.

"I agree with Anza. Being a basketball jock, for one." Diego wisely picked up the opening that Charlie's gaffe created, and gave Anza a conspiratorial smile.

Anza smiled back at him. Diego scored a point there. Veren felt a kick of irritation and a stirring of dislike towards Diego.

A cool breeze swept over them, making Anza shiver. She was the only one among them unprepared for the cold temperature. The thin shirt he loaned her was not enough to keep the chill away.

"Do you want my jacket, Anza?" Charlie offered, poised to remove his windbreaker, and redeem himself from the earlier mistake.

"There's no need," Veren said, stopping Charlie. He took the picnic cloth tucked inside his jacket, shook it out, and draped it over Anza's shoulder. The cloth retained the heat from his body. He took advantage of the opportunity and placed his arm around her, pulling her closer to him.

He could better protect her like this.

6 IN KEEPERSHIP

I*f I was a full Vis, a true Aswang with shape-shifting skills, my animal form would be a cat. No doubt about it.*

The cosiness of being cradled by Veren was purr-inducing, and she would have purred if she had been capable of it. His left arm was draped behind her, cushioning her back against the stone wall. She had laid her head on his chest. He smelled of that unidentified yet familiar scent of himself and night air. She closed her eyes to savour and drown her senses with the sensation of being close to him. It was also useful to pretend to doze off to avoid engaging with the three people who invaded their private moment.

She was comfortable, both inside and out. She could stay like this until morning. No conversations, just being together. The sound of the waves, the cool breeze that wafted from the sea, and the comfortable semi-darkness had a mellowing effect on her. Nothing Charisse or Charlie could say or do tonight could rouse her temper.

"Aww ... she's so sweet. The poor kid fell asleep," cooed Charisse.

Except that.

"Has she?" Veren asked with laughter in his voice.

She knew Veren was aware that she wasn't sleeping, that she just didn't want to socialise and this was her means of escape. The tension in her body would have been impossible for him to ignore.

A lull in the conversation followed. Her hair tingled at the sensation of eyes resting on her. Perhaps they were making sure she was indeed asleep.

"What do you do, bro?" Diego asked, breaking the silence.

Anza thought, *That's a good question*. She also wanted to know Veren's answer.

"I'm into asset recovery," Veren replied, a hint of mirth in his tone.

Asset recovery? That made her peek under her lashes.

"Cool ..." Diego clearly didn't know what Veren meant.

"You're in finance, then?" Charlie piped in.

"Not quite."

Veren's reply made her want to press him for more explanation herself, but she couldn't because she was pretending to be asleep.

"What type of assets do you recover? Properties? Vehicles?" Charlie persisted.

"Only those of extreme value," Veren replied. He rearranged the cloth that had slid down her back.

She wondered what valuables he was referring to. His response to the question didn't make his position clear.

"How long have you three been friends?" Veren asked, effectively ending that topic.

She could almost see his raised eyebrow, a habit of his when asking questions.

"Years," Charisse replied. "Diego and I have hung out together since grade school. Charlie and I met two years ago

through Diego." Charisse sounded glad to be directly conversing with Veren.

She heard Charisse shift in her position, maybe to find a more comfortable one, or to move closer to Veren.

"Are you and Anza related by blood?" Charisse's question was bold and direct.

Veren stiffened. Either it surprised him, or he didn't like the question.

"We're not." Veren's response was curt. It discouraged further probing.

She wondered if Veren's clipped response told Charisse he wasn't about to divulge any information about them. Hopefully, the woman was smart enough to pick up on the nuance.

"What *is* your relationship with her?" Charisse asked.

Apparently not.

"At the moment, I'm her keeper," Veren said. The muscle in his arm flexed. It felt like it tightened around her.

"Keeper? What is that? Like a babysitter?" There was a slight smirk in her tone.

"Or a bodyguard?" Diego asked.

"Anza doesn't need a sitter, and she can take care of herself," Veren said.

There was a tinge of pride in his voice, and a touch of disbelief, like it was a revelation to himself. It warmed her insides.

"So, what does it mean to be her keeper?" Charisse persisted.

"I'll let Anza answer that," Veren replied, evading the question.

"But she's asleep ... Can you just tell us?" Charisse cajoled.

Under her lashes, she saw Charisse reach out to touch Veren's knee. She wanted to slap it away, and didn't realise her hand, sandwiched between them, was clenched until Veren chuckled and squeezed her shoulder.

Veren shook his head. "No, that would betray our keeper-ship," he replied, chuckling.

Charisse released a slow breath of frustration. "How old are you, Veren?" she asked.

"I'm ... 23," he replied, surprised at the turn of Charisse's question.

"I'm turning 20," Charisse said, with a note of glee. "We only have three years' age difference between us," she continued. "My cousin and Charlie are closer to Anza's age," she added when Veren didn't respond.

Anza sensed Veren's puzzlement. He didn't seem to understand where Charisse was going with the question and statement. But she did—Charisse was using the age gap between Veren and her as a weapon. It sparked her temper and incinerated her natural inclination to be prudent.

"Are we comparing manufacturing dates? Measuring shelf life? Or counting down to our best before?" Anza questioned.

All eyes swivelled in her direction, their expressions of surprise identical.

Except for Veren—amusement danced in his eyes. A slight warning entered it when she roused herself. With hands linked, she stretched them overhead, pulling on the muscles of her back. The hard rock and the cold air made it sore.

"We were discussing birth dates ..." Charisse's tone sounded defensive, and a touch antagonistic.

"Were you?" she asked sarcastically, not caring if she offended the woman.

"Was that a good cat nap?" Diego asked in a pacifying manner. The smile on his face seemed genuine.

"Yes, it was ... stimulating," she replied, smiling back. Of the three, Diego was the only one she liked. Marginally.

"Was there enough time for a dream?" Diego appeared to be bent on easing the tension that had built up between her and

Charisse. He was a peacemaker, a true gentleman. Anza appreciated it.

"Alas, no," she replied.

"Would you like to stretch your legs?" Diego had stood up, offering her his hand. She hesitated. Her muscles were tight, but she didn't want to leave Charisse to monopolise Veren.

Charlie got up, too. "That's a good idea, Diego." He faced Veren and said, "With your permission, Veren, can we accompany Anza for a walk?"

Veren looked at her, waiting for her to decide.

"Let them go, Veren. My cousin and Charlie are harmless. They'll take care of Anza," Charisse said, touching Veren's knee again.

"Why don't we all stretch our legs?" Veren suggested, standing up and pulling Anza to her feet.

She didn't realise her butt had gotten numb from sitting for so long. She winced and gasped as the blood resumed its restricted flow through the veins at the back of her thighs.

Veren heard her. "Are you okay, little one?"

"Pins and needles," she said, trying to rub the sensation back on her rump. Veren grinned as he watched her. "I'm ready." She shook off her legs.

With her hand curved into Veren's arm, they walked toward the end of the ridge, their steps slow and meandering. Diego had situated himself beside her. Charisse, as Anza expected, had slid her own arm through Veren's other arm. Charlie, it seemed, had lapsed into silence, and walked a step behind them all.

She wished the three would leave them alone. She wanted to ask Veren some questions, specifically what he meant when he declared himself her keeper.

Was he just joking?

What does it mean?

Veren's patience was running thin. These three humans and their normal ways shouldn't have bothered him, but they did. He didn't like how Charisse treated Anza, or how Charlie insulted her. He was glad that Anza's reaction to a crushing comment made her hackles rise instead. Her first instinct was to fight.

But the most bothersome thing was that Diego got on Anza's good side. Veren didn't want to look too deep into why it displeased him, since Diego wasn't as obnoxious as the other two, and making friends would benefit Anza.

During her brief stint here in Basco, she would have a chance at every human experience to create enough memories to last her a lifetime—so, she wouldn't want to do this again. The most ideal situation was for her to make them while Veren was around to protect her. He could help her assess which ones she could trust, and which ones she should stay away from.

Anza's instinct with people was good, but her youth and perhaps her desire to make connections would make her vulnerable. And, if tonight was an example, she was attractive in every way a teenage girl could be. She would draw that kind of attention wherever she went, especially when she learn to use her feminine charms.

He wondered now if her father ever taught her how to defend herself. Most females of their kind, at least the *Vis* he knew, had some basic training. It was part of the drill.

Anza didn't look trained, her body slim and slight like a normal human teenager. She didn't strike him as athletic, either. Maybe it was the combination of her physique and innocent face that made him want to make sure she was safe, unharmed, unhurt.

Anza's chuckle drew him out of his own musings. She was

laughing at whatever joke Diego told her. The boy was getting more successful in drawing her out by the minute. It chafed at him, but he didn't react. He would let Anza enjoy herself. This was temporary since she wouldn't see Diego again after tonight.

"I think my cousin and your ward are getting along fine. Don't you?" Charisse's comment was pointed as she leaned closer to him.

He could smell the pheromones emanating from her, but her wish would remain unfulfilled. He wasn't into one-night stands, and his work ethic forbade playing while on a job. Unlike the other males of his kind, he wouldn't dally with female humans just because it was common practice. *Brevis Amorem* may be a habit to most *Viscerebus* males, but it was not his.

The *Tribunal's* rules may justify the indulgence for brief affairs, since they were expected to keep relationships with female humans brief and impersonal, but it was not something he liked to do. He wouldn't add more parentless children in this world. No child of his would be a *Vondenad* left to survive alone in this world.

Charisse tugged at his arm, prompting him to respond to her earlier question.

"Anza is a friendly girl," he said with a glance at Anza and Diego. Anza's hand was still hooked on his arm, even if her attention was on Diego. That made him feel connected to her still. On an unconscious level, it anchored her to him.

"My cousin likes her very much. Charlie does, too. But, since Anza seems to prefer Diego, Charlie has stepped back," Charisse observed.

"We'll see. In the meantime, Diego had better behave himself. Anza is under my care." He said it loud enough for everyone to hear. It was a warning that he wanted Charisse to know, and for Diego to heed.

Anza and Diego stopped at the edge of the ridge and looked at him. Then, Anza pulled off the tablecloth draped around her shoulders and laid it on the grass. Charisse was quick to sit at Anza's right side after Anza took the first seat. With Diego at her left, they sandwiched Anza between them. Charisse's intention was obvious: the vacant space beside her was for Veren.

Veren opted to be behind Anza. An exasperated Charlie sat beside him.

Undeterred, Charisse twisted around to face him instead. Her disinterest in the incoming sunrise was made clear. Veren sighed, finding her persistence tiresome, although he couldn't help but be impressed by her extreme self-confidence—she ignored all the signals he was giving her. She seemed like a woman unused to getting rejected. Either that, or her manner of succeeding with them was by railroading their objections.

"So, Veren, do you have a girlfriend?" Her forwardness wasn't unexpected.

"No, I don't have a girlfriend."

Anza overheard his response and twisted to look at him. He placed his hands on her shoulders and made her face forward with a light pressure on her shoulder blades to keep her there. He rubbed gentle circles to reassure her.

Of what, he wasn't sure.

"What traits do you find attractive in a woman?" Charisse asked in a tone so saccharine, it was cloying. All her affectations were so unnatural—it was off-putting.

His response was a gentle shake of his head and a smile. Charisse pouted, unable to hide her irritation at his evasion.

Rays of sunshine started peeking out from the horizon, lightening the dark sky. The midnight blue hues transitioned to red violet. They were all transfixed at the sight. A welcome spate of silence enveloped them. Veren dug out his mobile

phone and gave it to Anza, handing it to her from over her shoulder without an exchange of words. She glanced back at him with a grateful smile.

Another blast of cold air swept through them, making Anza shiver. Without a word, he grasped Anza's waist and pulled her back to him, close to his chest. His bent legs served as her armrests. She leaned back on him. His body protected her from the wind, warming her. Her silent sigh of contentment echoed his.

His chin rested at the top of her head, her back flat on his chest. They watched the sunrise on the horizon in complete silence. Anza held his mobile phone, her elbows propped on his knees. His arm hung loosely around her middle.

As the half globe of the sun showed, Anza aimed the camera at the view, watching the sun through the screen. The colours of the horizon transitioned from varying shades of violets to reds and yellows. Her eyes focused on the display, her fingers clicking at a furious pace.

"Two more minutes, Anza. You have enough beautiful shots," he whispered in her ear. A puzzled frown formed on her face as she glanced at him.

"Why?" Her question came a breath away from his cheek.

"So you can experience the sunrise—the photos can never capture that," he replied. "Be present, little one."

She nodded and lowered his cell phone. And for the succeeding minutes, they watched the sunrise until the whole globe of it emerged. The rays of yellow radiated from the centre sphere and painted the surrounding areas, layering them with red and orange.

It was breathtaking.

Anza took a deep breath and released it in gradual degrees. He felt her smile on his cheek, which triggered a smile of his own. "Shall we go?" she whispered.

"Yes. Let's get some breakfast along the way," he said. With a swift motion, he got up, pulling her too to her feet.

The rest of the group got up with them. Anza seemed surprised at their presence. He couldn't blame her. The complete silence and their shared moment earlier made him forget them, too. That wasn't a good thing if he was to become a great *Iztari*. Losing awareness of the surroundings could be deadly to a warrior.

"Are you guys leaving?" Charisse asked, stepping off the cloth as Anza tugged at it.

"We have to be on our way," Veren said. He took the cloth from Anza and folded it.

"Where are you off to next?" Diego's question was directed at him, but his eyes shifted to Anza.

She shrugged. Anza was waiting for him to speak for them.

"We'll decide along the way," he replied. He understood that Anza was as eager to leave their company as he was.

"Can we tag along?" Charisse asked.

He saw the spark of temper in Anza's eyes. She was close to saying something rude. He squeezed her fingers to stop her.

"We have a few things we need to accomplish. So, goodbye to you now. It's been a pleasure." He held out his hand to Charisse. She looked at it, unwilling to accept his handshake of farewell. Charlie grasped it instead.

"The pleasure was ours. Thank you, too," Charlie shook his hand. "Guys, I believe we have to get going, too. We've imposed our presence on them long enough. We don't want to take up more of their time."

Veren's dislike towards the guy lessened. It seemed he wasn't *that* self-absorbed.

Diego offered his hand to Anza, saying, "It was great meeting you and spending time with you, Anza."

She shook his hand and replied with a benign smile, "Likewise."

"Can I ask for your number? Maybe we can get in touch when we get back to civilization?" Diego's gaze and crooked grin seemed hopeful.

Anza hesitated.

"Anza doesn't have her phone right now. Give me your number and she can get it from me later," he said.

Diego hesitated for a moment, but dictated his number anyway. As he saved it on his phone, he wasn't sure if he could be selfless enough to give Diego's number to Anza after. He could only hope that Anza would forget to ask for it later.

"Can I have yours, Veren?" Charisse asked, her phone at the ready.

He gave her his number without hesitation. It was a burner phone, with a burner SIM card. Training protocol required that they destroy the phone and the SIM card after every case.

The three walked them to their bike. Just before Anza got on the bike behind him, Diego stopped her. "Call me, Anza, okay? I'd like to get to know you better as a... um... friend," he said. His hand clasped hers once more.

The warrior in him didn't like the feeling that bloomed in his chest at the sight of Anza's smile. It made him impatient to leave. The feeling faded as they zoomed out of the parking lot and onto the road, away from Diego, Charlie, and the persistent Charisse.

Veren stopped at a roadside eatery half an hour later. On the menu were fried rice, eggs with fried flying fish and the crispy, dried pork dish they had the night before. The meal came with

dark coffee and brown sugar. It was served outdoors—the weather was perfect for it.

As they set the plates down, Anza's mouth watered at the aroma of hot, garlic fried rice. Intrigued, she watched Veren pour a quarter of his coffee on the rice. Veren laughed at her expression.

"You should try it. It's fantastic. I learned this from the Batangueños. They all pour coffee on their fried rice." With an excited lift of his eyebrow, he tucked into his food with enjoyment.

She copied him with more caution. She spooned some of her coffee over a bit of rice. Combined with the egg and flying fish, she had to agree with Veren. The smokiness of the coffee complimented the flavours and neutralised whatever oiliness there was in the fried rice and egg.

"That was delicious!" she said as the first mouthful assaulted her taste buds.

It was such a simple variation of a commonplace dish. Just a tweak. And yet, it brought her a new understanding of it, a new appreciation that made it more enjoyable.

"That's what travelling does to you. It enables you to experience other cultures. And the best way to do that is through their food," Veren said. "Have you travelled outside of the country before?"

"Yes, every year, with my parents." Somehow, her trips with her parents didn't have the feel of a novel experience or an awakening. With them, it was conventional, like a continuation of a routine, just in a different location.

He frowned at her lacklustre response. "Did that not make you perceive the people and their cultures in a different light?"

"It's hard to learn more about people when you encounter them at a distance, or to appreciate something new if your parents restrict you the whole time." She sighed. "It doesn't

matter where we go, which attraction we visit, which restaurant we eat in: I feel like I still view my world through the narrow lens my parents set me up for."

Veren's intent gaze revealed his contemplation, as if her viewpoint was something he hadn't considered.

"I think we view the world through a narrow lens of our own experience," he stated, "and for most of us, each lens is different, but the size of that lens is within our individual control. Yours is a distinct case, I've got to admit."

They ate in silence for a minute or two as she weighed whether she would raise her next question now or later. Her impatience won.

"Veren, why did you say you were my keeper?" She had been itching to ask him the question since she first heard him say it.

Veren chewed, slow and prolonged. It appeared deliberate, as if he was buying his time to think of a decent response. "Well, that's the role I see myself having in your life..." It was a very casual response; it was almost evasive.

"What does it mean ... to be my keeper?" That he saw it as a role in her life implied permanence. Considering the limited time they had together, the statement confused her.

"Like a bodyguard, I guess. A mentor, a guidance counsellor, a friend ..."

"All of those require a constant presence." She had to point that out. When he left Basco, she would still be here. *How could he be my keeper if he's somewhere else?*

Veren stared at her. There was a line of strain around his mouth, as if he was in pain. It disappeared when he smiled at her, yet there was a touch of sadness to it.

"That's true, but with technology, there's really no way to lose contact with anyone you care about," he said.

A stab of sadness hit her. Once he leaves here, there would

be no way they could keep in contact with each other. For as long as she was hiding from her parents, she couldn't turn on her phone. She planned to hide for a year. She doubted that Veren would still remember her.

"For some people, yes. In my case, that wouldn't be possible," she said.

Veren's frown deepened. "Why? Don't you want to be friends with me?"

"While I'm in hiding, I *cannot* turn my phone on. That means I won't be able to text you, either." Even if she went back home, her parents would never allow her to form a relationship with a human like him.

"What about when you return home? Can't we keep in contact then?"

"No. My parents would never let me be friends with any human ... being." In the *Vis* world, she would go back to her isolated life. She didn't want to go back to that.

Veren was quiet once again. He turned contemplative, then took a deep breath and continued eating. When she didn't do the same, he prodded her. "Eat up, little one. Your food is getting cold."

She complied, but she had lost her appetite. There was no resolution, but it was no use forcing him to respond if he didn't want to. She had heard and witnessed his evasive moves last night. He was skilled at it.

Ten minutes later, as they were preparing for the ride back, a thought came to her: "If you are my keeper, does it mean that I'm your keeper in return?"

Veren paused from fixing her helmet. "When I'm ready to have a keeper, you'll be my first choice," he replied. "There you go—all done." He avoided her gaze and turned to straddle the bike.

She had no choice but to follow his lead. She got behind

him, like before, with her arms around his waist, her thumbs hooked inside his belt loops. But this time, while it was the most natural thing to do yesterday, today it felt awkward.

Just before he put his own helmet on, Veren looked back at her and said, "Little one, you need to hold on to me a little tighter. You've had no sleep and I don't want you to fall off during the ride."

"Okay." She leaned closer to him, her stomach pressed to his lower back, arms firm around his midriff, hands crossed and thumbs hooked on his belt loops. Her action became automatic; the awkwardness faded with his command.

Veren strapped on his helmet and away they zoomed along the picturesque country road. Like yesterday, they zigged and zagged past the stone, earthen and wooden homes; the mixture of blue sea and sky, the lush green of the hills, and the local people going about their daily chores.

She was content—something fundamental to her well-being settled in her heart. The hum of the motorcycle hypnotised her, and her last conscious thought was the hope that she could smell him through the helmet. His scent reminded her of home.

The silence and the stillness woke her up. Disoriented, she realised they had arrived back at the inn. She was still pressed along Veren's back, and his left arm was pressed on her right, left hand clasping her elbow.

Veren straightened when she moved. His hand loosened, but he didn't remove it, anchoring her to him still.

"You awake now, little one?" He asked over his shoulder.

"Yeah—Sorry. You were right. I needed the sleep ..." She straightened up. Her legs were wooden. She gasped when the

rush of returning sensation attacked her limbs. Veren looked back at her in alarm. "Pins and needles," she muttered.

"Don't move," Veren said.

He manoeuvred his long legs off the bike, removed his helmet and then hers. The strap had left a mark on her chin, and Veren massaged it away. He then grasped her by the waist, lifted her, and set her gently on her feet.

She winced as the painful sensation of recirculating blood flowed to her veins, making her hop on each foot. Veren's hands remained on her waist, steadying her. Soon the prickles faded, allowing her to stand on her own. Veren's gentle fingers combed through her hair, ruffling it.

By instinct, she touched his hand, but before she could ask him what he was doing, he said, "Helmet head," and his hands dropped away.

"Thanks." Her hair must have looked like a bird's nest. "I think it's time to hit the shower. I'm starting to stink..." She needed a brief respite from her rioting emotions. Her resolution to treat him like an older brother was melting like ice cream in the midday sun.

"Yeah, me too. It's a wonder you were able to fall asleep on me like that. You must think I smelled like hell and the devil's ass combined." He ruffled his own helmet-flattened hair.

"No, the helmet was on the way," she blurted.

Veren laughed. She felt her cheeks heat up.

"Okay, so that redeemed this helmet from its hair flattening flaw." He chuckled.

"I guess," she said. "Are we going somewhere else later?" she asked to divert him from the reddening of her face and neck.

It was mid-afternoon. There was still the rest of the day, and Veren might have other plans for them. She needed re-energising. She felt lethargic.

"None for the day, but I'll meet you here later at six. Let's go out to dinner," he said.

"All right, I'll see you later ..." She proceeded to her room. She had a ton of things to do and so little time.

Her clothes needed to be washed, or she would have nothing to wear tomorrow. She had worn her two t-shirts, and if she wore this pair of jeans one more time, it might grow its own culture. Perhaps she would have enough time to go to the town centre and get a dress. She could afford one if she didn't spend over five hundred pesos.

As she got into the bathroom, she realised she was still wearing Veren's long-sleeved shirt. She rushed into the shower for a quick rinse. She wanted enough time to wash the clothes, go out to buy a dress, and come back in time for dinner.

To save time, she washed her shirt, underclothes and Veren's shirt under the shower using the hand soap that was provided in the room. It took a while as the soap wasn't foamy or meant for washing clothes. But it was all she had. She hung them on the verandah of the room to ensure that they would dry by morning. She would return Veren's shirt clean.

With her wet hair combed into place, she rushed out. She needed to get to the town square as fast as she could. It would be a good fifteen-minute walk, and she had about three hours to get ready for dinner. She wanted to have as much time as possible to make herself presentable.

Veren jogged down the stairs, checking the piece of paper he had and the written instruction on it. The front desk staff had given him directions to the town centre's best shop. He wanted to get Anza her own jacket. As he got out of the lobby and

turned left, he saw Anza up ahead, hurrying towards somewhere.

Where is she going?

He followed her.

She might get into trouble.

Three blocks on, Anza turned left to the main street. The shop he meant to visit loomed over the horizon. He had kept the one-block distance between him and Anza, but lessened it as he realised he might lose her inside.

She just entered a clothes outlet when he got to the entrance. Anza disappeared through the door. He stayed out of sight and watched through the windows as she flicked through the hangers in the clothes rack. The racks were shoulder-height, and he could see every expression that crossed her face. There was an impatient frown on her forehead.

She was looking at dresses.

He realised Anza was a dress-wearing kind of girl, even if he hadn't seen her wear anything but jeans and a T-shirt since he met her. He supposed that, when she came with her parents for their holiday in their log cabin up in the mountains, a dress would have been inappropriate.

Anza had picked up a beautiful light and flowy, grey sleeveless summer dress with a tank top bodice and soft pleats under the breast. It had a profusion of tiny red, yellow and blue flowers embroidered on the hem that looked like it spilt from a basket.

Her eyes sparkled as she held it against her to check the fit. It was in her size. Then Anza looked at the tag. Her face fell. With a sigh, she put it back on the rack and walked away, but she glanced back with longing at the dress one more time. In her characteristic grit, she squared her shoulders and continued on to the rack closest to the wall.

He watched her pick up a short, blue eyelet blouse and a

skirt set. She held it against herself and examined her reflection in the mirror. She asked for another colour. The saleslady informed her there were three choices—blue, yellow, and green, then came back with what looked like a sea-foam green pair. The lady pointed to the dressing room to her left. Anza walked over and disappeared inside.

I should let her shop in peace and not spy on her like this.

Yet, he was compelled to keep watching. But his vantage point was bad. He couldn't see her well from this location. He entered the shop and headed towards the male section, then navigated between the racks of clothes for women and children. The shop was crammed and dusty. Grimy, beige linoleum covered the floor. The place smelled of plastic, floor wax, and packaging. The men's section was a little further at the back, close to where various shoes were on display.

"Good afternoon, Sir. How can I help you?" An eager saleslady approached him.

"I want to browse first. Can I go around for a bit? I'll call you when I need you." When the saleslady didn't respond, he asked, "Is it all right?" while exerting his charm. The saleslady blushed, nodded, and left him.

He positioned himself among the hanging clothes. Not looking, but waiting with bated breath for Anza to come out. To his disappointment, she wasn't wearing the new dress when she got out. She smiled at the waiting service staff and confirmed that she would get the set.

After she paid, Anza walked out, but not before throwing one last longing glance at the grey dress she had looked at earlier. With a sigh, she left the shop.

With her gone, he bought what he came here for—something warm for Anza to wear. He found a blue hoodie with a zipper closure on the front. It was the thickest he could find. On impulse, he bought the dress that Anza liked.

Satisfied with his purchase, he tucked the shopping bag inside his jacket and got out of the store. He hurried back to their inn, and within minutes, from a distance, he spotted Anza going the same direction.

He remembered the blouse and skirt pair she bought and wondered if she would wear it at dinner.

———————

An hour and a half later, he sat in the lobby, waiting for Anza to show up. He was looking forward to seeing her in her new purchase.

Ten minutes in, he wondered what was taking her so long. She was uncharacteristically late. He approached the counter to call her room, but no one answered.

She could be on her way down now. It's a pity that she's not using her cell phone.

After another ten minutes without her, he got worried. He knocked on her door. There was no answer. For a moment, he felt tempted to kick the door in. Instead, he got the lock picking set that he always carried with him. A remnant of his childhood and a reminder of his troubled past, of what he had escaped from, what he overcame.

Every time he looked at it, it made him grateful for what he had, where he was, what he had achieved and the people who helped him. Today, he was grateful for it for a practical reason.

Within a minute, the door opened. Anza was lying on one of the two beds in her room, curled on her side like a child. Asleep. He felt a quick rush of relief to find her safe, but he saw the flush on her cheeks and realised she was running a temperature. He approached her and touched her cheek. Her fever was high. Heat emanated from her body.

She had laid out the clothes she bought at the edge of the

other bed, and beside it were the jeans she wore earlier. She was wearing the same oversized T-shirt. *It must be the one she borrowed from her cousin.* It was a good thing, as it was long enough to cover her. She was lying on the top of the sheets, shivering.

He whipped the cover from the other bed and draped it over her. He was tucking her in when Anza woke up, disoriented. She looked confused when she saw his face. Her eyes darted around.

Alarmed, she rasped, "Am I late?" She tried to get up but swayed even in a seated position.

"You're fevered. We're not going anywhere, so you're not late for anything." He pressed her back to the bed with gentle force and tucked her in.

"Give me a few minutes' rest, then I'll be fine," she said weakly, her eyes already closing.

"Have you taken any medicines?" He prodded her.

She shook her head. Her body trembled.

He phoned the reception and asked for some fever medicine. He didn't carry any—something he must rectify in his first aid kit. While he waited, he lay down behind her and pulled her close, infusing her with his warmth to stop the tremors that wracked her body.

The doorbell rang. It was the front desk clerk, with two paracetamol tablets in hand.

"Sir, these are the only two tablets we have. Do you need more?" the clerk asked.

"Yes, please," he said, giving a nod. "Can someone buy them for us?" He didn't want to leave her. The clerk nodded. "Is there a doctor on the island, just in case?" He didn't want to think about it, but it was best to be prepared.

"Yes, Sir. Should we call him?" The clerk peeked over his shoulder to ogle Anza.

Veren moved to block his view. He felt protective, and ... possessive.

"Not yet. Let's see first if the medicine works. If we need to call him, how soon can he come?" He wanted to plan, to prepare.

"If he's not at another house call, around ten minutes. His home clinic isn't very far from here."

"Okay. Thank you very much." He dismissed the clerk. Anza needed the paracetamol in her system as soon as possible.

He lifted Anza's upper body and slid behind her, leaning her back on his chest. Her body was scorching.

Holy Prometheus, she's on fire! This medicine better work.

He roused Anza with a gentle shake. She blinked up at him, her lids heavy. "Take this, Anza. It's for your fever."

He pushed the tablets through her lips. She complied, but it seemed to have taken most of her strength. She could barely swallow the tablets and the gulp of water.

He kept her pressed close to his chest until her shivering subsided. But her fever was still raging. He eased out from behind her. His body heat was adding to her temperature. She needed to cool down.

He realised she had unplugged the air conditioner in her room. No doubt—she didn't want to use it to save money. He turned it on to full blast, hoping it would help cool her down. He toed off his shoes and sat on the other bed, to stand guard and watch over her.

This was how it was to be someone's keeper—to be in charge of their physical, mental, and emotional welfare. It was such an enormous responsibility; he was unsure if he wanted it, but at that moment he had no choice. And, if he was honest with himself, he would have no one else care for her but himself.

For half an hour, he waited for the medicine to take effect, to control her fever.

Anza twisted in a sudden movement and flung the covers off. A long moan came out of her mouth. Fear struck his heart. He tried to rouse her, but she was insensible. She was close to convulsing. He picked her up and hoisted her over his shoulder to keep one hand free.

He went to her bathroom, turned the shower on and tested the water. She was burning up to a dangerous level, but the water couldn't be ice cold, just a few degrees cooler than her core temperature. He let her slide down his body until she was on her toes and anchored against him, his arm around her to support her limp body.

Heedless of his own clothes, he stood with her boots under the shower. The water flowed over both of them for a few minutes. One big hand held her head by the neck, so the cooling liquid could cascade from her crown to her feet without getting into her ears.

The water drenched them both, clothes and all. But it worked—Anza's fever abated, although she remained unconscious throughout. He reached behind her and turned off the shower. Still clasped against his chest to keep her upright, he pushed the hair off of her face. Anza stirred and briefly opened her eyes.

"Veren," she mumbled, then fell back into unconsciousness.

He walked her out of the stall where her towel hung. Beside it was the bathrobe provided by the inn. He took both. He wrapped the beach towel around her, and laid her on the bed. Her feet dangled over the edge. He knew he would have to get her out of her wet shirt. While he was concerned about her sensibilities, right now it was more important to keep her dry. Without a second thought, he took the damp towel from her body, revealing the soaked T-shirt that was almost transpar-

ent. With his eyes averted, and with quick movements, he pulled the shirt off of her, and her underclothes followed. Her wet clothes landed on the floor with a splat. With determination, he pushed away every thought that had nothing to do with Anza's welfare and covered her with the dry bathrobe.

He didn't realise he held his breath while undressing her with averted eyes until he had to inhale. The air conditioner was blowing fiercely at him and sent shivers up his frame. He also needed to get out of his own sodden clothes. He peeled them off and pulled on the second bathrobe that was hanging in the wardrobe. It was thin, but it would do.

He collected their soggy clothes and dropped both sets on the bathroom floor. He towelled Anza's hair dry and ran her comb through the wet tresses. Tangled hair would greet her in the morning, and he was sure she wouldn't like that.

He fit her properly into the bathrobe, lifted, and placed her back on her bed. He pulled the covers over her and spread her damp hair on the pillow. She still had a mild fever, but her temperature was under control.

Thank Prometheus for that!

He was on his way to her bathroom to take care of their wet clothes when the doorbell rang. It was Mrs. Bassig, and she looked scandalised when she saw him in a bathrobe.

"Please, don't jump to conclusions, Mrs. Bassig." He stepped aside to let her in.

Mrs. Bassig walked in, speechless. She looked at him from head to toe, the raised eyebrows laden with questions and judgmental thoughts she dared not voice out for fear of having it confirmed.

"No doubt you came here because you heard Anza is sick." He glanced at Anza, still deep in slumber on the bed. "Her fever spiked so high, she was a second away from convulsion. I had to put her under the shower to lower her temperature."

Mrs. Bassig continued to stare at him. He could tell that she was trying to curb her own initial assumption. The older woman's considerable bosom heaved.

"Mr. Albareda, as far as I know, you just met Anza the other day in my lobby. Why are you suddenly so close to each other? What are your intentions towards this little girl?"

Mrs. Bassig's questions were direct. His impression was that she would not swallow a lie, and nothing would get past her sharp eyes and instinct.

"Mrs. Bassig, my intentions are pure. I assure you, I have done nothing, nor will I do anything that would harm her. All I want is to protect her and keep her safe." He infused his truth with as much sincerity as he could.

"But why are you doing this? What are you to her?" Mrs. Bassig asked.

"I'm her keeper." His reply was quick, automatic.

He could utter no truer words at the moment. And no one could make him unsay it.

Not Mrs. Bassig. Not even Anza's father.

7   THE REVELATION

"Who are you, really, Mr. Albareda?"

Mrs. Bassig's tone told him she wouldn't leave the issue alone until he answered all her questions to her satisfaction. At his hesitation, Mrs. Bassig's hands went to her hips. She bristled with authority.

"And don't tell me you're her keeper. *I* can take care of our young patient. She's staying in *my* inn. *I* have offered her employment, she's more *my* responsibility than yours."

Alarm streaked through him at her words. She threatened to cut his access to Anza if he didn't tell her the truth of who he was, why he was here, and what his connection to Anza was. He needed to tell her an acceptable variance of the truth.

He sighed. "Okay, Mrs. Bassig. You win ..." He sat down so he was at eye level with her. "My name is Veren Albareda. Anza's father, Manuu Soledad, sent me to find her, watch over her, and convince her to go home."

"Her father sent you?" Mrs. Bassig raised a disbelieving eyebrow. "How come she doesn't know you? She told me she

met you here when you first checked in." Her tone sounded thick with suspicion.

"Because we have never met before." He glanced at the bed to check if Anza was still asleep. He didn't want her to overhear anything.

"Why send you? Are you a private investigator? You look too young to be one," Mrs. Bassig questioned.

"Do you mind if we move outside to talk? I don't want to disturb Anza." he said.

Mrs. Bassig gave his attire a pointed look. He shrugged. His clothes were wet, and he couldn't care less if people saw him buck naked.

After some hesitation, Mrs. Bassig nodded and opened the front door. He followed, barefoot and in a bathrobe. They stood in the hallway.

"Anza's father is a friend of my ... family. I just graduated from the military academy. I've been away for my studies. That's why Anza and I never met. Her dad asked me to convince her to come home. They didn't want to send anyone they don't trust."

He didn't create that brief explanation on the spot. It was part of his training to cover all kinds of situations. He had thought about this scenario before, except in his head, he was saying this practised statement to Anza.

"I gather Anza doesn't know yet who you are, and you don't want her to know..." Mrs. Bassig guessed correctly. Her objection to his strategy was plain in her voice. "So, what *is* your plan?"

"I want to ensure her safety while she's here and convince her of the merits of going home. She'd be more receptive to a neutral viewpoint. If she finds out who I am, that I'm part of the family, she'll put a wall between us. She'll dig her heels in,

out of stubbornness." The reasoning was sound, and true. That had always been their concern about Anza.

Mrs. Bassig's indecisive stance softened. He could see that his explanation made sense to her. Finally, she nodded and said, "Okay. I'll keep your secret. But you can't take care of her dressed like ... that." She gestured to the bathrobe; her own thoughts had scandalised her.

"I was going to hang my clothes to dry and put them back on later. This was the only thing I could use for the moment. I wasn't planning to walk around your establishment wearing this robe. I just need this for the meantime."

"Give me your clothes and I'll have someone run it in the dryer."

Mrs. Bassig shooed him into the bathroom to get the wet clothes. He scooped them out into the damp towel and handed the entire load to her. Arms full of sodden clothing, she called something out over her shoulder, then added, "I'll send up some hot soup in an hour ... or so."

"Thank you, Mrs. Bassig."

He closed the door.

Anza was still deep in sleep. He touched her forehead. Not bad. He sighed and sat down on the bed, his back against the headboard. He wondered what caused the sudden onslaught of fever. The high temperature was the body's response to an infection. Hopefully, it was just a minor one.

His stomach rumbled. He was hungry. They both missed lunch earlier. He also wanted to get a spare change of clothes from his room, but the need to keep Anza in sight, not to leave her alone, was stronger. He would have to be in this bathrobe until Mrs. Bassig returned with his dry clothes. Maybe Anza would sleep on until then. He didn't want her scandalised like Mrs. Bassig.

Now that their innkeeper knew about him, the deadline to

accomplish his mission and tell Anza about himself loomed nearer. While Mrs. Bassig promised to keep his secret, she might make a mistake and slip up with Anza. He didn't want her to find out from someone else.

And to ensure her safety, he would make a bargain with Anza's father. To prepare her for the eventual life that she would live outside of her family, Manuu Soledad *must* give her more freedom. He must allow her to meet new people, to make friends, have a boy—experience life outside of her family, even in short bursts.

The thought of Anza being exposed to other people, other men in his absence, disturbed him.

Anza woke up just when the soup arrived, together with the food Veren had ordered for himself. She seemed confused, wanting to get up for whatever reason. He pressed her back on the bed with gentle and persistent force until she calmed down, her eyes focused on him.

"Are you hungry, little one?" he murmured.

She blinked up at him, glanced at the soup tray, and swallowed.

He smiled. "I'll take that as a yes."

He propped her up and spooned some into her mouth after blowing on it. She ate little, but the soup's saltiness made her drink a lot of water. He suspected Mrs. Bassig designed it so.

She was breathless afterwards, and dropped back to sleep like a tired child. He took the opportunity to eat. He had a hunch it would be a long night for him.

It was a good thing her room had two beds. He wouldn't have to suffer the small sofa or the floor.

Hours later, Anza kicked off her covers and shifted in her sleep. Her violent movement woke him up. He approached her bed to take her temperature. Her skin was clammy. She was drenched in sweat, her hair stuck to her forehead and neck, her pillow damp. She was on her side; the lamplight showed that the back of her bathrobe was wet.

He would have to change her into dry clothes. Since he would have to re-dress her with his eyes closed, his discarded bathrobe would be the easiest thing to change her into. With a sigh, he sat her up, her damp back supported by his chest. He kept his eyes focused on the ceiling as he peeled the bathrobe off her shoulders, one arm around her upper chest, his fist closed. He was careful not to touch her anywhere else. But glimpses of her creamy skin flashed in his line of vision.

With his free hand, he pushed the damp robe down, and pulled the other bathrobe over her naked back. He pulled her arms through each sleeve and wrapped the front of the robe around her, securing it. She had better be well-covered if she was going to keep kicking the bed sheets off.

That done, he pulled the damp robe from her and dropped it on the floor. He discovered her entire bed was almost soaked. She must have tossed and turned for hours. He put her on the other side of his bed, then whipped off the damp cover sheet from her bed to let it dry.

He took his place beside her and smoothed the hair off her face, spreading it on the pillow. Feelings of tenderness suffused him as he looked at her. This slight slip of a girl, with her innocence, grit, and fighting spirit, had penetrated his defensive wall. She was like a kitten, wide-eyed and soft. One couldn't help but melt inside while looking at her.

For now, she was his kitten. One he needed to take care of. Anza shifted and turned towards him, then huddled to his side. Her damp hair rested on his arm. He dared not pull her close—his body heat might increase her temperature again. So, he closed his eyes to savour the inner connection, this tenuous strand of understanding that had developed between Anza and himself.

It was precious, beautiful, fragile, and daunting.

"Veren ..."

A gentle prod on his side woke him up. Anza's sleepy gaze was on him as he opened his eyes. He was on his side, one arm slung over Anza's waist. He must have moved last night, as Anza's position was the same before he fell asleep.

"How are you?" His voice came out in a whisper. He pushed himself on his elbows and looked down at her.

"My throat hurts. I'm thirsty," she replied, her voice raspy. Her hand touched her own neck.

He stood up and got her a chilled bottle of water from the refrigerator. He helped her sit up, and she drank it fast. It drew a long exhale of relief from her. The hands that handed the bottle back to him trembled. Her breathing was short and quick, as if the action sapped all her remaining strength.

"Better?" he asked. At her nod, he touched her cheeks and forehead. She was cool to the touch.

"You need to eat—you're weak." He grasped her hand as it shook when she tried to reach for the bottled water again.

"I'm not hungry. I'm just thirsty," she said shakily.

"No, let's give you something easy to eat." He called the front desk to order some Arroz Caldo, a chicken and rice porridge for her, and some bacon and eggs for himself.

"Did you watch over me the entire night?" Her voice came out soft, her expression one of curiosity and concern.

"Yes, little one, I did." He nodded as he sat on the other bed. "I came looking for you when you didn't show up and found you asleep, and burning hot. Don't you remember?"

"No." Anza was trying to dredge her memory, but it must have come up blank. "The only thing I remember is taking a nap."

He pushed the limp hair off her pale face and pressed the cool, damp towel on her forehead, cheeks, and neck. Her eyes closed in bliss.

"Do you have any injuries? You might have an infection," She frowned in confusion at his question. "I'm trying to find out the source of your fever," he explained.

"No injury, but ...... my throat is sore," she replied, and swallowed. "It feels swollen, too."

He tipped her face up by the chin. "Say ahh."

She opened her mouth wide as he peered down her throat. Her tonsils were red and inflamed.

"Okay. Let's see if the swelling goes down within the day." It didn't look too bad. He was relieved. The island wasn't equipped for serious medical cases.

"Veren ..." she called as he stood up to go to the bathroom.

He looked back and waited for the rest of her statement. "Yes, little one?" he prompted.

"You don't have to pay for my fee, since I can't accompany you on your trip today," she said.

"Oh, don't be silly. You're keeping me company."

"No, you're nursing me. There's no need to charge you for the privilege," she said. Her attempt at humour made him smile. She was on her way to recovery.

"Let's discuss that later, little one—when you're strong enough to argue with me."

There was a knock on the door. Their food had arrived. He strode to the door and took the food tray in. "For now, you and I will eat."

Anza insisted on eating by herself. Despite her pronouncement on her disinterest in the food, she almost finished the porridge. This pleased him. As expected, she got sleepy after the meal. He was reading a book while Anza rested when his phone rang.

Edrigu was calling.

"Good morning, Sir." His mind debated with his heart whether to tell Edrigu about Anza being sick.

"How's everything, Veren? I'm due to call Manuu in half an hour, so I need an update from you," he said.

He understood Edrigu was asking not just for the truth of the status of his mission, but he also wanted a plausible statement they could give to Manuu.

He stepped out of Anza's room for privacy. "I have established a rapport, Sir. But I'm not yet confident that I can influence her enough to make her change her mind."

This was an accurate statement. Anza's reason for leaving was rooted deep, and he didn't think he would have enough influence on her decision.

"Is there anything you need to hasten the process? Manuu is worried and restless," Edrigu said.

"Yes, I think there is. I think it might be the only thing that would convince Anza to return and ensure she won't run away again. I need a commitment from him, Sir." He needed Edrigu to champion his cause, Anza's cause, to ensure her safety.

"What kind of commitment?" Edrigu sounded intrigued.

"He needs to promise to allow Anza to make friends with humans, to establish long-term friendships and ... relationships," he said. There was silence on the other line. "Sir?" he prompted.

"Is that what Anza wants?" Edrigu asked.

"Yes, Sir," he sighed. "She feels out of place in her own family, being the only Erdia among them. She can't take part in any of the things they do as *Vis*. Even so, her father treats her like a *Vis*. They all do."

He had to sway Edrigu to this cause. "She's not at all like us. She doesn't want to live her brief life unanchored, as our kind does. We have the longevity to do this, she does not. She does not want to waste her short lifespan living the *Vis* life when she doesn't have the years to sustain it."

"I see ..." Edrigu said.

Those two words carried so much understanding, it made his heart pound.

"Can you help me, Sir?" He heard the plea in his own voice. "I don't think Mr. Soledad will listen to someone like me, but he will with you."

"Veren, Anza is sixteen. In *Vis* years, she's practically a baby. She is his father's only child, daughter of his great love, the centre of his life. Therefore, he is understandably over-protective. While I see your point, a father's love is something we cannot question," Edrigu said, his tone gentle.

"Sir, it is the only thing that would convince her to come home, and stay home. Without that promise, Anza might just run away again. I believe Mr. Soledad is due for *Transit* next year. Anza might just do it again then. And this time, she might get lucky enough to disappear completely. It's the only way to keep her safe." The desperation in his voice was obvious to his own ears.

"Okay, that's a good argument. I will do my best to persuade Manuu to give her that." Edrigu sounded convinced.

An enormous rush of gratitude flooded his heart. "Thank you, Sir!" He could breathe easier now. Anza would be safe

when he'd return to his training. He could focus on the rest of his life goals and not worry about her while away.

"So, what update can I tell Manuu?" Edrigu asked.

"You can tell him I have covered leads in Naidi and Vayang, and I have not found her there. I'm going to Valugan next," he said. This was half true. Those were the locations that he intended to visit with Anza.

"Okay. That will work. I don't expect him to say yes immediately, but I will convince him of the merits of your plan," Edrigu said. "I'll call you in a day or so. Earlier if I succeed with Manuu on my first try."

Waves of confusing emotions washed over him when he realised that if Edrigu secured Manuu Soledad's commitment tomorrow, he could reveal himself to Anza and convince her to go home. And, if she agreed, perhaps in two days they would part ways.

My time with her would end.

I should be glad.

I should be happy that I'm so close to completing my mission.

Instead, he felt deflated.

Anza woke up in the dim lamplight.

Did I sleep all day?

She glanced at the other bed and saw Veren asleep, an opened book lying face down beside him. He looked peaceful and boyish.

This must be what he looked like before the troubles he took upon his shoulders weighed on him. At twenty-three, he struck her as more serious than he should be. Despite his light-

hearted manner, there was something grave that underpinned his actions.

She stretched out and her tight muscles protested. She had been abed for far too long and needed a shower. It propelled her to go to the bathroom. After a short, cool rinse, she put on the same bathrobe she wore earlier. The feeling of cleanliness and the scent that lingered in the bathrobe gave her a sense of well-being. She sniffed at the robe, trying to remember where she had smelled it before.

She padded out to the verandah and sat on a cushioned rattan lounger. The cool sunset breeze soothed her. The fresh and fragrant scent of sea, jasmine, wet grass, and some unfamiliar vegetation perfumed the air. Day birds had changed shift with their nocturnal kin, their call now dominated the night air. The cricket chirps accompanied their song.

She sat curled up and hugged her knees close, enveloped by the comforting darkness. The first week of her journey for independence had been eventful. Fate seemed determined to show her, at first instance, what it would be like on her own. If Veren didn't show up, she would have been sick alone, in a bed space, with no one to help her.

Her life wasn't in danger, but if something direr had occurred, it would devastate her father. If he never ever found her, or her body, he would suffer for a long time not knowing what became of her. Her impulsive action to run away was irresponsible, and selfish. She knew that she needed to rectify it, that she must relieve her parents' anxiety about her health and safety.

The door behind her slid open with a thud, startling her. A frantic Veren followed. His eyes were wild and furious.

"What the hell, Anza!"

Veren loomed over her. His body vibrated with menacing

energy. She looked up at him, confused by the anger on his face.

"What did I do?"

"I woke up, and you were gone. You ... I looked all over for you ... I thought ..."

"I'm sorry, I wanted some air. I didn't realise you would worry ..."

He stood looking down at her for a while, fists clenched. He exhaled, and the tension bled out of him. With a sigh, he tapped her leg to make her scoot over so he would have room to sit down. She did. Veren dropped beside her.

"Why didn't you wake me?" His tone was calm. The light from the bedroom no longer illuminated his face, darkness hiding his expression from her.

"You were sleeping. You needed your rest too." She tucked her legs under herself to hide her toes. The night air had turned cold.

Veren scooped her into his lap. One hand covered her bare feet. The heat from it warmed her toes. She went rigid for a moment, but soon settled into him. She curled into his chest and laid her head at the curve of his neck. This felt right, being cradled in his arms. It was safety, comfort, affection all rolled into one warm cocoon.

Ahh. The smell is Veren. He wore this before I did.

This realisation made her heart hum. It still had that elusive whiff of something familiar yet unknown embedded in the robe, but she was too content at the moment to delve deeper into her memory bank.

"You scared me, little one," he murmured.

"I'm sorry. I didn't mean to." She inhaled deeply. With this breath, a decision solidified within her, borne out of the insight that came to her tonight. "I seem to have a habit of unintentionally scaring the people who care about me."

Veren's body tensed. She could sense his eyes on her.

"Did you come to an epiphany during your fever?" he asked.

That made her smile. "Not quite an epiphany. Just a realisation that I've been selfish. I didn't think about how much my father and my family would worry about me when I left like that."

"Wait—does this mean that you've changed your mind about your plan? To be independent and live away from them, I mean."

There was a hitch in his voice that she didn't quite understand, but she let it go.

"Not quite. I still want to achieve independence. But I need to amend my methods, so I won't worry my parents unnecessarily. I guess they still see me as a child."

"You can do it gradually, Anza. Not like this—not cold turkey."

"Right," she yawned. "Not cold turkey."

Veren felt Anza's weight settle on him as she fell asleep. The hand that rested on his chest slid down to her lap. Her breathing became an even cadence. She slept like a child— complete, trusting, vulnerable.

This had become a habit between them. Him watching over her slumber as she dreamed. He wouldn't have it any other way.

He took in a deep breath, then released it. Every molecule of air flushed away the remnants of the fear that had gripped him earlier when he thought she'd wandered off in a fever-induced sleep. He went on a frantic search for her in the hall-

ways. And the stairs, half afraid that he might find her broken body at the bottom.

He was in the garden when he looked up and saw someone smoking on a verandah. He realised he didn't check the one in her room. The only thing that stopped him from climbing the verandahs from the front was the smoking guy. It would shock the man to see him scale the building one verandah after another. That could cause a ruckus.

He rushed back to her room. His relief when he found her curled on the small couch overwhelmed him. Then he got angry at himself for overreacting.

Anza had carved a space in his heart, a fact that he found alarming. She was too young for him, and he had no time for love in his life right now. Her impulsiveness, her drive for independence, required someone who would watch over her constantly while allowing her to grow.

He couldn't afford to be derailed. His path was set and the timetable for each milestone, fixed. This case was supposed to be a stepping stone, but she turned out to be a divergence from the direction he had chosen since childhood.

His frustrated sigh echoed her sleepy one. She shifted in his lap and straightened her legs. He looked down at her sleeping form and cradled her closer, rocking her. Holding her like this, entrusted in his keeping, somehow soothed his anxiety. It made him believe that life would sort itself out in the long run.

It gave him hope.

Their conversation earlier showed him the time to convince her to go home had come; she was ready for it. She had loosened her grip on her idea of independence. She was ready for a compromise.

He knew he could convince her to go home before the end of the day tomorrow if he applied himself. And they would be on her trip back home the day after. She would be with her

father then, and he would be on his way. It would be 'Mission Accomplished' with a day to spare. His schedule would return to normal, but the rest of his life never would.

Anza sneezed. It alerted him to the dropping temperature and reminded him that she was still recovering. He stood up and carried her with ease back to the room, then laid her down on the bed, tucking her in.

He stood by her door as he fought the desire to stay. The knowledge that he had another day with her made him close the door and walk away.

If he must learn to let her go, he might as well start now.

Pangs of hunger woke Anza up. She was disappointed when she saw the empty bed next to hers. Veren must have decided last night that she didn't need to be watched anymore.

The sky was just lighting up now with the morning sun. She wondered if the kitchen was already open. Her stomach growled. She felt normal, but her hands trembled a little. *Must be my hunger.*

To revive herself, she took a full shower to wash away traces of her illness. She put on the sea-green eyelet dress she bought the other day. She was going to wear it the night she fell ill. Now that she felt better, she wanted to look good.

She got downstairs and found that the coffee shop had just opened for the day. The staff was turning on lights and setting tables. The kitchen wouldn't be ready for another hour. They offered her coffee while she waited. She accepted it and took it with her as she walked to the bakery located two blocks away. An hour was too long to wait. Also, she wanted fresh air—the walk would do her good.

A block in, she was out of breath and reconsidering the

wisdom of her decision. She rested and weighed the pros and cons of continuing to the bakery—she was halfway there already—or going back to wait for the kitchen to open.

She was gauging the distance between her two options when she saw Veren hurrying her way. His expression was thunderous. And she knew the reason for that look. She waited for him to come closer and as he loomed over her; she gave him her best heartfelt smile. It worked as intended. Veren faltered mid-step and forgot whatever he intended to say at the sight of her beaming face.

"Good morning, Veren. What brought you out this early?"

He blinked at her. Twice.

Resigned, he asked, "Why are you out this early, Anza?"

"I was hungry. I want to buy bread." She pointed to the bakery.

"You're not recovered enough yet to be walking this distance." He led her to a wooden bench at the corner of the street. "You wait here. I can get you what you want. Anything in particular?"

"I can go with you ..."

"No. You're already breathless. Just sit there, and I'll be back shortly."

He sounded like her father whenever he didn't want any argument or negotiation. It made her smile.

"So, what do you want?" Veren persisted.

"Some pandesal? Or anything with meat in it, like meat pies, or sandwich buns. Anything savoury ..." Veren's eyebrow raised in surprise. "I'm hungry," she said in her defence.

He reached out and touched her cheek, smiling. "That's a good sign. Your appetite is back. And your temperature is normal." With one last appraising perusal, he departed.

She watched him jog to the bakery. Her heart fluttered.

How exactly did Veren see her apart from as a little sister? His affection and concern for her warmed her soul.

The sound of jogging feet made her turn her head. It seemed there was another early riser today. To her surprise, she recognised him as Diego. He skidded to a stop in front of her, jaw going slack in surprise.

"Anza!" The delight in his face was clear.

"What are you doing here, Diego?"

"Jogging. We're staying four blocks away from here." He pointed in the bakery's direction. "I'm on my way back to our hotel."

"What a coincidence!"

"Where are you staying? And why are you here?" Diego's questions were tripping over each other.

"I was going to buy bread from the bakery. Veren is doing that for me."

"Oh ... So, he's still with you?" His frown seemed wary.

"Yes. He's my keeper, remember?"

"Yeah, I remember. Although, I still don't know what it means," Diego said, his tone inviting an explanation from her. He would be disappointed, as she had no inclination to do so— she didn't know how to define it herself.

In perfect timing, her keeper approached, a brown bag full of bread in his hand.

"Good morning, Diego. It's quite a coincidence to find you out and about this early in the morning." Veren's deep voice lacked much intonation, but still sounded thick with meaning.

"Good morning, Veren, and I agree. It's quite a pleasant shock to encounter Anza here. But it makes my day."

"It looks like you were out jogging, so we won't keep you. Anza needs to eat and rest for now." Veren may have been polite, but he was also dismissive. He grasped Anza's elbow,

clearly intending to bring about her eating and rest as soon as possible.

The highhandedness annoyed her, but she had no energy to argue with Veren in the street, and certainly not in front of an audience. "Bye, Diego," she said in a cheerful voice as she waved at him. "It was nice to see you again."

Diego had no choice but to nod. His expression reflected his unvoiced protest.

She and Veren walked back to their hotel, bag of bread in hand. They settled on a chair set outside of the coffee shop. Veren took out the contents of his purchase. The smell of freshly baked bread made her mouth water.

A pandesal and a beef bun later, she was a new woman. The coffee was the perfect pair for the pieces of bread. Veren consumed the rest, and when the staff informed them that the kitchen was ready to take their order, he asked for scrambled eggs.

"You're still hungry after all that bread?" His appetite amazed her.

"I'm a growing boy," he joked. "Plus, the jog to the bakery sapped my energy."

"Oh, that reminds me ..." Her earlier annoyance at his domineering manner returned. "I dislike it when people decide for me."

His eyebrow raised. "Did you not need to eat and rest earlier? You braved the distance just to get something to eat, and you were breathless in the effort. That shows you were both hungry and tired."

"Yeah, but that's beside the point."

"Well, you can discuss your point when you're well and have enough breath to argue," Veren said, ending their discussion on that topic.

It was hard to sustain her annoyance when he had a valid argument. She would let it slide, for now.

Anza and Veren spent the morning by the garden under the shade of the trees, with Anza dozing off a few minutes at a time. But she was on the mend, and her recuperation satisfied him. He wanted her recovered for their talk about her homecoming.

The day was breezy; the garden was fragrant with jasmine, the sky blue and cloudless. His heart felt full of emotions as he watched her nap against him. Anza looked better in a dress. She looked less like a child in it than in jeans and oversized shirts. She was on the brink of blossoming into full womanhood. It pained him to think he wouldn't be there to watch it happen.

For now, he needed to finish his mission, to fulfil what he meant to do when he came looking for her; to convince her to come home.

The opportunity came over lunch. He had food delivered to her unit and set it all up on her verandah. He wanted the perfect ambience and privacy for their talk.

Anza ate well. She even had a hankering for dessert, so he ordered some fruits for her. Over her ginger tea and his coffee, he raised the question that was at the surface of his mind.

"Anza, last night you mentioned changing your plans to achieve independence. What changed?"

"I want my parents to know that I'm well," she said.

"How would you do that?"

"I'd like to borrow your phone for a start, so I can text them and tell them I'm okay." Her eyes held an appeal for him to say yes. "I plan to send them regular messages later, perhaps once a week, once I get a new phone."

"Anza, a text message once a week won't stop your father from worrying. Only one thing would do that. And you know what that is." He could relate to her father's anxiety. The thought of leaving her here alone and unprotected was knotting his gut into pretzels.

"I can't give up on my independence, Veren. It's crucial to my future ..." Her response carried defiance, desperation, and regret.

"You wouldn't have to give up on your quest. There's a better way to do this."

"How?"

"Negotiate with your dad. Tell him why you want to do this and then ask him to allow you to make friends and establish relationships with people outside of your family."

Anza digested his suggestion, determining the viability of it. "Do you think my dad would agree?" Hope glinted in her eyes.

"You're in a better position to answer that, Anza. I don't know your father ... as well as you do." He took a gulp of his coffee. "But, given his bitter experience this past week, he would know you're serious and that it's worth considering."

Anza went quiet for a while, chewing on the inside of her lower lip as she contemplated her circumstances and the options available to her.

"It might work ..." She nodded to herself, then sighed. "I wish I had asked him before I ran away."

"Well, look at it this way. The pain of the past week added weight in your favour to sway him to your cause."

She smiled. "You have a good point there."

"So, are you ready to go home tomorrow?" He wanted to bring her to her father himself, to ensure that his last image of Anza was that of her surrounded by the people who loved her.

"Yes, I am," she said with a nod. "How about you? When are you planning to leave here?"

"I was thinking that we can travel together; fly back to the mainland tomorrow."

"Why would you cut your visit here short?" She was perplexed.

"I want to make sure you get home safe and sound."

"Veren, I don't want you to cut your holiday short on my account."

"I can come back here anytime," he reassured her. "Besides, I need to go to the mainland tomorrow. There's something I need from there that I can't get here." He needed his *sustenance*, since his *vital hunger* was surfacing. He could feel his *Crux* weakening. The telltale tightening of his core had begun this morning.

"Are you sure?" She looked doubtful. "You're not just saying that because you're taking your role as my keeper seriously, are you?"

"No, I'm not saying that because I'm your keeper. However, I *do* take that role seriously." He pressed her mouth closed with his forefinger when she was poised to argue. "So, it's settled. We're flying out together tomorrow."

Anza looked unconvinced, her eyes narrowed as she seemed to be readying herself for an argument. And he remembered their last exchange. His chest tightened with the effort not to coddle her, like her father did.

"Anza, I am not deciding for you in this instance. I am choosing for me. And I really want to fly with you. Will you let me?"

She looked at him intently, then a slow smile appeared on her lips. She nodded. "Okay." She went back to eating her fruits.

Warm feelings invaded his heart as he watched her eat. He

wondered if he should tell her who he was, why he came here. It was an unnecessary barrier between them.

Will she be angry at me for deceiving her? Maybe I should warn her father not to divulge who I am to her.

"After lunch, why don't you go take a nap? I'll go to the airport and buy our tickets."

"Okay, but let me give you money for my fare." She jumped up to rush off.

He held her arm to stop her. "It's okay, little one—I can take care of it."

"I insist, Veren. Besides, I don't have to pinch pennies now. I'm going home." Her mouth had a stubborn curl to it.

"Okay." He let her go; the determined glint in her eyes brooked no argument.

Anza came back soon after and handed him the money.

"I should call my dad first. He could be in Manila," she said, thinking aloud.

"He won't be," he said on impulse.

Anza looked at him, surprised. "How would you know?"

"Well, um... if I was your father, I would stay where you left me, in case you return."

She paused and considered that. "I guess so."

He got up and kissed her forehead. "Bedtime for you, little one. I'll take care of our tickets."

On the way to the airport, he battled regret, sadness, gladness, hope, and some other emotion that he couldn't name. It was too alien for him to identify.

All he knew was that it stemmed from the reality that he was parting ways with Anza by tomorrow.

8 THE KEEPER, THE VISCEREBUS

The mixed feelings that ruled him as he completed his task weighed in his heart. He had secured the tickets. The inevitability of their parting was now tangible. He was both reluctant to hurry back and wanting to take his time. With the moments ticking by, he wanted to squeeze every second with Anza, and yet, not seeing her felt like he was holding back time.

As if Fate wanted to rub it in, his phone rang. It was Edrigu.

"Good afternoon, Sir," he said. Edrigu's call was another dose of reality.

"Good afternoon, Veren. How are you doing with your mission?"

"We're flying to the mainland tomorrow. Anza agreed to go home." His heart weighted down by that declaration.

"Congratulations. I knew you could do it." Edrigu's pride in him should have lifted his spirit, but it didn't. "Did she make a fuss?"

"No, Sir. She came to her own resolution when she got sick.

But the idea of negotiating a measure of freedom from her father convinced her, ultimately."

"Well, she won't have a hard time. Manuu agreed." Edrigu sounded smug.

That was welcome news, but that information was like the closing of a door.

"What did he agree to, Sir?"

"We didn't discuss the details. Just that he would allow Anza to make friends with humans, and keep in contact with them. I trust Anza can handle it herself. Based on your reports, she's got pluck."

"Yes, she's got that in buckets." He was proud of her. Anza would hold her own against her father.

"So, does she know who you are? Have you told her?"

"No, Sir. To her, I'm a friend she made here on the island. Her first human friend. A temporary keeper."

"A temporary keeper ... I see." A brief silence ensued. Edrigu seemed to have understood the pain in Veren's heart. "Should I expect you to be back here by tomorrow as well?"

"Yes, Sir, I booked a flight in the afternoon."

He had today and tomorrow with Anza, and he planned to make the most of it.

He was perusing the tourist brochure for a place to take Anza to dinner later that evening when someone tapped him on the shoulder.

"Hi, bro." Diego stood beside his table, uncertain yet defiant.

"Diego"—Veren stood up, surprised—"What brings you here?"

"I was looking for a place to eat, and ..." Veren's direct look

made Diego falter. "Fine. I came here looking for Anza. I saw you guys go in here earlier."

"Why are you looking for Anza?" There was no use in prevaricating, in pretending he was unaware of Diego's interest in her.

"I'll be honest with you, Veren. I like Anza very much and I want to be her friend." Diego's straight reply and unwavering gaze impressed him. Most guys wouldn't challenge another male if they could help it.

"Diego, I can't stop you from pursuing her. Only Anza can, frankly." This truth was obvious to them both, but he knew Diego wanted to hear it from him.

"So, you won't stop me?"

Diego was asking for his permission, he realised. As much as Veren would have liked to deny Diego the pleasure, he didn't have it in him to impede what would be beneficial for Anza.

"Of course I won't, but you must accept the responsibility for what your actions would do to her. Anza's young—a sixteen year-old. She had a sheltered upbringing and she's naïve. If you take advantage of her, if you hurt her, you'll colour her view of life and men from then on." He paused only to take a breath. "So, are you prepared for that?"

He was daring Diego to give him his word, to prove to him that he was as honourable as he seemed to be. Diego stared at him, gauging his sincerity, it seemed.

"Yes. My intention is pure. And if friendship is the only thing she wants at the moment, I'll be a friend to her." Diego's statement conveyed that he wanted more.

Part of him wished Diego had backed down. Emotionally, Anza was a blank slate. If a human like Diego showed her kindness, she might just fall in love with him. Veren felt a twinge of fear. But he couldn't put his self-interest above Anza's. Her welfare was more important.

"What she wants and what she needs might not be the same thing." Veren couldn't help but stress the point again. "Are you committed to putting her needs above your own?"

If Anza was going to go out into the world, it would help that she had another human in her life who wouldn't take advantage of her lack of experience. Especially since he couldn't be with her, to watch out for her.

"I have never taken advantage of anyone in my life, Veren. I'm not about to start with Anza." Diego's defensive response was empathic, but not enough for him.

"Diego, Anza needs someone who would allow her to experience life. She needs to make many friends, to develop relationships that would expand her horizon. Would you allow her to grow into her own person before making her yours?"

Diego stood still for a long moment; his eyes never left him. The understanding that dawned on Diego's face chafed at Veren's insides. It made him feel raw and exposed.

"Is that what you're doing, Veren?"

Diego's question struck him with the force of a sledgehammer. His jaw tightened. He had to swallow to loosen the knot in his chest.

"Can you do it?" He asked, ignoring Diego's question.

Diego nodded and released a long in-drawn breath, then held out his hand—a man's offer of his commitment. Diego had just accepted to take his place in Anza's life as her keeper. Veren shook the other man's hand; it was the sealing of a pact, the passing of a baton.

And it was a blow to his heart.

"When can I see Anza?" Diego asked, clearing his throat.

"Not today. We're leaving Basco tomorrow." He wanted all of Anza's remaining hours here to be only his. Every single second.

At Diego's expression, he took a piece of paper and wrote

Anza's phone number down. "Here you go. Anza's number. Her phone is off at the moment, but she'll turn it on when she returns to Manila." He handed it to Diego. "I'll tell her to expect your call."

Diego looked at it and considered him, "Thank you, Veren." He pocketed the paper. Then, with a nod, he turned and left.

His borrowed time with Anza was bleeding away fast. With grim determination, Veren proceeded to where she was.

Anza was still napping in her room when he entered. He watched her for a while, memorising the curve of her shoulders, the relaxed, half-opened mouth, the lashes that threw a slight shadow on her baby-soft cheeks, and the gentle rise of her body as she slept. He would commit this to his memory, etch it in his heart. This child-woman that destiny threw in his path continued to create chaos in his soul without knowing it, and with so little effort.

He laid down the dress he bought for her a few days ago at the foot of the bed. He hoped to see it on her tonight.

It would be his one and only chance.

———

Mrs. Bassig allowed them to use her vehicle when she found out he was planning to take Anza to Fundación Pacita for dinner. She didn't want Anza exposed to the chilly night air, which she would be if they rode his rented motorbike.

When Anza showed up wearing the grey rayon dress, it rendered him speechless. She fixed her hair into relaxed waves, and she was wearing makeup. She gave him a glimpse of what she would be like as a woman, when she'd be old enough for him.

Emotions choked him up.

"You look stunning, little one," he said through a tight throat. His voice sounded rusty, even to his own ears.

"Thank you," Anza said, throwing him a bemused look. "And thank you for this dress. How did you know I wanted it?" The glitter in her eyes was challenging, and a tad suspicious.

He swallowed a kick of panic in his constricted chest. "I saw you look at it in the shop a few days ago."

One delicate eyebrow quirked with warning. "You were following me?"

"No. I was going to the same shop... to get you a hoodie, so you won't be cold when we travel." His pulse was rioting while he waited for Anza's response.

Her eyebrow lowered and erased the suspicion in her eyes. She smoothed the dressed down. Her smile was shy, and grateful. "Thank you, again."

"You're welcome." He gulped down his relief. "Shall we?"

She took his offered arm and walked with him to the waiting car.

"No bike tonight?" Anza asked, surprised. She looked around for the motorcycle.

He smiled at her. "No. Mrs. Bassig doesn't want you to get too exposed to the night air."

"Oh! Does that mean we're going somewhere far?" Her eyes were alight with excitement.

"Not far, but somewhere special," he replied, and ushered her to the passenger seat.

"Where are we going?"

"You'll like it. You'll see."

A garden glittering with hundreds of tiny fairy lights greeted them. Fundacion Pacita was perched atop rolling hills, with a

three-hundred-sixty degrees of amazing view. The beautiful stone building made her think of a small castle ruling over a compact kingdom. It had an otherworldly ambience.

Veren booked a table for them on the verandah with the view and the sound of the wind-swept ocean. Their illumination came from the glass lamp set on one corner of the table. They sat side by side, allowing them to enjoy the scenery and talk at a comfortable level.

Few words were exchanged between them during dinner. Veren seemed content. He gave her smiles, affectionate little touches, and pleased looks. As for her, she was just happy being there with him, in this peaceful setting. Time was fleeting, and words seemed to make the clock move faster. Silence was the best way to savour the moment.

She recalled when she woke up earlier that day, thinking of the grey dress that she regretted not splurging on. It was like a miracle to find it there, draped at the foot of the bed. For a moment, she thought she dreamt it. It could only be Veren who got it for her. She thought it an odd coincidence that he picked up the one dress she really liked in the shop. But then, the shop was small, the choices weren't varied and the grey dress was the best among the selection.

It was not the most expensive dress she had ever owned. Not even close. But to her, this dress was invaluable. Veren gave it to her at the time she wanted it most. It made her look and feel like a woman, or at least older than her current age. And, with the aid of make-up, she felt worthy of the opportunity to breach the age gap between her and Veren tonight.

As she glanced his way, she caught him studying her, a look of indecision on his face. But he took a deep breath and his smile chased it away.

"Why were you looking at me like that?" She wanted to know what was on his mind, to see if she read him right.

"What do you mean?"

The flickering light of the lamp made it hard for Anza to read his thoughts as the shadows danced across his face.

"Earlier," she explained, "you looked like you were weighing your options, and whatever it was, you decided against it."

"I was weighing ... whether I was going to order dessert or not, but I had enough ... food already. It was just ... greed," he replied.

She sensed he wasn't referring to food, but she let it pass.

"What's our plan tomorrow? What time do we leave?" The thought of going home and seeing her father again gave her butterflies in the stomach.

"Eleven a.m. We need to leave the hotel by eight. Will you be ready by then?"

"Yes—all of my possessions fit in my backpack." Packing her bag had brought the finality of her decision home. "Where are you staying in the city?" She was compelled to ask him. She didn't want to cut their connection short.

"I don't know yet, but I can escort you to your home, to your father." He covered her hand in assurance.

"You don't have to. I can call him. He'll want to pick me up at the airport." She didn't want him to feel obligated.

"I want to do this, Anza."

Why? "As my keeper?"

"As your keeper."

"How long are you going to be one, Veren?" She leaned closer to read his expression better.

He paused before answering, "For as long as it takes."

It was still a vague, unsatisfactory response, but the promise of a future reassured her. If her father agreed to her bargain, Veren would be her first official human friend. And she

couldn't have done better. Her father wouldn't fault her judgment on Veren.

An icy breeze swept over them, making her shiver. Veren took off his jacket and draped it over her shoulder, grasping the front of it close.

"Shall we go?" he asked, tapping the end of her nose.

She nodded.

As she stood by the entrance, Veren stopped. She glanced up at him, wondering why.

"I've got a request, little one." Veren smiled down at her, tucking the wisps of hair behind her ear.

"What is it?"

"Can I take a photo of you?" He held up his phone, crooked half-smile on his face.

She didn't expect that. *Veren wasn't the selfie-taking kind.*

Bemused, she nodded. With the fairy-lighted garden as a backdrop, Veren took a photo of her on his phone. The seriousness in his face as he took the shot made her smile—the satisfied glint in his eyes as he looked at his picture widened it.

On the leisurely drive back to their hotel, Veren stopped by every lookout point along the way and took more photos. It was like Veren was trying to capture all their moments together as much as he could, cram as much of it in the remaining time they had together, and record them all in his phone for posterity.

"You have to give me copies of those shots, Veren," Anza said in jest. It was her attempt to drive out the unsettling emotions from her heart.

"Of course. I can transfer them to your phone later. Have you turned it back on, by the way? Or called your father, for that matter?"

"No, not yet. I was planning to do it tomorrow when we're

at the airport." The thought of calling her father made her stomach ache.

Veren squeezed her hand. "Everything will be okay, little one."

Somehow, she believed him. His certainty gave her confidence.

They got back to the hotel just before the wind changed. The downpour that followed made their shared coffee on her verandah cosy and heart-warming. There was something soothing about being together while watching a storm rage outside. It made the turmoil in their hearts seem inconsequential.

They spent the late hours of the night and well into the early hours of the morning talking about life, anything, and everything. During the moments of silence, they were in accord. No conversation was necessary.

Veren held her close to him for hours. They remained awake and witnessed darkness turn into light. They listened to the whispering wind that turned into a howl as the morning came and the rain intensified. Flashes of lightning made the swaying streams of rain visible. Stormy weather had never looked as fascinating or compelling. Dark clouds hid the sun, giving them the illusion that night refused to give in to morning, that it was here to stay and prolong their remaining time together.

The moment was broken when Veren received a text message. His serene expression turned into alarm as he read it. His grim silence and the hardness in his expression unnerved her.

"What happened?"

"They cancelled our flight because of the poor weather." Veren's flat tone scared her. It seemed to have created a panic in him.

"It's not too bad ... isn't it? We can re-book tomorrow, or the next day ..." Her voice faltered as the dread in his eyes grew. He didn't seem to hear her. Her heart hammered violent beats against her chest.

"Anza, I have to go ... somewhere. I need to do something. Stay here. I'll be back later," Veren said, then rushed out of the door. He didn't wait for her response.

For the first time in her life, she was frightened. Of what, she didn't know. It was a premonition of something terrible, and it settled like a boulder in her stomach.

Veren phoned Edrigu multiple times, but the signal was bad. He sent him a text message, just in case. It was a disaster to be stranded here today. There was no *Tribunal* source of *victus* here in Basco. The population was too small. No morgue or hospital to steal fresh human heart, liver or kidney from.

His *vital hunger* was rising. His *Crux* was strong because of practice and training, but he didn't know how long he could delay the *Auto-morphosis* into his *Animus*, his animal hunting form.

Once he turned into a panther, his vital hunger would force him to secure the viscera he needed. Hunting humans remained a capital crime in their laws, and he didn't want to unleash his beastly nature in this island paradise. It would ruin the peace.

The weather, which seemed beautiful earlier, now appeared like a sign that all things that could go wrong just did. His only consolation was that people would be less likely to

come out in this storm. There would be fewer victims and potential witnesses to his crime.

The safety of the people on the island would depend on the protection that he would erect around himself. He hoped his text to his mentor got through and *sustenance* would be on its way within a day or so. He would try to hold off the *Automorphosis* for as long as he could.

If help failed to arrive in two days, he dared not think about the choices left to him. To kill a human, a capital crime punishable by death; consume his own liver, which would make him insane; or end his own life.

The result for him would be the same—death.

For now, it was time for his defensive plan. He had scoped the area the first day he arrived for a potential shelter just for an incident such as this. The old grain barn, made of stone and clay tucked at the back of the compound just behind the hotel, was the ideal place. And as was his training, he brought everything that he would need with him. His *Impedio*, some sedatives, and a muzzle. He would restrain and barricade himself there until *sustenance* arrived.

His pounding heart threatened to deafen him. He took deep breaths to calm himself down, to slow his heartbeat and tap into his *Crux* to determine how many hours he had left before he would lose complete control of his *Animus.*

Six, maybe eight hours before my Crux breaks down.

He needed to be away from Anza before then. He had enough time to prepare the barn, to protect the people from him. And hopefully, he would have some time to spare to reassure Anza.

She would be alone during his confinement. He didn't want her to think that he had abandoned her.

Veren had been gone since six a.m. It was past noon now, and he still wasn't back.

He wasn't in his room, nor was he in any of the public areas of the inn. No one had seen him, and they doubted he went anywhere outside since it had been pouring rain since dawn.

Where is he?

Anza couldn't shake the hunch he was in trouble. Something dark loomed, and it would affect them both.

The verandah, which she grew fond of because of the moments she had spent with Veren, was now restrictive. A single text message wiped away the serenity they had enjoyed just a few hours ago. She could not stay there, just waiting and worrying about him.

Despite their connection, she knew little about him. He could be a fugitive from the law or a psychopath. But even as she enumerated every possible dire and dangerous scenario about him, she couldn't disregard the fact that he had been nothing but caring to her.

She was a runaway, and he knew about it. He could have done anything to her, and no one would have found out. He could have taken advantage of her many times—at the Lighthouse, when she was sick, and even last night. There were plenty of times she was alone with him, and if he had wanted to do her harm, it would have been easy for him.

She was pacing in her room when a knock sounded. She rushed to open it, but to her disappointment, Mrs. Bassig greeted her.

"Good afternoon, Anza. I heard they cancelled your flight." Her cheerful voice grated on her nerves. Mrs. Bassig was carrying folded bedsheets, towels, and pillowcases.

"Good afternoon, Mrs. Bassig." She stepped aside to let her in. "Yes, Ma'am. I think they rescheduled it for tomorrow."

Mrs. Bassig handed her fresh bedclothes, and paused by the bed when she saw the backpack.

"All packed?" Mrs. Bassig said over her shoulder as she stripped the bed of its sheets with a quick, efficient motion. "You must be excited to go home to your family," she continued as she took one of the fresh sheets from her and redressed the bed.

"Yes, I am."

"I'm glad Veren was able to convince you to go home. While I would have loved for you to work with us, I was quite worried about you, as you are very young." Mrs. Bassig prattled on as she stripped the pillows' old cases and replaced them with fresh ones.

"And thank you for your generosity, Ma'am. I truly appreciate that you offered me the job." She would never forget how the older woman came to her rescue with no qualms.

"Did you call your father yet? He must be waiting for your homecoming," Mrs. Bassig mumbled as she stripped the second bed and peeled the cases from the pillows.

Anza shook her head. "Not yet, Ma'am. I need to charge my phone still. It might be flat." She found the tediousness of their exchange grating. She was worried about Veren and would rather go look for him.

"Oh, I'm sure Veren has informed your father already," Mrs. Bassig said as she fixed the new sheets on the bed. "He's an efficient emissary," she added as she tucked the ends of the sheets under the mattress.

Emissary?

"What do you mean, Mrs. Bassig?" Anza had taken a step closer to the older woman, unable to believe her words.

"I'm sure your father made the right decision in sending Veren ... I like that boy," Mrs. Bassig continued, unaware of the

upheaval she created. She was busy shaking a pillow into a fresh case. She fluffed it and dropped it on the bed.

Anza's heart, already beating fast because of her anxiety over Veren's unknown whereabouts, stopped and sank like a leaden weight inside of her stomach.

My father sent Veren after me? That can't be true.

She had to find Veren to talk to him, to hear the truth from him. Maybe Mrs. Bassig misunderstood, or Veren just said that to protect her. There were a thousand other reasons that could have prompted Veren to say that to Mrs. Bassig.

She rushed out of her room to search for him and left Mrs. Bassig without a word, driven by undefinable emotions. The horror that Veren might have played her echoed in her head as she rushed to his room, but he wasn't there. His backpack was also missing.

Did he leave me? Her heart pounded even harder at the thought.

She ran down to the lobby. Like earlier, no one had seen him. She felt crushed and bewildered, but told herself not to jump to conclusions until she had spoken to him.

Where did he go?

Short of running around in the rain, where else could she search? She had no choice but to go back to her room.

Just as she turned the corner of the stairway, she noticed movement in a small stone building at the end of the hotel compound, close to the herb garden. Someone slipped inside the structure. She didn't see who it was, but her gut told her it was Veren.

She sprinted downstairs and ran the distance from the back door to the stone building. The pouring rain drenched her, but she didn't care. The heavy wooden door was ajar. She pushed it in, just enough so she could squeeze through. It was dark, musty, and smelled of grain and damp stones. A barn.

Unable to see the interior, she cautiously paused by the entrance and waited for her vision to adjust. But she sensed a movement inside, which raised the hairs at the back of her neck.

The sound of a panting man echoed from inside. It was Veren. Then another sound came from the depths of the dark interior. It was something unknown to her. It sounded like the whimper of a wounded beast.

She took a step forward, but faltered when a harsh voice stopped her.

"Anza, no!" An agonised call came from the corner, behind sacks of grain piled high like a wall. "Stay there!" The guttural command wasn't enough to dissuade her.

Her eyes adjusted to the dark, and she could now see the heavy sacks that had partially barred the door. It looked like Veren had created a floor-to-ceiling barricade, to keep himself inside. Judging from the uneven height of the stack, it was unfinished, likely from a lack of material.

"Veren," she whispered.

"Anza, please ... leave me ..." Veren's harsh voice reverberated against the stone walls.

His plea went straight to her heart. It propelled her to climb atop the unfinished stack. Veren was curled on his side. His entire body shook—it looked like he was in horrible pain. He had a dog muzzle on, and he had shackled himself to the stone wall with chains attached to a thick leather vest strapped tight around his torso. That familiar contraption, an *Impedio*, one that she had seen in every *Viscerebus* household, explained everything to her.

Veren is a Viscerebus.

An Aswang like her entire family.

That one item confirmed everything Mrs. Bassig said to her

earlier. Anger bubbled up inside her, threatening to explode. In its wake, the pain of betrayal.

He was her keeper because her father sent him. He meant to take her home because it was his mission to do so. And he was to gain her trust, her friendship, to convince her to come home.

She stood there, rooted on the spot by the competing urge to lash out, and to leave him, never to see him again.

"Anza, please go ... you can't be here," he pleaded through pain that roughened up his voice.

The tortured tone broke through her fury. She realised he was protecting her from his *reflexive transformation* because she was the closest viscera source around. Her thoughts cleared like a cloud blown away by the wind.

If she ran to hide and left him to his fate, he might break away from his shackles. His wall of grain sacks was incomplete. Escape from this barn would be possible. If that happened, he would be in danger of attacking one of the staff in the inn. The humans would go after him in retaliation. They would kill him.

But even if he escaped them, an attack like this, in a place like this island, would make national news. The *Tribunal* would consider this a direct violation of the *Veil of Secrecy*. They would end his life, because he had just exposed the *Viscerebus*.

Veren would be in trouble no matter what.

By instinct, she knew what had to be done. All her life, she had prepared for and imagined doing this to her family members—to give out the only valuable thing she had to offer them: her viscera.

The clock had run out on Veren. There was no way for the *sustenance* to arrive on time.

She was his only chance.

She jumped down from the sack and rushed to Veren's side.

He recoiled, crawling away from her. He held out his hand to ward her off.

"Anza, no! Stay away ... Go to your room. Please, I can't—"

"Shut up, Veren! You need my help."

She started looking around for tools to use. She might need to go back to the kitchen and get a sharp enough knife, and the first aid kit.

"How much time do you have before you shape-shift?" She heard the urgency in her own voice.

"I don't know ... An hour or less," Veren replied, giving her a confused look.

"Okay, I need you to hold on. I'll go to the lobby and ask for their first aid kit. And a knife." She turned away from him. "Hopefully, a very sharp knife," she muttered.

Veren's hand shot out and captured hers, stopping her.

"I have those in there," he gasped out, pointing at his backpack. It was lying unnoticed behind her.

She reached for it and dug for the kit inside, conscious of the time constraints. She took out two soft bags marked with a big red cross. The smaller one contained two small bottles of pills. Sedatives and antibiotics. She zipped that one shut.

The bigger one was what she was looking for. Inside it, she found three hard plastic cases. The biggest contained a scalpel, some surgical clips, clamps, a pair of scissors, and various suture needles and surgical threads.

The middle-sized one was the heaviest. It held a bottle of antiseptic, a smaller bottle of alcohol, plastic-wrapped bandages, and cotton pads.

A longer but slimmer case carried two individually packed sterile syringes and needles, and two tiny glass vials.

"Anza, what are you planning to do?" Veren asked. His face reflected his dawning suspicion and was aghast.

"You're going to *absorb* me, Veren. It's the only way to save you."

The firmness of her tone hid her own misgivings. She didn't want him to doubt her intent, or to argue. If he fought her in this, she could lose her nerve.

"No ... Anza, you don't have to do this." Veren's weakened denial was hopeful, contradicting his words.

"Veren, don't argue. I've made up my mind. This is the best option. You'll end up killing a hapless human if we don't do this. And they'll murder you in return."

She had taken out the scalpel and bottle of antiseptic, then hiked her t-shirt up, exposing her abdomen. She realised she didn't know how to start.

"Veren, I need you to help me, too. You'll have to guide me on where to make the incision."

Veren's sharp intake of breath made her pause. He must have seen the determination in her eyes, saw her fear of what she needed to do, and her anticipation of pain.

"Okay," he said. "Let me do it."

He took off his muzzle and fumbled at the straps of the *Impedio*, but he stopped. He kept the *Impedio* on. After a moment's hesitation, he took out the bottle of alcohol from his kit and squirted it on his hands, rubbing them vigorously. Then he grabbed the bottle of antiseptic from her. With shaking hands, he ripped open a package of cotton pads, twisted the cap off the bottle, and moistened the pads with it.

"Lean back, Anza, and hold your shirt up."

She half reclined against a sack of grain. He wiped her upper abdomen, under her right rib cage with the antiseptic-moistened cotton pad. With efficient motion, he took a syringe, fitted a needle in it, and took one glass vial from his kit. He began siphoning the contents into the syringe.

"This is anaesthesia," he muttered through gritted teeth.

Thank Prometheus for that.

She nodded in acknowledgement. Her breathing became shallow.

"Are you sure, Anza?" he asked again, his expression pained.

She swallowed and nodded once more. "I am. Hurry, before you run out of time."

She was conscious of the possibility that he could transform at any moment. She wouldn't have the strength to stop him should the *Impedio* fail to keep him restrained.

The first puncture was quick, like an ant bite. He dispensed a quarter of the contents of the syringe. She felt the liquid spread through her muscles in tiny tentacles, radiating outward from the puncture point. Three more injections followed, then it was done.

She breathed out in relief. Sweat beaded her forehead.

"How long before the anaesthesia takes effect?"

"A few minutes... I'll make this quick. But I have another vial if we need to ..." He was unable to finish his sentence.

While they waited in the pregnant silence, Veren busied himself by preparing the suturing needle he would use later. He fished out a towel in a sealed bag from the bottom of his backpack. She marvelled at his level of preparation, despite her efforts to regulate her breathing to arrest her growing panic.

"How come you have all these medical tools with you?" she asked to distract herself and lessen the tension in the air.

"It's part of an *Iztari* medical kit. A standard issue." He couldn't meet her gaze. "Tell me when the area feels numb."

Finally, she felt the numbness in her upper stomach.

"Veren, it's time."

He poured antiseptic on his hands and rubbed them together. He then took the scalpel from her, squirted alcohol gel on it, and spread it all over the blade.

163

"Ready?" he asked. His thumb and forefinger pressed on the area where he would make the incision.

She swallowed and nodded. "Yes." She took a deep breath; braced herself for the cut and averted her face so as not to see the blood.

The sharp end of the blade cut deep into her flesh. She winced, not in pain, but at the strangeness of skin and muscles getting sliced, and the flow of warm blood that poured out of the cut and ran down her torso. Then she felt a sharp twinge of pain as the blade reached deeper and cut through the sheath that surrounded her liver. It made her gasp and jerk.

"Sorry," Veren mumbled, his voice as pained as hers. One hand held her down to minimise her movement.

Her hands clenched on the t-shirt she held up while her body trembled at the pain, her abdominal muscles locked with tension. Tears leaked out of her tightly squeezed eyelids.

It was unlike any pain she had ever experienced.

"Relax, Anza. Deep breaths ..."

Veren's calm voice alerted her to her shallow breathing. With extreme effort, she followed his direction. He widened the cut to expose a bigger portion of her organ. Thankfully, the cutting of her muscles didn't hurt, giving her reprieve.

However, when he cut through her liver, though it was quick, she screamed. The sound reverberated in the barn. The pain almost made her lose consciousness. Through her fading alertness, she heard Veren slurp the piece he had taken from her. She was vaguely aware of Veren pinching the wound close; of his warm tongue as he licked the wound to stem the blood flow.

Cold sweat covered her body, her efforts not to hyperventilate forgotten. Every puncture of the curved needle as he sewed her up made her appreciate the power of the anaesthesia. But at every moment, she expected the return of the pain.

Veren worked quickly. His movements were practised and quick.

After what seemed like an eternity, he cut the excess suturing thread from the wound. With a gentle touch, he wiped her torso clean with the towel, then poured antiseptic on the cut. The last thing she remembered was Veren pressing a square bandage on the wound.

Then everything faded.

Veren panicked when Anza's body slackened. His thumb touched the pulse on her neck. It was strong and fast, but it slowed down to its normal pace after a while. He breathed a sigh of relief. She was fortunately unconscious.

His awareness of their surroundings came back. It was still pouring rain outside; the howling wind would have masked Anza's scream. His strained muscles loosened somewhat. The effects of Anza's liver strengthened and energised him, fortifying his *Crux*.

Then the enormity of Anza's sacrifice dawned on him. Gratitude and something else he couldn't comprehend engulfed him. It was his undoing—his tears flowed.

His bloodied hand picked up hers, and he kissed it with reverence. Every emotion he had inside him, he poured into that kiss. This child-woman in his keeping became his keeper. He was supposed to save her, and yet she became his saviour.

She did not know it, and she probably never would, but she would always own a part of him that no other person in this world ever would.

He unshackled himself from his *Impedio*. There was no need for it now. Her liver gave him a week before he would need *sustenance* again. He got out and washed the bloodied

towel in the rain. He returned inside the barn to make sure Anza was comfortable. While she slept, he put away his things in the backpack and started dismantling his sacks of grain barricade, returning it to its previous location—stacked at the back of the barn.

He kept a close eye on her wound. It had stopped bleeding. When the rain abated, he slung his backpack on over his shoulder and lifted Anza in his arms. He was thankful that they didn't encounter anyone along the way as he carried her to her room.

He realised this was the second time he would have to undress her. Her shirt and jeans were damp from earlier. Like before, he kept his eyes averted, but this time, he didn't dress her in a bathrobe. He covered her with the sheet. Her cut bled a little. The blood seeped into the bandage, staining it. It would be easier to dress her wound if she had no clothes on.

After replacing the bandage, he took the shirt to her bathroom and washed it. There were spots of blood on it. He hung her jeans and wet underclothes to dry. His mind was occupied with worry and prayers that her wound wouldn't get infected.

He was thinking of getting to his room to change out of his own damp jeans when his phone rang. It was Edrigu.

"Veren, I have been trying to call you, but you were out of range. I was informed that your flight was cancelled. How are you doing?" His questions came out in a barrage. Edrigu knew he was due for his *sustenance* today.

"I'm well, Sir," he replied. "The storm made it hard to get a signal." He didn't know how to tell Edrigu what Anza did for him.

"Can you still hold on for another day? I will try my best to fly in *victus* for you tonight. Although, I'm not sure if our team in Tuguegarao can brave the weather," Edrigu said, forewarning in his tone.

"There's no need for it, Sir," he began. "Anza offered ... her liver to me." He choked down the emotions that rose in him.

"What? Wow!" A low whistle followed his words. "How is she?" Edrigu asked after a momentary silence.

"She's resting," Veren said. He didn't want to voice out his concern about infections, for fear he might manifest it into a reality.

"Do you have antibiotics in your supplies?" Edrigu asked, his perception of the situation clear. His calm tone implied that everything that happened was commonplace.

"Yes." Edrigu's question had bolstered his confidence.

"Good. Give her two doses as soon as she wakes up. Now, you need to call Manuu to assure him you're taking Anza home in another two days," Edrigu said.

His mentor's brisk manner reminded him not to be emotional, to think like an *Iztari*. That sobered him up.

"Should I tell him ... what Anza did for me?"

"I think it is Anza's decision to make. Ask her when she awakens," Edrigu advised.

"Okay, Sir. Thank you," he said. The load on his shoulder lightened with the support of his mentor. "By the way, Sir, if I need a chopper, just in case, would you be able to arrange one?"

"Yes, just let me know if, and when, you need it. I'll have one on standby," Edrigu assured him.

After he ended the call with Edrigu, he took a deep breath and dialled Manuu Soledad's number. Their call was formal, his emotions held in check, no trace of the agitation that ruled him. He assured Anza's father that Anza agreed to go home and that he would arrange it in two days when the weather improves. As expected, Manuu was impatient and wanted to send a helicopter to pick them up, but he told him the weather could make the trip dangerous.

Manuu asked to speak to Anza, perhaps to reassure

himself. He got out of it by telling him Anza was still unaware of him being an *Iztari,* which was technically true. He pacified Manuu with two promises: that Anza would call him after she learned the truth about him, and that he would call Manuu by tomorrow afternoon to reconfirm they got a flight back to the mainland for the following day.

Anza stirred awake a few minutes later. He rushed to her side. She tried to get up, but the wound on her abdomen made her flinch and flop back on the bed.

"How are you feeling?" he asked. The pallor of her skin worried him.

Anza touched the bandage and realised she was naked underneath. Her cheeks flamed in embarrassment.

"Anza, on my honour, my eyes were closed. I kept you undressed because it's easier to change your bandage, should I need to," he said in haste.

His agitation calmed Anza as she looked back at him. Her abashed expression faded and transitioned to a serene, assessing one.

"Veren, I need an explanation." Her quiet words were loud in his ears.

He sighed and nodded. "Yes, you do. I'm an *Iztari,* and your father sent for me to find you …"

"My father asked for you specifically?"

"No. The *Chief Iztari* appointed me because I was the closest to your age. Your father told us you know how the system works and you would expect *Iztaris* to come after you. Your father didn't want to force you to come home. He doesn't want you to run away again. They ordered me to work undercover."

"So, the friendship … all to get me to trust you? To convince me to go home?" Anza's tone was clipped.

"No …" He swallowed, took a deep breath, and grasped her

hand in his. He wanted to be completely honest with her. She deserved nothing less. He caught her gaze and held it. "In the beginning, the goal was to get your trust. The friendship came naturally." He hoped that his sincerity got through her defensive wall. The indecisiveness in her face hurt. He rubbed his chest to ease the pain of it—losing her regard might be the price he had to pay.

"Is that why you called yourself my keeper?" Her question came after a long silence. She sounded uncertain.

"No, Anza. That, like our friendship, was unplanned, unexpected. It just happened, and I wouldn't have it any other way."

Anza's eyes held his. In earnestness and without words, he pleaded with her to believe him. He felt tears prick behind his eyes, and he swallowed hard to push them back. Anza's gaze softened. She smiled and reached out to touch his cheek.

He closed his eyes at the relief; the gratitude at whichever god in the universe had gifted Anza with such a generous heart. He caught her hand and pressed a kiss at the centre of her palm. Her hand closed on that kiss and pressed it to her own heart.

To him, that small action was the most beautiful, most excruciating thing he had ever seen in his life.

9 THE HOMECOMING

Veren watched Anza sleep in silence. He had given her antibiotics and pain medication from his kit; and requested the front desk to get some ibuprofen from the doctor nearby for her use in the succeeding days. He told Mrs. Bassig that Anza was suffering from a bad toothache. It was an acceptable reason for her not to question why Anza would be in her bedroom for most of the next two days.

The next morning, with the sheet wrapped around her, he assisted her to walk around her room for a few minutes. The surgery exhausted her, so Anza spent a lot of time sleeping. Her wound was healing well. Her *Erdia* genes helped heal her cut faster. Not as fast as someone like him, but it was still quicker than a human's.

He spoon-fed her, even when she refused. He also made her do breathing and coughing exercises every time she was awake to ensure that she didn't develop pneumonia. By the evening, Anza was begging him to allow her to take a shower. He would hear none of it.

They compromised with a partial sponge bath.

Just before bedtime, he convinced Anza to call her father. He moved to the verandah while father and daughter conversed. He wanted Anza to have the time and privacy to express to her father how she felt about her life, and what she wanted to do.

The call wasn't long, and Anza was crying by the time it ended. Worried, Veren went back to the room to comfort her. A tremulous smile accompanied her tears.

"Did everything go well with your father?" His heart was full of hope for her.

"Yeah, I apologised. He accepted it. I told him we'll go home the day after tomorrow. He wanted to send a helicopter for us, but I convinced him not to—I told him the flight is confirmed," She said, her tone light. She looked relieved.

"Did you tell him about the *absorption*?" He wanted to be ready when he faced Manuu Soledad.

"No." She shook her head, her eyes intent on him. "That was my decision. It remains mine alone," she whispered.

"Okay." He wasn't altogether sure if he agreed with that decision, but as Edrigu said, this was her province since it was her liver. *Absorption* was always a personal decision. He realised he hadn't thanked her yet, even if he felt it in his soul.

"Veren, what happens after?" Anza asked, her eyes focused on the corners of the sheet she was twiddling with her fingers.

He understood what she was asking about, what she was asking for.

"I don't know, Anza. I have to go home, and I have military training to focus on." He had three more weeks of holiday before he was due. He was torn between spending it with her or using the time to fortify his emotional defences against her, which she had demolished with ease.

"Will you keep in touch?" Anza asked after a while. She

seemed to have accepted the fact their lives would diverge, if not the day after tomorrow, soon after.

"Yes. I will," he said, response automatic. "If that's what you want," he added, not knowing if she wanted this friendship to continue.

The slowly widening smile on her face soothed the ragged edges of his bruised heart. "Yes, I would like that. Very much, actually."

He knew what the promise would cost him, but there was no question about giving it to her. He would keep in touch for as long as she wanted him to. The power to dictate how much of him she wanted in her life would be in her hands. He wouldn't hinder the spreading of her wings, no matter how it might lead her away from him forever.

Hopefully, she would need him until she was ready for the kind of love that he could give her. And she would still be there when he became ready to love her the way she deserved to be loved.

Loving an *Erdia* like her would be a short-lived bliss for an *Aswang* like himself. Most of the males of his kind knew this. That was why most of them avoided it—why he should avoid it still.

It was a heavy price to pay for the surrender of one's heart for eternity.

The hour of their flight back to the mainland flew by despite Anza willing for time to slow down. Veren was solicitous, almost overly so. He refused to let her carry anything, not even her backpack. He hovered over her like a mother hen. She allowed him to, because she knew it was his way of thanking her.

Her wound was healing well. It still stung, but compared to the remembered pain of the surgery, it was negligible. Apart from the inner soreness behind her ribs, no doubt from her traumatised muscles and injured liver, there was nothing wrong with her.

They had left the wound free of the bandage after the first night to allow it to heal faster. Today, Veren placed a plaster over it so it wouldn't get chafed by her blouse during travel.

She thought about what she did and asked herself if she regretted it. Her response was an easy no. The reason she did it had a logical justification for it, but why she gave it to Veren was harder to answer. It just felt instinctive. No rhyme or reason to it.

They sat in silence, side by side. Her head rested against his bicep by force of habit. It was the most natural thing to do when she felt like dozing off. Her heart hummed with her head on him like this, surrounded by his familiar warmth and smell. As she inhaled, she recognised the elusive scent she had been trying to identify in Veren—the telltale musk of a *Viscerebus* male.

Her heart smiled, and something settled in her like a missing puzzle piece found.

After a few minutes, Veren lifted his arm, settled her head against his chest, and pulled her close. His action was spontaneous, and nothing new between them. What she didn't expect was Veren's larger hand clasping hers up as soon as they sat down. He linked their fingers together, palm resting in palm. His hand tightened on hers periodically during the flight, as if he was reassuring her and himself.

Two hours on, they both declined meals. She wasn't that hungry, and she didn't want to relinquish his hand. He didn't seem inclined either.

The jolt of the touchdown registered in her heart, like a

final curtain call. Her father would be at the airport to pick her up. Veren would wait for his connecting flight to Manila. And, they would part.

They kept to their seats until they were the last passengers in the aircraft. They had no check-in luggage, nothing to delay the parting. As they walked on, they slowed their steps as much as they could. Before they turned into the arrival area, Veren stopped her.

"Anza"—he dropped her hand as he dug his phone out from his backpack—"here's my number. Take it as we might not have time to exchange numbers later when we see your father."

She grabbed her phone from her bag and typed it into her phone. "Shall I give you mine?"

"Text or call me later and I'll save it." He wanted to keep to his internal vow to let her take the lead in their relationship.

She dialled his number, her eyes on him. The phone rang, confirming the number he gave her. That was a burner phone, with a burner number. Normally, he would discard it after a case, as was their training, never to use it again. This time, the phone would remain in his possession. It would be his lifeline, a part of him that only she would own.

She smiled at him, satisfied. Then, she took a step forward, but he stopped her with a hand on her elbow. There was one more thing he had to do, and it required going against his own interest.

"Anza ..." He inhaled then let out his breath. "Remember Diego?"

She nodded. "Yes. Why?"

"He might call you in Manila ..." he mumbled. "I just wanted to warn you." He couldn't look her in the eye. He had

given Diego the chance to usurp his position as her keeper. He could only hope that Anza wouldn't take him up on it.

"Okay." Her response was dismissive.

She took the information like it was of no consequence to her. He didn't know how to process her reaction. Then Anza grabbed his hand and pulled him toward the arrival area, where he knew her father would be waiting.

Her welcoming entourage was a party of four: her father, stepmother, a male cousin, and an uncle. They all enveloped her in warm hugs, their circle complete and exclusive.

And Veren was outside of that circle. Out of place. He watched them admonish her gently in between kisses and hugs. These people clearly loved her. She would be safe and well-cared for.

"Mr. Albareda?" Manuu Soledad broke off from the group to shake his hand.

"Yes, Sir," he said. He kept his face impassive to quell the pain inside of him.

"Thank you for all the help. For getting her back to us. We owe you an enormous debt of gratitude that we cannot repay. If there is anything I can do for you, just say the word." Manuu Soledad's effusive gratitude rubbed him raw.

"Please, don't mention it, Sir. No gratitude is necessary." It was time to restart his life. "I have to go, Sir, as I have my Manila flight to catch." He shook Manuu's hand.

He turned towards the departure area, his back ramrod straight. As he walked away, he kept his eyes forward—he didn't want to look back and see Anza's face. He felt panicked at the idea of saying goodbye to her, and mournful for not being able to.

One regret was eating at him, he just realised.

He had wanted to kiss Anza, maybe since the first time he saw her. He never allowed the thought to surface, to even

consider it. Her age, his age, their situation—all had stopped him.

At this moment, he would have given anything for that one brief kiss. But it seemed the kiss would have to wait for the right time, the right circumstances.

Just as he turned the corner towards the departure area, compulsion made him steal a last glance towards Anza. Her family still surrounded her, but through the gaps between the multiple arms wrapped around her, their eyes connected in the distance. There was a question in her gaze and a promise in his.

For his life, she willingly gave him a piece of her liver, an organ that she could regenerate. For her sacrifice, he gave her his heart.

Unfortunately for him, he couldn't regrow a heart.

10 THE RETURNING HEART

SIX YEARS LATER.

Veren was on the third day of his first-ever holiday since he became an *Iztari*. They had promoted him: a reward for a hard two years of war to subdue a rebellion among their kind. It was an arduous battle. He almost died during two encounters, but he fought on. The vow he made to himself made him want to live.

The war ended, but the danger of another one was never far from their minds. It caught the *Supreme Viscerebus Tribunal* unaware and, as a result, it endangered the lives of every one of their kind from the humans that outnumbered them.

His mentor, Edrigu Orzabal, had formed a small band of *Iztaris*, designed to work in complete secrecy to spy, and to preempt any other potential uprising.

Before they started their official operation, they were all given a chance to rest, recuperate, and fulfil any unfinished business they had left behind. Veren intended to do all of that. If there was some-

thing the previous war had taught him, it was that time was fleeting, and he shouldn't let it bleed away without doing everything in his power to achieve the personal happiness that he craved.

He selected this location for his first Transit, not for the scenery or the lifestyle. His reason to be here was more compelling. He was on a search and recovery mission—a personal one.

And according to confidential records, Anza had moved here.

After the war, he needed to find her. He realised that he had searched for her every day in the most elemental of levels. His work may have occupied his waking hours, but she was never far from his thoughts. She was with him during the lull of each day, the minutes just before he fell asleep, and most often, she appeared in his dreams.

In the early months of their separation, her messages were friendly, sweet, and innocent. She filled it with accounts of her days, which made his heart ache with longing, and the worst parts were when she reminisced about their days in Basco. That broke his heart every time.

As he had promised himself, he adopted the same tone as her messages, but with fewer details. He didn't want to clip her wings as she learned how to fly, nor did he want to anchor her to the ground when she needed to soar.

The frequency of their exchange dwindled as the contents of her messages changed. It became filled with mentions of other people in her life, new routines and activities. She stopped communicating with him after one year. That is, after Anza's family left for their Transit.

He wondered if she had changed, if she was still into photography, music, and poetry. If she still thought about their days in Basco.

Now, six years after the fact, he was hot on her trail. One of Edrigu's gifts to him was access to the Soledad family's *Transit* file. He knew she was here in Madrid, but not her exact address. He would have to do some digging from the local *Tribunal*. One lead was the Biblioteca Nacional. He had a gut feeling that would lead him to Anza.

Intuition led him to her that first time. Hopefully, it would guide him to her this time.

Anza closed the book *The Matriarchy—Five Hundred Years of Progressive Viscerebus Existence in the 21st Century*. For the past five years, she read as much as she could about the lives of the *Viscerebus* to make up for the years she ignored that part of her heritage.

She grew up with her *Aswang* kin, bound herself to the *Veil* that ruled them, yet she had never attempted to get to know them deeper. That was a mistake. She limited herself to knowing her immediate family, but not into understanding them at a core level. She knew their laws, but not why the laws became necessary.

Her thoughts, as usual, dealt with Veren, her Keeper, whenever she touched upon the subject. She wondered what he was doing at the moment. They had lost touch five years ago when her old phone fell into the sea when they boarded the cruise ship to Europe. It was a holiday before they settled in New Zealand for their *Transit*.

She was frantic about it when it happened, but she realised maybe it was meant to be. His previous replies to her messages had become shorter and impersonal. The last one was a single word—"Okay," which took him two days to send. Perhaps he

got busy with work as an *Iztari*. It could be that he moved on with his life. One that did not include her.

She then focused her attention on enjoying the freedom she won from her parents. It was hard fought, but it was well worth it. She now lived the life of a human. Her father had given her a reasonable amount of autonomy, with just one caveat—none of her family members would be photographed, mentioned, or recorded in any of her correspondence and social media, except in the most superficial of ways. Also, she needed to spend at least three months a year in Auckland with them.

When they *Transited*, she had a choice to keep in contact with her friends by phone, but not with her social media. She kept that account active for two years, hoping that Veren might contact her there, but at his continued silence, she relented and deactivated it.

Two years after they settled in New Zealand, she moved to Madrid to study. And here she had stayed since. She'd made close friends here, a circle of five girls including Elyse and Rizzi. They had maintained their friendship since high school. Elyse and Rizzi elected to study in Madrid and she found the idea attractive. Summer had been crossing over from Paris twice a year.

She spent her days on her creative endeavours—writing and composing songs for some upcoming singers in the country. Her life became more balanced, more satisfying. Richer and nuanced. However, the sense of contentment that she was trying to recapture remained elusive.

Veren resurfaced in her consciousness and had taken up much of her thoughts in the past two years, because of the political crisis that assailed the *Viscerebuskind*. The conflict had escalated to a degree that it almost became a full-blown global war. Her concern for Veren's welfare became constant.

Reading the *Tribunal Journal* as soon as it got released became a priority. She scouted for news about the *Iztaris*, about him.

She put the book back on the shelf. It was time to meet her friends near Puerta de Alcala. A glance at the overhead clock in the library told her she was running late. She would have to walk as fast as she could to arrive on time. Diego, a long-time friend, had flown in from Manila and she didn't want to make him wait.

All her friends rooted for Diego. They thought it very romantic that he always came to Madrid at this time of the year for his annual holiday. Diego hadn't been secretive about his desire to be more than friends with her since the very beginning, but she felt she was too young for a relationship back then. Also, she had to admit that her memories of Veren hindered her inclination towards other boys her age. They all seemed too juvenile, too shallow, too insubstantial.

Diego was selfless enough to accompany her through her journey of personal growth and learning about the world and its human inhabitants. He had been a good and constant friend over the years, and he was one of the few humans she maintained contact with after the *Transit*.

Her close relationship with her cousin Xandrei balanced her view of the two kinds of people in her life, and she realised she was quite lucky. She lived between two worlds, allowed to cross either at will. Most of her *Vis* did not have that freedom, and the humans didn't even know of the other. Diego remained ignorant of her nature and her family, so trust between them never deepened.

As she walked down the stairs of the library, she thought that if she was going to have a boyfriend now, she could do no better than Diego. Attractive, smart, kind and steadfast. She trusted him, and she knew Diego loved her.

Her mind was preoccupied with the thoughts of the past,

present, and wishes for her future as she rushed towards her destination.

Anza traversed the streets by instinct while she sent a text message to her friends to inform them she would be ten or fifteen minutes late. She was familiar with the streets of Madrid, and had walked them almost every day since she moved here. She slid her phone back into her bag and turned into the corner of an alley that would cut her travel time in half.

As Veren turned the street corner, a woman crashed into him, almost bouncing off of him. By instinct, his hand shot out to steady her. That simple touch electrified him. His entire being knew before the woman looked up.

Anza.

Her gasp of recognition echoed his sharp intake of breath. His brain reeled, dizzying him as his world staggered to a complete stop. He didn't know how long he stood there gazing at her. She looked equally stunned and thunderstruck. Her eyes locked onto his.

All his senses focused on her and her sweet face. Familiar, yet new. The baby soft cheeks were less so, her eyes were still as wide, and her lips had the same plump pout. All those years apart, the tame, friendly messages in the early months, and the complete silence in the last five years, came rushing back to him.

The pressure in his heart bubbled over, and a burst of instinct overpowered him. He pulled her flush into his arms, her hands flattened between them, palms rested over his pounding heart. His mind had only one overwhelming thought: to kiss Anza. *Finally.*

His iron control was stretched taut. His sense of honour

compelled him to ask for permission from her. But the words wouldn't come. His lips were almost touching hers, his shuddering breath an entreaty as he waited in pained silence for her.

Anza's own breath trembled before she breached the hairline gap between their lips. Her agreement was like an explosion to his senses. That was enough.

His lips fastened onto hers like a man dying of thirst. It was a fierce, demanding, pleading kiss. Anza's indrawn breath was lost in his mouth, her head cradled in his hand as he anchored her for his kiss, savouring the texture of her mouth.

Her scent enveloped him; the softness of her clouded his vision. She still smelled the same, still felt the same. Except that she was a woman now. Ready for the love he wanted to give her. And his heart quickened as she kissed him back with equal intensity. The same longing flavoured her kisses. The same feeling of homecoming suffused them both.

All the emotions he had bottled up inside, so he could function during those years of radio silence, all the feelings he refused to shine a light on as a matter of self-preservation, converged into this one single moment.

He ripped his mouth off from her when the pressure on his chest threatened to burst. He leaned into her; their foreheads touched. His arms wrapped like tight bands around her. His very being wanted to absorb her into himself, never to part with Anza again. He kept his eyes closed. To look into hers would unman him.

"Anza," he breathed out into her mouth. His throat refused to move for the words he wanted to say to her. He swallowed to loosen it.

"What took you so long?" She rested her cheek on his chest.

"Life goals ... You needed to grow up, and I needed to be ready for us."

"And are you ready now?" Her voice came soft as a whisper.

"Yes ... No more wasting time."

Her sigh of contentment went straight to his soul.

And everything in his world righted itself. In her presence, he felt his heart grow back.

THE END

Dear reader,

We hope you enjoyed reading *The Keeper* Please take a moment to leave a review, even if it's a short one. Your opinion is important to us.

Discover more books by Oz Mari G. at https://www.nextchapter.pub/authors/oz-mari-g

Want to know when one of our books is free or discounted? Join the newsletter at http://eepurl.com/bqqB3H

Best regards,

Oz Mari G. and the Next Chapter Team

WORLD OF THE VISCEREBUS
GLOSSARY
THESE ARE THE VISCEREBUS TERMS MENTIONED IN
THE NOVEL.

Absorption—or ***Zurugatzen***—the voluntary practice of offering one's own viscera upon death to select Viscerebus loved ones. This is practiced by Viscerebus, Veil-bound Erdias, and in rare cases, Veil-bound humans. The offered organs are consumed or 'absorbed' by the Viscerebus recipient. This is an act of love and faith that once absorbed, the donor, or *Rugat*, becomes part of the recipient, or the *Zurugat*, forever. The ritual is usually between parent and child, siblings, life partners and lovers. (*See Zurugatzen – The World of Viscerebus Almanac*).

Animus (Heart or Instinct Animal) or Spirit Animal — the true animal form of a Viscerebus. All Viscerebus have one, although not all would discover theirs. An *Auto-morphosis*, or *reflexive transformation*, usually reveals to a Viscerebus their Animus. Some Viscerebus transform into one animal all their lives and discover that their Animus was a different form.

In some Viscerebus families, it was part of their tradition to deny sustenance to the child of twelve to force an Auto-morphosis. This is usually done under the supervision of the adults. The practice lost favour over the centuries because it often resulted in injury to the child and usually the said child would elect to transform into the animal form they habitually turn into, thus defeating the object of discovering their Animus.

Now, the term is used erroneously by modern Viscerebus to refer to their animal form, whether it is their true Spirit Animal or just their hunting form. (*See Auto-morphosis. See Spirit Animal, Reflexive Transformation – The World of the Viscerebus Almanac*).

———

Apex – A super shapeshifter. A very rare Viscerebus that can transform into a winged animal, either chiropteran (bats) or avian (birds) form. They can transform fully, or partially. Other special Apex skills that previous ones have manifested are echolocation, sound blasting, and magnetic field manipulation.

Natural facial alteration for disguise is a skill Apex Kazu Nakahara discovered. For an Apex that becomes skilled in turning on their brain's theta waves, they can read other people's brain waves and influence them.

It is said that the full skill set of an Apex has not been fully revealed yet because new skills keep getting discovered by each successive Apex. (*See Shape-shifting – The World of the Viscerebus Almanac, Dawn of the Dual Apex*)

———

Aquila—the other name for the giant eagle named Aetos Kaukasios, one of the two primary mythical gods to the Viscere-

bus. The other is Prometheus. The Viscerebuskind attribute the beginning of their race to the two gods. According to the legend, Zeus sent Aetos to devour the liver of Prometheus every night as his eternal punishment for giving fire to humans and for tricking Zeus to choose a less valuable sacrificial offering from humans. The Viscerebus' need to eat viscera is attributed to the saliva of Aetos believed to have contaminated the liver of Prometheus, which was used by the latter to create the Viscerebus.

Aetos was the offspring of two other Titans, Typhon and Echidna, the father and mother of mythical monsters in Greek Mythology. (*See Prometheus. See Origin – World of the Viscerebus Almanac*).

Aswangs – The Filipino term for Viscerebus. Of all the countries in the world, the existence of Viscerebus is the most entrenched in the Philippine culture for two reasons:

First, the Filipinos launched the most aggressive campaign against the Viscerebus. Their Venandis were the most experienced. The Venandi practice, which started as a family endeavour, became traditionally and habitually passed on to the next generation. There are still active—albeit a lesser number of—Venandis operating in the country.

The superstitious nature of the Filipinos allows them to believe that Aswangs still exist, albeit in exaggerated and erroneous form. Many books have been written, and movies made, featuring Aswangs as evil creatures, usually depicted as the minions of the devil.

Like every culture, the existence of the Viscerebus has been relegated into myth and lore, and the term Aswang is used as a blanket term for almost every man-eating and blood sucking ghoul in the country.

Second, the local tribes in the country were also the first to accept the Viscerebus into their midst and established a collaborative and symbiotic relationship. Native Viscerebus in the Philippines were the only ones sanctioned by the Tribunal to work openly with the human tribal members. Their Veil-binding applies only to humans that were not part of the tribe. (See *Venandi – World of the Viscerebus Almanac*).

Auto-morphosis – also known as *Reflexive Transformation* is the involuntary shape-shifting into the animal spirit of a Viscerebus. The vital instinct to hunt and secure *Victus* or *sustenance* triggers this transformation. It triggers the vital instinct when a Viscerebus fails to consume human viscera for over three days.

It is possible to induce an Auto-morphosis through practice and meditation. Some Viscerebus do this to discover their *Animus*. (See *Animus, Crux, Reflexive Transformation, See Shape-shifting – World of the Viscerebus Almanac*)

Brevis Amorem—or short love. A label used by the Vis community for a temporary romantic relationship or affair between a Viscerebus male and a human female. The chief characteristic is the initial intention of the male to conduct a short-term relationship with a female from the outset, regardless if the female is aware of or in agreement with it.

Most male Viscerebus use the Veil of Secrecy law to justify having multiple brevis amorems. It was normal and acceptable. The community called Viscerebus males who practise this as a

Hedonis. It had the same connotation as being a player, or a playboy in the human world.

In the most recent history, female Viscerebus embraced the practice as well, and claimed equal rights to conduct brief affairs with males, whether Vis or human. The fundamental distinction was their refusal to have kids with the males. It started as a way of rebelling against the societal expectations for females to give birth to a new generation of Viscerebus.

To call a female *Hedonis*, or a **Hedonna,** was derogatory. Most female Viscerebus resented the label. However, the stigma falls away the moment a female Vis gives birth. The Viscerebus society considers them to have done their duty in the propagation of their kind. A woman could return to Brevis Amorem practice and never again be looked down upon.

Recent times, however, revived the title, and the Viscerebus women wear it proudly. (*See Hedonna, Hedonis – The World of the Viscerebus Almanac*)

Crux—the subconscious inner control of a Viscerebus to stop or start shapeshifting into their animal form. A Viscerebus could call forth their Crux into consciousness to prevent an *Auto-morphosis* or *reflexive transformation*. A Viscerebus can strengthen their Crux through meditation and constant practice.

It is common training for *Iztaris* and some individuals to embark on regular vital fasting to flex and strengthen their Crux.

The Crux is similar to human willpower. (*See Auto-morphosis, Reflexive Transformation, See Vital Fasting – The World of the Viscerebus Almanac*)

Erdia—an Erdia is a half-blood, born from a Male Viscerebus and a Female human. Erdias are very human in their nature except they would be slightly stronger, faster and live longer than their human counterpart. They may inherit some enhancement on their senses. They don't inherit the shape-shifting and need for human viscera.

Most Erdias who use their enhanced strength and speed become athletes. Erdias who inherit a superior sense of taste and scent usually become renowned chefs, perfume makers and other professionals that maximise their abilities.

The knowledge of the Erdias about the Viscerebuskind would depend on whether the Viscerebus father tells his offspring. If the Erdia was told, they would be bound to the Veil of Secrecy just like their Viscerebus parent, and they become part of the Viscerebus world.

A significant number of Erdias are unaware of the Viscerebus world because the Viscerebus father abandons them from infancy. These Erdias, being non-Veil-bound, are treated as human. They live normal human lives, unaware of the existence of the Viscerebus. (*See Eremite, Mejordia – World of the Viscerebus Almanac*).

Gentem — (nation in Latin)–the current country of residence, or the immediate, previous country of residence of a *Transitting* Viscerebus. A Viscerebus can have between six to ten Gentems in their lifetime. This is not to be confused with **Patriam**, which is the country of birth of a Viscerebus. (*See Patriam – World of the Viscerebus Almanac.*)

Impedio – a leather vest and chain contraption meant to restrain a Viscerebus from attacking humans during Auto-morphosis, or reflexive transformation. It is strapped tightly to the body of the Vis; the chains are attached to a firm foundation, like a wall or a tree. And when appropriate, a muzzle is part of the set. Every Vis is required to own one and carry it with them when they travel to remote places, especially if they travel for over three days.

The modern Impedio has a Tracking Device that is automatically triggered when the Distress Transmitter is turned on. The Distress Transmitter can be activated manually and automatically by the change of the heartbeat in a Vis during complete transformation.

The transmitter signals the nearest Iztari office that someone needs human viscera. The Iztaris are then deployed to rescue the unfortunate being.

It is illegal to activate a Distress Transmitter as a joke or a prank. The punishment comprises a huge fine, and a demerit point on their record. (*See Auto-Morphosis, Reflexive transformation, See Demerit System – The World of the Viscerebus Almanac*)

Iztari—the law enforcement of the Supreme Viscerebus Tribunal. They are embedded in the human armed forces, police and security community as a way of hiding in plain sight, acquiring military training and gaining knowledge on the human military and police system.

The Iztaris' main mandate is to implement strict adherence to the Veil of Secrecy. They are deployed to either a) hunt

Harravirs or Harravis, b) implement the Veil procedures, c) defend humans or other Viscerebus from Harravirs and Harravises, d) Find other Viscerebus communities.

The Iztari system is unique, as there are no ranks among the Iztaris. However, there is a Team Head appointed when a team is deployed. The only figure of authority is the Chief Iztari. The Iztari office employs both Viscerebus and Erdias with the right skills. Erdias are office bound and do analyst and research tasks rather than fieldwork.

Only the Viscerebus may go on field because of the inherent danger of dealing with a vicious Harravir and Harravis. Iztaris are well-trained and well-equipped for combat. The Iztari office uses the latest technologies that the human and the Viscerebuskind can offer. Ten per cent of the Viscerebi population are Iztaris. (*See SVT – World of the Viscerebus Almanac*).

———

Prometheus—A Greek Titan and the god of creative fire and the creator of men. He was the son of Titan Iapetus and the Oceanids, Clymene. His siblings are Atlas, Epimetheus, Menoetius. He is known for his intelligence, as the author of human arts and sciences, and a champion of humankind. His name meant "Forethought".

According to the Viscerebus legends, while he created humans out of clay, Prometheus made the first Viscerebus couple from his own liver, the soil and rocks of the Caucasus mountain where he was bound and tortured.

With his DNA, the Viscerebus inherited godlike traits of super strength, speed, senses, healing abilities and long life. Prometheus also imbued them with the ability to shape-shift so they can hide themselves from Zeus.

It was said that he created them out of his need for companions to distract himself from the pain of having his liver eaten every day by Aetos, and the loneliness during the regrowing of the organ every night.

During the day, the first Viscerebus were in their animal form, a feline and a canine, but they transform into their human form at night to keep Prometheus company. This is also why cats and dogs were regarded as the closest companions to humans. (*See Origin – World of the Viscerebus Almanac*)

Reflexive Transformation – also referred to as *Auto-morphosis*, the involuntary transformation or shape-shifting into the animal spirit of a Viscerebus. The vital instinct to hunt and secure sustenance triggers this transformation. This instinct, in turn, is triggered when a Viscerebus fails to consume sustenance, weakening the Crux, the subconscious and internal control of a Viscerebus to retain their human form. Once weakened, a Viscerebus' human form becomes unstable. Once sustenance is consumed, Crux control is regained, and the Viscerebus can shift back to their human form with ease.

It is possible to induce a Reflexive Transformation through practice and meditation. (*See Auto-morphosis, Impedio*)

Shape-shifting – one of the primary traits of a Viscerebus. This is closely related to their need to consume human viscera. The viscera stabilises the human form of a Vis. The prolonged absence of a victus, usually three days, triggers the vital hunger and kicks in vital instinct to hunt. Once vital instinct is triggered, the Vis transforms reflexively into their Animus. A Vis

has a conscious control of their shape-shifting at most times, through their Crux. (*See Auto-morphosis, Reflexive Transformation. See All about the Vis – World of the Viscerebus Almanac.*)

Supreme Viscerebus Tribunal – or the SVT. This is the primary ruling body of the Viscerebus. It is composed of previous and current Matriarch and Patriarchs from different Gentems all over the world. SVT functions as both the main legislative and judicial body of the Viscerebi. The execution of the laws, however, is the responsibility of each Gentem's Tribunal. Members of the body meet bi-annual, where laws proposed by members are discussed and voted on. The main mandate of the Tribunal is to oversee the compliance of every Gentem in the upholding of the Veil of Secrecy. The SVT is the ultimate rule of law for the Viscerebi. (*See Veil of Secrecy. See 5000BCE Constitution, Implementing Rules and Regulations – World of the Viscerebus Almanac*).

Sustenance– or *Victus*. The blanket term used by Viscerebus to refer to human viscera that they take regularly. This is crucial to stabilising the human form of a Viscerebus. This is the term used by modern Viscerebus, as the term does not invite unnecessary questions and explanations. (*See Crux, Auto-morphosis, Reflexive Transformation. See Victus, Vital hunger – World of the Viscerebus Almanac*).

Transit—The program of relocating a Viscerebus and his/her family to maintain the Veil of Secrecy. A Viscerebus can be under a Life Transit, a mandatory, scheduled relocation every thirty years; or a Forcible Transit, unscheduled relocation because of the Viscerebus' violation of the Veil. A Forcible Transit is equivalent to an exile in human government.

A Transitting Viscerebus is required to cut contact with any of their *non-Veil-bound* human or Erdia friends, relatives and connections. But they can keep contact with other Viscerebus and Veil-bound Erdia friends, relatives and connections.

A Transitting Viscerebus may keep his or her old name and profession, or may take on a new one. The new Transit location has to be in a different country or continent. A Transitting Viscerebus can return to their *Patriam* or previous *Gentem* after 100 years to ensure that any human they had a relationship with before are already dead. Visits to the Patriam and previous Gentems are permitted on brief holidays and only once every ten years. Veil of Secrecy restrictions apply. (*See Veil of Secrecy. Gentem, See Patriam, Transit Program – World of the Viscerebus Almanac*)

Veil of Secrecy—the inviolable law of the Tribunal to keep the existence of Viscerebus a secret from non-Viscerebus. The Law made exceptions to a) Human spouse; b) Human kids. However, the exceptions apply only if the above people prove themselves loyal to the Viscerebuskind and to the Veil.

The strict adherence to the Veil guides every interaction of a Viscerebus with humans and non-Veil-bound Erdias. The violation or breaking of the Veil would entail severe punishment that could cause the death of the human or the non-Veil-

bound Erdia, and the violator is expected to execute the punishment. (*See SVT, or Supreme Viscerebus Tribunal. See 5000BCE Constitution – World of the Viscerebus Almanac*).

Victus – colloquially called as *Sustenance*. This is the blanket term for human viscera, heart, liver and kidney, that a Viscerebus must consume regularly to keep their Vital Hunger at bay and prevent involuntary transformation to their animal form.

This term had become less popular than its colloquial counterpart as humans who overheard ask question what it means. The Tribunal encourages the use of the term *Sustenance* in a public setting to avoid the questions. (*See Sustenance, Crux, Auto-morphosis, Reflexive Transformation, Vital Hunger*)

Viscerebus/Viscerebi (pl.)—or Viscera-eaters, colloquially known as ***Vis***. They are a different species of human. They live two to three times longer than a human, are stronger, faster, and have quick healing abilities.

Physically, they look exactly like humans, but they can shape-shift into a land-based predator. The Viscerebus need to eat human viscera to stabilise their human form. To normal humans, they are monstrous man-eaters.

Viscerebi are known by many names in many cultures. And the descriptions vary because of the dilution of the truth engineered by the Tribunal to bury the existence of the Viscerebus under myth and lore. The common thread among these lores is the shape-shifting and the viscera-eating.

Most modern human societies have completely ignored the lores, but the belief persists in some pockets of rural communities all over the world. This is especially true in Asian countries, particularly the Philippines, where stories about Aswangs, the local name for Viscerebus, are still told to this day. (*See Aswang*)

Vital Hunger—the term used to refer to the need to consume *Victus,* or *sustenance.* The sensation is similar to physical hunger, but it pertains to the need of a Viscerebus to secure sustenance to keep their Crux strong and prevent an Auto-morphosis. This manifests if the Vis has neglected to consume sustenance for at least three days. This triggers the *vital instinct* to hunt, which, in turn, triggers the Auto-morphosis, or reflexive transformation.

The symptoms are usually a loss of energy and physical weakening of the Viscerebus. Some Vis develop physical hunger-like symptoms, like shaking and trembling. Vital hunger itself is not painful, but the accompanying pain comes from the battle between the body's Crux and the vital instinct. (*See Auto-morphosis, Crux, Reflexive Transformation, Vital Instinct*)

Vital Instinct—the basic survival instinct of a Viscerebus to consume *Victus,* or human liver, heart or kidney. While this could be interchangeable to the term *Vital Hunger,* this refers to the instinct to hunt rather than the hunger to consume. This surfaces when a Viscerebus fails to partake of human viscera for over three days. At this point, there is a battle between the Vital Instinct and the Crux of the individual.

The stronger the Crux, the longer the Viscerebus can control the transformation. However, inevitably, the Vital Instinct wins, thus forcing an Auto-morphosis, or the reflexive transformation into the Viscerebus' Animus. Once the Vital hunger is quenched, it restores the Crux control of the Viscerebus. (*See Crux, Auto-morphosis, Reflexive Transformation, Vital Hunger*).

Vondenad (Vondenada, f, Vondenado, m) – from the Dutch word "vondeling". The Viscerebus term for "foundling." This refers to the Veil-bound offsprings of any male or female Viscerebus and Erdias that were abandoned by their parents. Although the term used is not the same as an orphan (*Aulila*) or a runaway (*Reneweg*), they are all taken into custody and become a ward of the Supreme Tribunal.

Unlike in human practices, most Vondenados and Vondenadas are immediately taken into the custody of the Tribunal. And they are assigned a foster family, or a *Thetadom* within thirty days. It is illegal to treat a Vondenado/Vondenada as an outsider while they are within the care of a foster family.

Foster parents (*Theta and Thetos*) are expected to care for their ward like their own child and teach them the ways of life and the rules of the Tribunal. They function like a mentor and a parent combine. A Viscerebus or Erdia family could only take on a maximum of one Vondenado or Vondenada every five years. Exceptions are made for siblings. They are usually placed together in one home.

Most foster parents end up adopting the child in their care. Adoption would only be approved when the child reaches the age of eighteen. However, the choice is left to the child whether they would like to be adopted or remain to be a protégé. More

than half the Vondenado/Vondenadas opt for the latter because they do not feel like they belong, or they prefer the independence. (*See Aulila, Reneweg, Thetadom, Thetas and Thetos – The World of the Viscerebus Almanac*)

Note: All novels in the World of the Viscerebus series contain a glossary of terms used in the respective books. The full glossary of terms and other information can be found in the WORLD OF THE VISCEREBUS ALMANAC.

AFTERWORD

Dear Reader,

I have built the World of the Viscerebus as richly as I could with stories that are exciting, entertaining and stimulating to the mind. Viscerebus is my global word for the viscera-eaters that are prevalent in various cultures, especially in Southeast Asia. They are known as Aswang in my country.

In this fantasy world, there is the main storyline, a trilogy: Rise of the Viscerebus, First Chronicle; Dawn of the Dual Apex, Second Chronicle, and InEquilibrium, Third Chronicle.

Then there are the companion novels namely Beasts of Prey, The Keeper, and two others that are still works in-progress.

To improve on this fantasy world further, your feedback is valuable to me. If you can please leave a review of my book on Amazon or through the email listed below, I would appreciate it very much.

Or, if you wish to be part of the select early readers of my

works, please let me know via email at marigr8@yahoo.com. And follow me at Twitter @GraceGranlund, Instagram @Gogranlund, or Facebook Oz Mari Granlund

Thank you.

Oz Mari G.